MW00947477

ECHOES OF
SKELETONS PAST

by

C. K. Phillips

Echoes of Skeletons Past is a work of fiction. Names, characters, places, and incidents are either the product of the author's imagination or are used fictitiously. Any resemblance to events, locales, or any person, living or dead, is entirely coincidental.

Dedication

Echoes of Skeletons Past is dedicated to the many true scientists who toil day after day, often without compensation or even a word of thanks, in order to discover truths about our present and past civilizations.

Echoes of Skeletons Past is also dedicated to the many people who helped me and gave me suggestions for making the book better. Thanks to the early readers and reviewers: Cheryl Dalton, Steve Robinson, Dr. Joy Yates, Sally Standifer Russell, Sandy Kovacic, and Sherry Bagley. Your thoughts were invaluable to me.

Again, I am in the debt to Joe Spencer for the help and advice that I received from him. Joe knows more about what makes a good story than anyone I know. Joe has been from my first book a cheerleader, an advisor, and a tough critic, not afraid to tell me what he thinks.

Saving the best to last, I want to thank my wife Cindi. As in the first book, she helped guide the plot and character development so that I could produce a story that I hope you will enjoy.

# # #

Cover Design: Kent Holloway

For a billion years the patient earth amassed documents and inscribed them with signs and pictures which lay unnoticed and unused. Today, at last, they are waking up, because man has come to rouse them. Stones have begun to speak, because an ear is there to hear them. Layers become history and, released from the enchanted sleep of eternity, life's motley, never-ending dance rises out of the black depths of the past into the light of the present.

Hans Cloos in "Conversations with the Earth"

Chapter 1

Kim opened her eyes as she tried to spring up from her sleep. She felt the hand clasped over her mouth and heard Shannon as she quietly whispered, "Shhh! I heard something. Somebody's out there.

"What time is it?" Kim said, as she struggled to see out the mesh window of the darkened tent. "What did you hear?"

"I'm not sure. It sounded like someone was sneaking around the camp." She looked at her luminous watch and said, "It's only five-thirty, much too early for Dr. Yates to be back."

"Maybe it's Dr. Smith," Kim said, referring to Dr. Yates' associate.

"No way; he sleeps so soundly he never gets up before sunrise." As she spoke, she pushed the power button on her cell phone and prepared to send the emergency SOS. She jumped as the bright light suddenly blinded her.

"Well, well! What do we have here? Looks like we have us a couple o' fillies." The man guffawed and moved into the tent so that his partner could join him inside.

Takeshi shook his head and pointed the handgun at the girls as they started to scramble away. "Stay where you are and make no sound if you want to live!"

Kim grabbed Shannon and held on as their eyes grew large and their mouths opened in a silent scream.

"What do you want?" Shannon said. "We don't have much money, but you can take it. Just please, don't hurt us," she pleaded. She shook as the man reached inside his jacket and pulled out duct tape and paracord.

"We don't want your money," Takeshi said. "Hurry and tie them up, Tynaka. But first, tape their mouths good and tight. Then, we'll decide what we want to do with you," he said as he leered at them.

Shannon felt Kim tense and whispered to her, "Do what they say; don't try anything right now." She silently pushed her thumb and sent the SOS before easing the cell phone into her back pocket.

Tynaka stepped up to the women. Now that he was in the light, they could see him clearly; his dark eyes glared at them. Shannon took note of his six-foot frame—a slim body that hinted at a deadly quickness. The light reflected off his shaved head; the only hair he had was a short thick goatee. She tried to get a good look at the other man, but the bright light he was holding placed his face in shadow. The girls jumped as Tynaka ripped off a couple of strips of the duct tape. He quickly ran the tape over each of their mouths and roughly pressed it tight. Shannon could smell the rank odor of his hands as he grasped her face and turned her on her stomach.

"Please don't hurt me," she prayed as he pulled her hands tight against her back. He took the paracord and expertly tied her hands, then her feet. He left her lying face down and reached for Kim. It took him only another minute to have her bound and helpless and laid out beside her friend.

"Leave them," Takeshi said. "Let's find the others."

Tynaka looked at them and smiled as his eyes roved over their bodies. "We may be back. Now, don't go anywhere."

They backed quietly out of the tent and silently approached the other shelter. They paused at the flap, and, then, on a signal from Takeshi, they burst into the room. They watched the man lying there, snoring, with no idea that he had visitors. It wasn't until he was roughly turned onto his back that he realized he wasn't alone. He shook his head and mumbled, "What is this all about? Who are you? What do you want?"

"Where is the other woman, the one in charge?"

He looked at Tynaka and said, "She's not here. She went into town last night to get some provisions."

"When will she be back?" asked Takeshi.

"I don't know—sometime around eight or nine. It's a long drive and she won't leave until it starts getting light."

"Which way will she come back into camp?" Tynaka shot the question while he looked at Takeshi.

"There's only one road out of here—she'll have to come in that way."

"Who are you?"

The man looked at Takeshi and answered, "I'm Dr. Charles Smith. I'm Dr. Yates' co-principal investigator for this project." He looked furtively toward the opening.

Tynaka noticed the look and hissed, "Don't get any ideas about running. And don't expect any help from your two little females over there." He chuckled as he added, "They are in no position to help you."

"What have you done to them? They are just volunteers—college students helping for the summer."

Takeshi replied, "They're okay—at least for the time being. Where does the good doctor keep her computer?"

"I'm sure it's with her; she doesn't go anywhere without taking it."

"Then I guess we'll just make ourselves comfortable and wait for her. Tynaka, look around and see if you can find some coffee while I tie up our good Dr. Smith."

Chapter 2

I followed Bill Lander through the trees, our horses carefully picking their way along the trail. The day had dawned beautiful and the temperature was in the mid-forties, normal for this elevation in the Colorado Rockies in mid-June. I looked at his six-foot-three frame as he sat on his horse. He was still lean and mean, not a lot different than when we had played basketball together in college, although his dark hair was now sprinkled with gray. Being only five-nine, I had been the point guard and had fed him the ball so he could score his many points—man, he could shoot! He could have gone to a larger school, but I was glad he hadn't done so; before we graduated, our team had won the first national championship for the division in which our school competed. After school, we had gone opposite directions. He had joined the service and became a Navy SEAL, completing many black-op missions. I had become a teacher and coach before I earned my doctorate and went into administration. After Lander tired of killing the bad guys, he had moved back to our small town in Tennessee and started teaching at the same college we had attended and we renewed our close friendship.

Recently, I had begun writing novels and I tapped into his knowledge and experience to help me. In addition to just being a fun vacation, this trip is doing a number of things. It is giving Lander the arena to teach me some "serious skills" from his SEAL training days and for me to get some onsite practice so that I can understand first-hand what I am talking about when I incorporate these techniques into my novels. As I see it, it is a win-win; I'm learning humility and he's learning patience. This first leg is focusing on survival skills in the wilderness; that's the reason we are using horses to get into the isolated Rockies. We also plan to work on rock climbing and rappelling while we are here; I've had some basics, but need to improve my techniques.

For Bill, these trips also add to his firsthand knowledge for his college teaching. North American Studies includes all aspects of the history of the U.S.; some of the most interesting topics revolve around the ancient Pueblo dwellings here in the Southwest. Throw in the rich environment for fossilized remains of the giant dinosaurs that once roamed this area of the country and it becomes a wealth of information that will add flavor to his classes. I tell him that he needs it if he wants to keep his students awake. After our backcountry camping, we are going to travel to the Durango area and explore some of the ancient dwellings in nearby Mesa Verde. We would like to fly to Phoenix and follow some of the paths of early prospectors looking for gold in the mountains. Superstition Mountains is reputed to be the location of the Dutchman's Lost Gold Mine and is a tentative destination for us.

The other important reason we chose to come to the mountains this year has nothing to do with our jobs. We both are into distance running and are planning to run another marathon this November. Last year, we ran the Rocket City Marathon in Huntsville and have registered to run the Chickamauga Battlefield Marathon this November. If we complete our training schedule, we also want to go back to Huntsville in December. Although our eight-thirty miles can't compete for the best times, we still want to improve our own records. It is our hope that training some at altitude will give us the edge we need to better our times. Durango is over sixty-five hundred feet altitude while our hometown in Tennessee is less than one thousand.

After a couple of more hours of riding, Bill said, "We'll leave the trail here and find a place to set up camp." He reined his horse to the right and mine followed.

I looked at the Aspens as we weaved among them. "Why do the trees have the black markings on their trunks?" I looked at Lander as I asked this.

"That's where the animals—mostly elk or deer—scar the trees with their antlers. Sometimes bears will scratch the trunks. Do you know why they are called Quaking Aspens?"

"Not really; it's something to do with the leaves, I think."

"You're right. The directions of the veins in the flat slender leaves allow them to shiver and quake at the lightest breeze." He looked at his GPS and said, "Let's find a spot around here. There's a stream about three hundred feet ahead of us. So, we'll be okay here."

"Why can't we just camp beside the creek?"

"Park Regulations. No one is allowed to set up camp close to a water source. That keeps the water accessible to other campers and to the wildlife. We have to be at least two hundred feet away from the water and we have to move our campsite each night."

We tied our horses off and within twenty minutes, our camp was set up. Bill looked at me and said, "Let's go get some water and then eat. After that, we'll find a rock wall to climb. Tonight, we'll work on something else. Use your topographical map; find the nearest stream and then mark our destination on your GPS. Take us the shortest way there. I'll follow you."

I accessed my iPhone GPS tracking app and looked at the map I had earlier downloaded; I could now use the GPS function without having to be connected to the Internet. I dropped a pin on the map and looked at the topography; I also marked the current location. The shortest distance required us to climb a ridge and go down the other side.

Bill said, "We'll take the horses so we don't have to carry water back to camp for them."

I moved off, with Lander close behind. I followed my GPS directions and we were looking at the clear stream within five minutes. We dismounted and let our rides drink while we filled our containers with water upstream from the thirsty horses; we dropped the purifying tablets into the water, waited a few minutes, and then drank. When we were satisfied, we topped the canteens off and Bill said, "Take us back to camp, but stay away from the ridge this time. See if you can identify edible plants on the way. We're not supposed to pick them but you still need to know which are poisonous to us."

I checked my GPS and moved off, staying away from the hills. After riding for a few minutes, I pointed at some flowering bushes. "What about those flowers? Could we eat them?" I asked.

We halted our horses; Bill dismounted, and lifted some of the flowers. He held them in front of me and said, "They're pretty, but deadly to humans. These are . . ." The sudden crack of a rifle shot stopped him in mid-sentence.

"I thought there was no hunting in this area," I said.

"There's not—at least not legally. Let's check it out. It sounded like it was pretty close to us." I watched Bill inspect his H&K .45, so I checked my Glock. Colorado has reciprocity with Tennessee, so we both had carried our handguns and concealed carry permits.

Our weapons ready, we mounted our horses and I followed Lander as he continued on the trail around the bottom of the rock ledges. We heard no other shots or no sound of any kind other than the noise we were making. Suddenly, Lander stopped and my horse had to veer off the trail to keep from rear-ending him.

"Look at that cliff, about half-way up," said Lander, as he pointed.

At first, I could see nothing. Then I spotted it. There was a body dangling from a rope. "Do you think that has anything to do with the shot we heard?" I asked.

"I don't know, but I would place odds that it does." He took his binoculars and looked closely at the swaying body.

I turned my horse toward the cliff and then said, "Let's go."

"Whoa! Hold on there, Kemo Sabe! There's no way to get to him from down here; his rope's too short. We'll have to get to the top of the ledge and use our ropes to get down to him." Before he stopped speaking, he had already started moving his horse. "Let's go!"

Food forgotten, I followed Lander as he quickly found the best way up the hill. Reaching the crest, we heard another gunshot and the tree next to my head exploded with bits of bark spraying around me.

"Take cover!" Lander yelled. We slid from our saddles and ducked behind the large Aspen tree. "Keep down," Lander said. He crawled across to another tree and slowly stood. As he did, two more shots rang out and then we heard a vehicle speed away.

Lander walked back to me and said, "They're gone. Let's check the body out." We found our horses close by and, after a short ride, Lander reined in his mount, hit the ground running, and stopped at the top edge of the cliff.

"Hurry, get the rope and tie it off on the base of that tree." He pointed to a pine a short distance from the edge. I watched him move to the left and saw another rope curling off the cliff. "This is his rope. We'll follow it down to the stranded climber. He either fell and hurt himself or he was shot. Either way, we need to hurry."

Lander went back to his horse and grabbed a rescue body sling while I hurriedly tied the rope off to the tree and carried the rest of it to the edge of the cliff. Lander grabbed it, pulled it to be sure the knot was secure, and dropped it over the edge. He rappelled down the cliff and stopped beside the swaying body. I watched him work with the wounded climber. I saw him jerk his head once;

then he looked back up to me and yelled, "We've got to go down from here. Take the horses back the way we came and meet me at the bottom. If you beat me there, get the first aid kit out. Oh, and keep your eyes open and your gun ready."

I untied both horses and mounted mine. Holding the reins of Lander's mount, I let my mare pick herself down the path we had come up. I saw or heard nothing out of the ordinary as I hurried to the base of the cliff. I pulled my horse to a stop when I saw Lander bending over an inert body.

"Bring me the first aid kit and some water," Lander said as I dismounted. "But, be sure to tie the horses—we don't want to walk out of here."

"How is he?" I asked, as I moved around Bill to get a look at him—and then stopped. It wasn't a he! As I watched, the woman raised her hand and removed her helmet. Her fingers came back bloody.

Lander said, "Meet Dr. Shirley Yates. This is Dr. Phil Kent," he said, pointing to me. "He is with me. Hand me the first aid kit."

Bill took the kit, removed some bandages, and spoke to Yates. "I need to clean this wound first. We heard a gunshot, investigated it, and then saw you hanging from the cliff. What happened?" As he asked the question, he soaked a sterile pad with alcohol and placed it on her forehead; she flinched as he applied pressure. "I'm sorry; I'll try to be gentle, but I have to get this blood out and it looks like you've got some rock fragments stuck in there as well." After a minute, he removed the top from some antibiotic medicine and squeezed some cream on a sterile pad and patted the bloody wound over her left eye.

As he continued to dress the wound, she began talking. "I'm a paleontologist and I have a crew—mostly volunteers—working a dig site not far from here. I left them last night to make a run to pick up some supplies. On my way back, I got an SOS message from one of the workers, alerting me that someone was in the camp. When I returned, I saw smoke coming from our campsite. I left my car to sneak up to the camp. As I got to the site, I noticed some strange men. I stopped to watch them, but they saw me and chased me to the top of the ridge. I was trapped so I tied my rope off and started down the cliff. About halfway down, they spotted me and fired at me. The shot missed me but a chunk of rock splintered off from the cliff and hit me in the head." She pointed to the wound. "I had nowhere to hide so I decided to play like I was hit from the bullet and lay out dangling at the end of the rope. They watched me a minute and then left. I thought they had come back when you lowered yourself to me."

"I guess you did." Lander rubbed his cheek and I noticed the fresh patch of red under his right eye.

"I'm sorry I hit you when you grabbed my shoulder," she said. "I thought you were there to finish me off."

She started to stand and said, "I've got to go check on my crew." As she stood, she swayed and looked as if she were going to pass out.

"Hold it! Not so fast there. You took a pretty good blow to that head," Lander said. "Where is this camp of yours? We'll go with you to check it out."

She looked at Lander and said, "I heard a couple more shots. They sounded like the same rifle that had fired at me. Do you know what they were shooting at?"

Lander nodded. "Yes, they were shooting at us. But as you can see, they missed. Now, let's check your site out."

"I don't want to get you involved; you've done enough already by rescuing me. I knew my rope was not long enough to get to the bottom. I intended to climb back to the top after they left, but I'm not sure I could have done that after the injury. Not good rock-climbing technique; however, I was desperate. And, as we know, desperation sometimes overrules logic. It's a good thing you happened along when you did; you undoubtedly saved my life."

"We're going with you. We've got good horses. You can double with me—that way, I can help support you if you are still dizzy." Lander stood and held his hand out to help steady her. "We'll take it easy so you don't get bounced around too much."

"My Jeep is just a short distance from the top. They boxed me in so I left my car and ran. I couldn't get back to the car so I tried to escape down the cliff."

Lander looked at me, then back to her. "We'll go check your car out first. It'll be easier on you than our horses." I began collecting the first aid supplies and put them back in the kit, which I then returned to one of the saddlebags on my horse.

Lander led the way up back up the slope. A couple of times, I saw Yates lean to the side and realized that had Lander not been right behind her with his arms around her to support her, she would have fallen from the horse. We found the car right where Yates said it was. It was a four-door Jeep Wrangler and at first sight looked to be in good shape. However, as we approached it, we saw that both rear tires were flat. I stepped to the ground and moved closer to it. "They've been sliced," I said, pointing to the cuts along the outside tire. "We'll have to use the horses to get to camp."

"Hurry," said Yates. "I don't have a good feeling about this."

I quickly climbed back onto my horse and we began to trot toward the site. Fortunately, Yates was starting to feel better now. We followed her directions and after about twenty minutes, she said, "The camp is just over this next hill."

It was eerily quiet as we guided our horses into the camp. We dismounted and watched Yates run into one of the tents. We followed and saw her drop to her knees and cry out.

Chapter 3

The driver turned his Range Rover off the road onto an old, abandoned fire trail. He eased it through the trees, scraping the sides of the vehicle with bushes and low-hanging limbs. Though the car was decades old and looked fragile, it had a new, powerful, eight-cylinder engine mated with a six-speed manual four-wheel drive transmission and could navigate the toughest terrain with hardly a strain. With its rough exterior, the occupants didn't worry about new scratches.

"We'll hole up in the cave for a few days; everyone around will be looking for us within the hour," Takeshi said, looking over at Tynaka. "I wish you hadn't used the rifle; that shot called attention to us, a lot worse than a call for help from the woman. Those two men were close to seeing us."

"How was I to know that there was anyone around? We didn't need to let her get away—she saw us and could identify us."

"Like the others couldn't?" spat out Takeshi.

"She won't be able to ID us now. I saw her head bleeding after I shot her. Even if she survived the bullet, she will bleed out before anyone can get to her." Tynaka refused to meet Takeshi's eyes as he spoke this. "The two campers didn't see us; my shots at them probably scared them out of the state."

"You'd better hope so. The Man will not be happy about this."

"He doesn't have to know, does he?" Tynaka looked at Takeshi anxiously.

Takeshi pulled the car behind some trees and shut off the engine. "Oh, he will know all right—even if I don't tell him. He has inside information to everything." He opened the door and said, "Let's go. Get everything out of the car—we'll leave it and walk from here."

When Tynaka started to lift out the covered package, Takeshi stopped him. "Leave that—I'll take it. You get the bags." Takeshi moved the package to a spot in front of the car and laid it carefully down on the ground. "Let's get the car covered."

He pulled the camouflage tarp from the cargo area of the car, then started to lock the doors, and paused. "Here, take these wipes and clean the inside of the car—don't leave a spot of anything; when you finish, carry the wipes with us," he directed Tynaka. When they completed the wiping of the car, Takeshi said, "Lock the doors and grab the tarp." They secured the covering to the front of the car, and spread it over the back. Takeshi took the remaining bungee cords, pulled the tarp tight, and tied it down to the back bumper of the car. "There! That should keep it out of sight unless someone just happens directly on it." He looked around, picked up the package, and motioned to Tynaka. "Follow me—and keep quiet. Step on leaves so you don't leave footprints."

The two men carefully and slowly made their way up the slope, stopping every few minutes to look around and listen for any evidence that they were being followed. The forest was quiet this time of day and the eerie silence noticeably bothered Tynaka. "It's like a tomb in here—it's scary."

Takeshi just stared at him and shook his head dismissively. "I told you to keep quiet. Sound travels and no telling who's close by. I would have thought that was a lesson you learned back there."

Tynaka hissed back. "I don't know why you are so upset. We got away, didn't we?"

"Shut up and walk!"

After forty-five minutes, Takeshi stopped in front of a rock bluff and pushed aside a large dense limb, revealing an opening in the stone wall. "Take our bags on back out of sight of the opening here. I need to make a call; then I'll join you."

He waited until Tynaka had disappeared and then powered up his SAT phone. He was glad he had invested in the satellite phone when the attack here in the mountains was planned. There were many areas where cell reception was non-existent. When he had connected his call, the first words he heard placed a knot in his stomach, "Why did you fire shots? And you didn't even make them count. You let people escape that can identify you!" He remained quiet through the pause on the other end. Then The Man continued, "The whole project may now be compromised. Did you at least get out with the package?"

Takeshi knew better than to question him. He had told Tynaka that The Man would know what had happened, but even he was surprised at how quickly that had happened. "I'm sorry about the shots. Tynaka panicked when the woman tried to escape down the cliff." He told The Man about the raid and their chase of Yates. He didn't mention the other shots at the two campers. "We got the package and it's safe with us. We're now at the hiding place; we'll stay here a couple of days while they look for us. They will expect us to be fleeing so they won't look for us holed up here in their backyard. Is our evacuation still on schedule?"

"Yes, be at the pickup spot in two days—at 9:30 a.m. Take care of the other matter and don't be late!"

Takeshi understood the implications; he didn't need to ask what the "or else" was, so he simply replied, "I'll be there." He ended the call, powered down the phone, and picked up the package. He looked around one last time and pulled the limb back over the opening. Using a small penlight, he made his way through the tunnel to where Tynaka was waiting for him.

"Grab that," Takeshi said, shining his light at the dead raccoon he had planted there a few days ago. "Take it to the back and drop it in the hole. We don't want any critters looking for an easy meal while we are here."

Tynaka replied, "Yeah, and we don't want the smell, either."

Takeshi followed Tynaka, easing the Ranger knife out of his pocket. As Tynaka tossed the raccoon over the edge, Takeshi silently opened the blade, reached around Tynaka, and, with one quick slice, severed his throat. An easy nudge and Tynaka quietly chased the dead animal down the hole. Takeshi cleaned his knife with a rag from his pocket, closed it, and placed it back in his jeans. "You won't make any more mistakes," he said, and a slight hint of a smile crossed his face. He peeled the facemask off and tossed it down the dark crevice . . . and Takeshi was no more.

Chapter 4

Yates said, "This is fresh blood," pointing at the dried spot on the tent floor. "It wasn't here yesterday.

"Are you sure?" I asked.

Yates' eyes flashed at me. "Of course, I'm sure. I've spent a life working with blood and evidence."

I thought, *Hmmm. What is your background? You don't deal with a lot of blood just digging up bones and fossils.*

I said, "I'm sorry—I didn't mean to insult you. What time did you get the message?"

"Five-thirty—almost five hours ago."

Lander interrupted us. "I've called the ranger; he should be here in about an hour. In the meantime, let's see if we can find your crew and figure out what happened here. What about the other tent? Is anyone in there?"

"Oh, my God! Dr. Smith! After I saw the blood here, I didn't even think about him." She was already moving as she spoke. Lander and I had to run to keep up with her.

We followed her into the tent. On the floor was the still body of a man, lying face down. Yates kneeled beside him and pressed her fingers to his neck. "He's unconscious but he has a pulse!"

Lander dropped to his knees and gently turned Smith over. He pointed and said, "He's been shot."

I looked at the circle of blood on his shirt and shuddered. "He was shot in the chest. Do you think the bullet hit his heart or lungs?"

"No, I don't think so. If it had hit his heart, he would be dead; if it had entered his lungs, he would be bubbling out blood every time he exhaled. But we have to get him to a hospital ASAP." As we watched, Smith moaned and tried to raise his head.

Yates pushed his head back down and said, "I'm here, Dr. Smith. Stay still. Help is on the way. Can you tell us what happened?"

We all strained to hear him as he muttered something. Yates bent closer as he spoke again. "Water," he whispered.

I looked around and spied a portable water cooler with paper cups sitting beside it. I filled one of the cups and handed it to Yates, who carefully tilted the cup so Smith could drink. After a couple of sips, he began to talk again—this time a little stronger. Even so, we had to bend close to him to understand. "I was sleeping when they came in; there were two of them. They were looking for you—or at least your computer. They were going to tie me up when we heard the girls running.

When the men started to go after them, I tried to stop them; that's when one of them shot me."

"Did the girls get away?" asked Yates.

"I don't know; I heard another shot, but then I must have passed out. That's the last thing I remember until just now when you all came in."

I looked at Yates and said, "Stay here with him; Bill and I will see if we can find the girls." I held out my Glock to her as I said, "Do you know how to use this?"

She stood to her feet and walked over to a locked cabinet in the corner of the tent. After spinning the combination, she opened the safe door. Coming back to us, she inserted the magazine and held out a Glock 21 for us to see. "I'm quite sure I know how to use one. I don't need yours—go see if you can find the girls."

Lander and I went outside. We started our search, walking around the tents in expanding circles, looking for any sign of the girls. On our third loop, we saw footprints and quickly followed them, both of us now holding our handguns. Behind a stand of trees, we spotted one of the girls lying face down in a pool of blood. We hurried to her and, while Lander checked her out, I searched the surrounding area for the other girl. Seeing nothing, I went back to Lander.

He looked up at me. "She's in bad shape—barely has a pulse. Go back to see if there is any kind of stretcher or a backboard of some type. I'll stay with her until you get back. But hurry!" I could tell from Bill's voice that her chances of surviving were not good.

I ran back to the tent. "We found one girl, shot and in bad shape. Do you have anything we can transport her on?"

Yates looked up at me with tears in her eyes. There's a board that we use to clean bones on; it's standing over there against that wall. For the first time, I saw a hint of weakness in her as she said, "Please bring her back alive."

I grabbed the board and ran back to the wounded girl. Lander looked at me and said, "She's hanging on, barely. She's still unconscious. I called the ranger again; he's getting a helicopter with medical personnel here to evacuate both victims. Let's get her on the board and back to the tent. She was shot in the back trying to get away. There's no sign of the other girl." We carefully lifted the girl onto the board and carried her back to the shelter.

"That's Shannon," said Dr. Yates, as we placed the board on the floor of the tent. "How is she?"

Lander replied, "She's in bad shape. A medevac helicopter is on its way. We'll try to keep her stabilized until help arrives. I field-dressed the wound while Kent came after the board. The bleeding has stopped, but she lost a lot of blood before we found her. Get something to keep her warm. I wish we had something to give her."

"We keep an extensive assortment of medical and emergency supplies," Yates said. "Being this isolated for a long period of time, we never know when someone may get injured." She went to the cabinet and retrieved the implements. "I studied Pre-med in undergrad school, so I try to be prepared for just about anything."

That answers my question about her background with blood, I thought.

In five minutes, she had an IV line started, bloody clothes removed, and a clean compress bandage pressed to the wound. "That's all we can do for her now. Did you see any evidence of the other girl?"

I answered her. "No, we lost the footprints in the woods. The good news is that I saw no other blood anywhere. Do you have any idea where she would have gone if she escaped the men?"

She surprised me with her answer. "Yes, I know exactly where she is if she got away from them." We looked up as we heard the car slide to a stop outside the tent. Doors opened, then someone yelled.

"Hello; is anyone here? If so, come out with hands up!"

We moved to the tent door. Lander leaned out with his hands visible as he called, "Ranger, we are coming out. I'm the one who called you. We have two injured persons in here that need immediate transport to the hospital." He walked up to the officer and continued. "Both have been shot. One has a chest wound with no evidence of vital organ injury; bleeding is stopped and he's conscious. A girl was shot in the back and lost a lot of blood before we got to her. She's unresponsive and barely has a pulse. We have the bleeding controlled and have an IV in her. She needs blood quickly."

The ranger triggered his radio and provided the information to his regional office. "They will contact the medevac and update them on the situation." He looked around and said, "That clearing may be big enough for the helo to land." He moved to the center of it, checked his instrument, and called out the GPS coordinates to his office. "That will save them time getting here," he said. "By the way, I am Tyler McKenzie."

We introduced ourselves to him and went back into the tent. Yates looked up and said, "They're the same. Still no sign of life from Shannon except the rapid, weak pulse." We looked at the pale girl struggling to breath. Yates continued, "Shannon's young and tough. She's gone through a lot in her young life and has a strong will; she'll pull through this."

While we waited for help to arrive, we filled the Ranger in on what had happened. In about ten minutes, we heard the thump, thump of the helicopter. McKenzie, Lander, and I went out to meet it. It landed in a swirl of dust and we watched as two men hit the ground running. Another man carrying a medical kit followed them. "Where are they?" shouted one. McKenzie pointed to the tent and two of the men rushed in.

The other came to us and introduced himself. "I'm Sheriff Jay Spencer. When I heard there was a shooting, I hitched a ride. What's going on?"

Ranger McKenzie answered him. "No time for the whole story right now. We have two gunshot victims and another young girl missing. We need to begin a search for her; there's a lot of territory to cover."

"Do we know who's responsible for the shootings?"

"No, all we know is that there were two men. The male vic said he thought they were foreigners. He heard one name but couldn't understand it clearly. He said it sounded like TieNoka."

One of the medics came running from the tent and entered the helicopter. In seconds, he jumped back to the ground carrying a backboard. We watched him reenter the tent.

Lander spoke up. "We may need to help them carry the injured to the helo," he said, moving toward the tent. McKenzie and I followed him. By the time we got inside, the medics had the wounded ready to go. Lander helped one of the medics and I assisted the other. Within three minutes, Smith and Shannon were secured in the passenger area. The pilot spun the rotors and the helicopter lifted off the ground.

I looked at Yates. "You said you knew where the other girl—her name was Kim, I think—would have gone. Can you get us there?"

"Yes, but we'll have to go on foot. Follow me." Before we could say anything, she looked at her phone and then she was dashing toward the trees where we had found Shannon. The rest of us looked at each other, nodded, and hurried to catch up to her.

Lander grabbed her arm and said, "Remember, there are armed gunmen out here, so we have to use some caution in our approach. You give directions and one of us will lead."

As he spoke, McKenzie pulled his handgun and moved to the front. "You tell me which way to go and stay back. These are my woods and I don't want any more bloodshed—unless it's the bad guys."

As we passed the spot where Shannon had fallen, I saw Yates look briefly at the bloodstains. The look on her face was intense, not of fear, but of anger and stoic reserve. "This is one tough lady," I thought. She directed us through dense undergrowth and paused at a rockslide, a group of huge boulders that had obviously fallen from the cliff before us.

Yates walked around one of the rocks and spoke in a low voice. "Kim, are you here?" She listened a minute and repeated the question. "Kim, are you here? It's safe to come out."

We heard a shaky voice say, "Dr. Yates, is that you?"

"Yes, are you able to come out?"

We watched as the young girl carrying a red hoodie emerged from the rocks and grabbed Yates. They held to each other for a minute before Kim asked, "What about Shannon and Dr. Smith? Are they okay?"

Yates lowered her head and replied, "Both of them were shot, but are still alive. They have been taken to a hospital. I'm sure both will be okay." She looked at us as she spoke, daring us to contradict her.

McKenzie spoke up, "Do you have any injuries? Are you okay?"

"I'm fine. I have a scratch on my wrist where I cut it getting loose. Thank goodness that man wasn't very good at tying me up." She looked at Yates and continued, "All that practice and the escape drills really paid off. Thank you!"

We looked at Yates, waiting for her to explain what Kim meant. She just nodded and said, "Let's get back to camp and check the damage; then we'll talk about all this."

Chapter 5

We made our way back to the dig site and entered the main tent. Although the medevac was on the way to the hospital we all shared a concern about the colleagues of Yates. Their chance at survival was iffy at best, especially Shannon. But one thing we did know for sure—we had a long sleepless time ahead of us, time filled with worry. When I noticed that Lander wasn't with us, I found him at the center of camp at the fire pit building a fire. "You plan on roasting marshmallows?" I asked.

"I don't eat that crap! And neither should you if you plan on keeping up with me, but since we can't go to the hospital until tomorrow and we won't be getting any rest, I figured it was a good time to make some strong coffee and do some serious collaborating and maybe come up with some answers—or at least some good questions."

I noted the anxiousness in his voice . . . so I began my quest for coffee.

Sipping the black coffee, we gathered back at the main tent. I glanced at Lander. "A little strong, don't you think? This could stand up on its own."

"Don't be a wimp. You're just used to that watered-down flavored stuff. When you make real coffee over a campfire, it's going to be strong—that's the way coffee is meant to be."

Dr. Yates retrieved some foldout chairs and we sat down. Sheriff Spencer said, "Okay, tell me what happened from the beginning."

McKenzie interrupted him. "Hold on a minute. Let me contact the office. We need to get some help out here to find those shooters." He went outside to make the call. After a couple of minutes, he returned. "Help is on the way. Now, let's see if we can determine what is going on. Dr. Yates, do you want to start?"

"As Ranger McKenzie knows, we are here because of a recent discovery of bones, quite possibly those of ancient dinosaurs."

Spencer asked, "Are you an archaeologist?"

"Actually, I am a paleontologist and am . . . "

"What's the difference in an archaeologist and a paleontologist?" I interrupted.

"An archaeologist is a person who studies past human culture and behavior; it includes analyzing human fossils and man-made materials from the past, things like tools and buildings. A paleontologist is a person who studies fossils, whether they are human, animals, or plants."

I replied, "So, I assume that since you are here with animal bones, you specialize in animal fossils?"

"Yes, to be more specific, my study is focused on the fossils of dinosaurs. At one time, I intended to be an archaeologist. I'm still fascinated by studying the way people used to live, especially ancient cultures that may have been as advanced as we are in many ways. But when I visited a dig site of a dinosaur, I was hooked."

"What about Dr. Smith?" asked Spencer. "Is he an archaeologist or a paleontologist?"

"Well, he is neither. He is an anthropologist. That means he studies human culture and behavior, past to the present."

I looked at Lander, who seemed as perplexed as I was.

"What's an anthropologist doing working with a scientist who studies dinosaur fossils? I wouldn't think those studies are typically connected, are they?" I asked.

Yates looked at me a minute before answering. I wondered about the hesitation and thought, *Was she unsure of us or debating about what and how much she should share with us?*

My feeling was proved right when she said, "First, tell me who you are."

"That's a fair question." I pointed to Bill. "This is Bill Lander. He's a retired SEAL who is now teaching North American Studies at a college in our hometown. We went to school there and played basketball together. After school, he joined the service and ended up in Special Forces. I went into education, taught and coached a few years, then retired after being a principal the last half of that life. Now I teach online courses and write novels."

"What are you all doing out here in Colorado?" asked Spencer.

Lander answered him, "We're on a working vacation. We spend a week each year in a different part of the country. I get information for my classes and also help Phil with survival techniques that he utilizes in his stories."

Yates considered this, came to a decision, and then answered the earlier question. "You're right. The two areas of study are not commonly related. However, this site—and it's supposed to be pretty secret at this point—may well prove to be an exceptional find. I must insist that any information I share with you remains away from the media." She looked at us expectantly.

We all nodded. I had no desire to see the story in print and I'm sure the others agreed with me. Besides, at some point in the future, I may get permission to include it in a new story.

Seeing our agreement, she continued. "We found evidence that the area may have been a settlement for the early Anasazi. Although most people think only the Fremont settled here, Dr. Smith is finding all sorts of artifacts that point to the Anasazi."

I said, "I've heard of the Anasazi, but I'm not sure who the Fremont were."

Lander spoke up. "The Fremont were an ancient tribe, somewhat like the Anasazi. They lived in caves and created villages and, although they did some hunting, they were mostly farmers. I think they grew about three different types of corn. They didn't build the elaborate structures that the Anasazi did."

Yates nodded and continued, "As I was saying, in addition to clues pointing to the Anasazi, fossilized bones of animals were discovered— bones that at least initially point to being an Epanterias."

"What's an Epanterias? I've never heard of it." McKenzie expressed my thoughts.

"An Epanterias is an extremely rare dinosaur—a giant, ugly beast that roamed North America one hundred thirty million years ago. It had jaws that operated like those of modern snakes and was so large and powerful that it could swallow a fourteen-hundred-pound dinosaur in a single gulp." She was animated and her eyes glowed as she talked about her passion.

"The Monster of Masonville," interjected Lander. "If I remember my facts correctly, it was only the third Epanterias ever found."

Yates looked at him with surprise before she replied. "This will be the fourth, if it proves out. These monsters grew to be over fifty feet long; it's estimated one Epanterias would eat about forty tons of meat every year."

Lander said to me, "That's almost as much meat as you eat." He was always after me to cut down on my intake of red meat. He turned back to Yates and said, "I certainly want to fully discuss this with you more at some point, but we need to see what was taken from the site." He looked at Ranger McKenzie and Sheriff Spencer as he said this. "What about the two girls? Why are they here?"

"Both of them are working on their doctorates and are fellows through the University of Colorado. Dr. Smith and I are funded through a grant from the National Science Foundation. Follow me; we'll see if anything was taken. Dr. Smith said they wanted my computer, but it was locked with a cable in the Jeep. We'll need to check that out. I should have thought to look earlier when we were there." She got up and moved to the exit and we followed.

Yates led the way out of the tent. "We'll check the dig site. There's really nothing of value except some tools and supplies in the tents." She picked her way down the excavation and led us to the west slope. "Over here are the bones we have been clearing," she said as she pointed. Suddenly, she paused. "Oh, no!" she exclaimed.

We looked at the spot where she had pointed. Even to us, we could tell it was a disaster. There were bone fragments all over the area, with almost nothing left intact. Yates picked up a piece of bone and looked closely at it. "This has been sawed. You can still see the pattern from the cut." She handed it to me and walked away, looking at other pieces. She collected a couple more fragments that she said also showed the telltale marks of a saw. "Why would they do this?" she said. "They could have stolen the bones and sold them for mega bucks."

"Maybe they only wanted samples of the bones," said Lander.

"That's what it looks like, but I'm not sure why," said Yates. "I would think it was just stupid kids vandalizing if it weren't for the saw marks on the bones. But it wasn't and we *will* find out who it was and why they did it." She slapped her fist into her hand and I could see the fire in her eyes.

A quick circle of the remainder of the excavation revealed the same reckless regard for ancient treasures; almost all pieces had been shattered. The scientist stopped and picked up a piece of pottery. "This was a complete vase, one of the few that had ever been found in one piece. Dr. Smith will be devastated." Yates shook her head sadly. "The only good thing is that we had really just begun and, hopefully, there will be additional bones and artifacts discovered as we dig deeper."

We made our way back to the pavilion. McKenzie outlined a plan and agreed that his department and that of the sheriff would share as lead investigators. As that decision was voiced, I thought of something. "What did Kim mean when she thanked you for the disaster drills?" I looked at Yates for the answer.

She said, "I got a warning a few days ago to be on the alert for trouble; another site—one in northwestern Colorado—was attacked last week. No one survived and it seemed as if all was destroyed."

"Maybe they need to go back to determine if a portion of a bone was taken there also. Was it the same type dinosaur?" Lander asked.

"No, this was an excavation of another animal, almost as rare. In fact, it is considered more exotic than a dinosaur."

"You were telling us about the preparation for trouble," Spencer said.

Yates started to reply, but it was Kim who spoke first. "Dr. Yates had told us about the other attack and warned that we could also have one. She set up some procedures in case something happened and made us practice them. If she were away and someone strange entered the site, one of us was to use the new phone app that sends an SOS and shows the coordinates for the sender."

Yates spoke up. "If Shannon had not sent that message, I would have just driven into camp and most probably would have been killed."

Kim continued, "We also had found a hiding place a short distance away. If we were attacked, we were supposed to get to that spot and wait for help. She also stressed that if one of us went down, the other was to keep going so that we all would not be captured. That's why I left Shannon; maybe I should have tried to carry her to safety."

Lander said, "If you had tried that, then both of you would have been hurt and quite possibly dead now." Kim shuddered at that realization.

McKenzie entered the conversation. "Those plans obviously kept this from being a multiple-murder investigation. We need to check your car, then get all of you to safety."

"I'll check the car, but then I'll come back here," Yates said. "I still need to secure this site." She looked at Kim and added, "You can ride to town with the sheriff."

Kim replied, "No way; if you are staying, then I am here with you."

Spencer said, "It's not safe for you to stay here without protection."

I spoke up, looking at Lander, "We'll stay here at the site with them until reinforcements arrive."

Lander focused his eyes on me. "What have you gotten me into?" Then, seeing the distressed look on Yates' face, he continued. "Private joke. Of course, we will stay here. We're both armed."

"So is Yates," I said. "We should be fine. We'll go back to the car and check for the computer, then come back here."

"You'd better check in with your grant director to let him know what has happened," said Spencer.

"Let *her* know what happened," corrected Yates. "I'll call Dr. Pasternak right away."

Chapter 6

We took McKenzie's Grand Cherokee to find Yates' Jeep. As soon as Yates opened the door, she said, "They cut the cable—the computer's gone!"

"How destructive is that to your program?" I asked. "Do you have backups?"

She smiled and said, "Of course. I have a backup on this. She grasped the necklace around her neck and pulled a flash drive from underneath her sweatshirt. Unfortunately, the only other site for the data is on the computer. Thank God, it is encrypted. We did not use a site in the cloud; we felt it was too susceptible to hacking." She then pulled her phone from her pocket, powered it on, and clicked a couple of keys. "There! That will erase everything on the computer as soon as it is powered on."

"Wow, this lady is good!" said Spencer. "We'll take you back to the site and call someone to replace your tires." He took a pen and a small notebook and bent down by one of the tires. "I have the tire size; you'll have new ones by tonight."

"I appreciate that, Sheriff."

"Can you run by our camp site so we can get our gear? There's a trail about three hundred yards from our camp," said Lander. "It's not far out of the way."

"Be glad to," replied McKenzie.

After McKenzie dropped us off at the dig site, Yates said, "Let's find something to eat first; then we'll talk."

I suddenly realized how long it had been since Lander and I had eaten. We had sausage, eggs, and hash browns cooked on the portable camp stove and I thought, *This is one of the best meals I have had in a long time.* For some reason, food always tastes better in the outdoors.

After eating, we spent an hour trying to salvage bones and artifacts. When we had cleaned up what we could, we went back to the tent and sat down. "Who discovered this site?" asked Lander.

"This whole area of the state is known as the Morrison Formation and runs from Colorado's Front Range deep through the southwest of Colorado. It is an area rich in fossilized remains. When Shannon was doing research for her dissertation, she ran across a discarded document that claimed that an old prospector had come back to town talking about giant bones he had seen. I am the chairman of her dissertation committee, so she told me about the claim. I ultimately discovered the location and did a preliminary inspection of the site. Encouraged by what I found, we began the process of finding funding for the excavation. It took us a year and a half to get all the pieces in place and we came back to the site two months ago. The most difficult part of the process was keeping the location secret."

"How many people know where the site is?" I asked.

"The grant coordinator, of course, Dr. Pasternak. She is really the only one that should know the exact location. Kim and Shannon were approved to work with Dr. Smith and me on an excavation project; they didn't have to provide exact location details. Oh, and Ranger McKenzie knew where we were. I guess that someone else could have tracked us here, but I'm the only one who has left the site since we've been here and I've been really careful to see that no one has followed me back here."

"What about the other site? Was it also a secret excavation?" Lander was following my lead in trying to pin down possible leaks to the project.

"I'm sure it should have been held close to the vest, at least until something substantial was unearthed. It was also an NSF project."

I asked, "Would Dr. Pasternak have been involved in that one, also?"

Yates thought about that briefly and then answered, "I'm not sure, but probably. I think she is in charge of all NSF excavation grants."

Lander replied, "Okay. We'll keep that under our hat for now. Talk to me about the Epanterias. I'm fascinated with the stories of giants, both human and animal."

I agreed completely with Lander and added, "That's really why we chose Colorado for our trip this year. We wanted to explore tales of the many giants that allegedly inhabited this part of the country—well, giants and the elusive Dutchman's Gold Mine."

"So, you plan to visit Superstition Mountains?" Kim stated it as a question.

"Yes, we are supposed to meet my wife in a couple of days over at Durango. We plan to ride the Durango/Silverton Narrow Gauge Railway, explore the area for a few days and then fly to Phoenix to check the Superstition Mountains out."

Yates looked at me. "Is she still in Tennessee?"

"No . . . but wait a minute. Did I tell you we are from Tennessee?"

"No, you didn't have to. I can pick that Tennessee sound out anywhere."

"I didn't realize my accent was that obvious." I saw both Yates and Kim smile at that. "Cyndi—that's my wife—grew up in southern California and moved away several years ago. Recently, she reconnected with her high school buddies on Facebook. They call themselves the Bond Sisters and they have gotten together a few times since. They are in Oregon now where one of the group lives."

Kim said, "She'd be worried about you if she knew what is happening here."

Lander laughed. "I don't think so. In fact, she would be surprised if we were together on a trip for a couple of days and nothing happened. Kent gets me into something pretty regularly."

"I guess so," I said. "We had a good time in Nova Scotia last year. The outcome was good, but it sure had the potential to be a disaster. So, I guess the training comes in handy for real life as well as in my novels; I'm more motivated now to learn the practical skills as well as the knowledge of them."

"I'll have to read the story. I'm sure you wrote about it in a novel," said Yates.

I smiled. I saw it wasn't necessary to confirm her statement.

Lander said, "The adventures he wrote about in *Comes the Awakening* served as a wakeup call for him. He *is* working harder developing his survival abilities and self-defense skills now. That's good-—I'm getting tired of carrying him . . . Okay, enough chitchat. Tell me about the Epanterias."

For the next hour, we talked about the giant dinosaur and even discussed the implications of the Anasazi being in this site. They were always thought to be neighbors to the Fremont in this section, but no one had ever placed them here. Lander said, "So, if these artifacts did belong to the Anasazi, it would be the first that proved they had inhabited this area?"

Yates replied, "Well, it's a little more complex than that. If we find only pottery shards, then we can't be sure that the Anasazi lived here. The Fremont may have traded for the items. We know—and are finding more evidence each year—that those ancient tribes participated in trade with others."

I enjoyed listening to an expert discuss her work and I knew that Lander was thrilled with the information.

After we settled in for the night, I lay awake for a long time, relaxing to the noises of the night woods and listening for the sounds of the attackers returning. We had discussed the need to rotate guard duty for the night, but Lander had convinced us that the men would not return. I believed him, but I still slept with my hand on my Glock and one eye open.

Chapter 7

He looked carefully out through the brush pulled against the opening. The day was breaking on what promised to be a bright, sunny day. He had slept well and heard no sound during the night. He glanced at his watch and moved out of the cave. Powering up the SAT phone again, he stood silently as he waited for the expected call. As soon as it buzzed, he answered, "Anything I should know?" he asked.

He could barely hear the reply. "There will be a manhunt today for you—rangers and sheriff deputies. You have to either stay completely hidden or get away from the area before they get started."

"What time will the search get underway?" he asked. He listened and replied, "That soon? It doesn't give me much time." He ended the call abruptly.

He then dialed another number. The Man answered almost immediately. He told him what he had just learned and listened a minute. "Yes Sir," he said and heard the connection end.

Plans had changed and he had only an hour to get to the extraction point; he quickly gathered his things. Within five minutes, he was leaving the cave and moving north. Frequently watching the GPS on his phone, he followed the directions. After thirty minutes, he heard the helicopter as it descended and he picked up his pace. Although The Man had told him that if he were late, the pilot would not wait for him, he knew he possessed the package that The Man had to have. He grinned to himself, knowing that, at least for the minute, he was in control.

He looked around carefully before he stepped into the clearing. He gazed up and watched the cable descend toward him. As soon as he could reach it, he grabbed hold and signaled the pilot. Immediately, the cable lifted him to the skid outside the open cargo area. The hand clasped his jacket and jerked him inside as the craft banked and lifted quickly away from the trees. He leaned back against the seat and relaxed. He was home free now!

Chapter 8

I looked at my vibrating iPhone and watched a message from McKenzie come in. I read it and looked at the others. "A manhunt will get underway in two hours. The men are gathering at the fire tower about a mile from here. If we want to go with them, we can meet them there."

Lander said, "Let's eat first; then we'll decide if we need to go."

As he spoke, Kim stood and said, "I'll be right back. I've got to go to the little girls' room."

After a breakfast of fried pancakes with syrup, the group sat drinking the last of the coffee. True to his word, the sheriff had sent help and had replacement tires on Yates' Jeep before dark last night. After getting a text message that relayed that information, Lander had left me with the ladies and hiked to retrieve the Jeep. He had returned to the camp about nine-thirty. Soon after that, we hit the sack; it had been a long day and we were all exhausted.

Lander looked as if he were going to say something, then cocked his head, and listened. Finally, I heard it—the unmistakable sound of a helicopter. We listened as it descended, paused, and then heard the sudden acceleration; in a few seconds, the sound had become a faint rhythm before it was completely silent. Lander said, "We won't find the men here; they just left. We might discover their vehicle and get some useful information from it, although I doubt it."

"Couldn't the helicopter be a part of the search team?" asked Yates.

Lander replied, "No. They wouldn't send in a helicopter until the men were in position to search. All it would do is send the shooters into hiding. That's the last thing they would want."

"If you're sure it's safe here now, do you think we need to join the search? From the sound of the helicopter, we at least know the direction to look for them." I posed the question while looking for a reaction from Yates and Kim.

Yates said, "We'll be fine. I have a weapon and am on high alert now. Take my Jeep and go find them."

Lander said, "I appreciate the offer of the Jeep, but I would rather go into the woods with our horses." He looked at me and said, "Let's get saddled up."

As we picked our way through the trees, we were now much more focused; our simulation had become a reality show! My senses had never been as acute. I could hear the least of sounds: the squirrel high up in the tree; the vibration of the leaves in the trees; the crunch of each footfall on the leaves. I could feel the slight breeze as it washed across the exposed areas of my skin. Every shadow stood out and I searched each one. Although it was not intentional, my thoughts cycled through each sense, looking carefully for anything out of the ordinary. In twenty minutes, we reached the fire tower. I noted that it was east of where we had heard the sound of the helicopter. The sheriff and McKenzie met us as we dismounted. Lander asked, "Did you have a search helicopter a little west of here an hour or so ago?"

"No, we didn't. We have one coming, but it will not be here until this afternoon. Why do you ask?" Spencer's answer did not surprise us.

I replied, "There was one that came in, hovered a minute, and then quickly moved out to the west. We think it picked up the shooters."

McKenzie thought a minute and then replied, "We can't be sure of that. We need to continue with the search."

Lander agreed with McKenzie. "At least we should find their car. Maybe they were careless and left something we can use to identify them. I estimate the helo was about three quarters of a mile to the west of here. That's where we need to start the hunt."

Spencer quickly agreed. "Let's spread out and move in that direction. If you see anything, use the radio I gave you to alert the others." He handed one to Lander and me. We quickly nudged our horses and moved out with everyone else close behind.

Chapter 9

The helicopter set down on the pad behind the house. Romonov hopped to the ground, carrying the package. He ducked his head under the still-spinning rotor blades and moved quickly to the back door of the home. The door opened before he got to it and a burly man held up his hands. "Stop right there; you know the drill."

"Popov, you should know me well enough by now to realize that I am not carrying anything when I come to see The Man."

"Perhaps it is because we know you so well that we need to check you. Now, put the package on the floor, spread your legs, and lean against the wall there." Popov waited until Romonov complied; he first ran his hands roughly over his body and then waved a wand over him to be sure he was carrying nothing electronic.

"I'm not stupid. I don't want anything to do with harming the person who pays me a great salary to perform a few minor tasks for him."

Popov ran the wand over the package lying on the floor, picked it up, and handed it over to Romonov. "He's waiting for you; you know the way."

Romonov entered the door and walked left down the hallway, portraying a confidence that he did not feel. He thought to himself, *I can't keep this up for long. The Man is too good; at some point, he will see through me.* He passed two additional guards before he came to the last door on the hall. He knocked and waited.

"Come in," came the gruff reply.

After opening the door with false swagger, Romonov entered the room. It was completely dark save for a faint glow; it gradually brightened and revealed the man who sat in the overstuffed leather chair. As Romonov approached him, an overhead spotlight came on. Romonov squinted at the sudden beam bathing him in a bright light. He looked at The Man, and, as was always the case, even though The Man was staring at him through a video monitor, Romonov was completely intimidated by him. A huge man with a shaved head and a mouth full of gold teeth stared back at him. Standing at six feet, four inches, he topped the scales at over three hundred pounds. But his size was the least of what scared Romonov. The Man was an accomplished Black Belt and could kill with one blow, a skill that Romonov knew he enjoyed. He knew this because he had seen him first hand do so with great gusto on more than one occasion.

"Let me see it." The deep bass seemed to resonate at a level almost undecipherable by Romonov.

Romonov carefully unwrapped the package and held the object out toward The Man. Romonov ventured to say, "It's just what you wanted—a six-inch piece of the femur; in good shape, I might add."

The big man said, "Turn the bone and let me look closely at it from different angles." Finally, he looked up and growled, "Yes, this is what I ordered. Did you take care of the other matter?"

"Yes, his body is at the bottom of the pit in the cave; he'll never be found."

"Can the ones you allowed to live identify you?" The Man's eyes bore into Romonov's as he waited for the answer.

"No, I wore a disguise. They think I am Japanese. I wore my mask and we let them 'accidentally' hear my name. Takeshi disappeared in the cave with his friend. The authorities are now looking for two Japanese men in the mountains."

After what seemed an eternity, Romonov heard the words he was waiting for. "You did well, my friend. Now, you must accomplish the next step. Take this and wrap it well enough to protect it against any threat. Collect the other items and then carefully divide each into three identical pieces. Pack each set into secure, waterproof, airproof containers. You must guard them with your life; they could very well be the most important items ever shipped . . . anywhere. One set must be delivered personally in five days to your contact in New York. You know where to take the other sets." A quick gesture with his hand and another man stepped from the shadows. He handed Romonov an envelope and a set of car keys. Romonov placed the envelope in his pocket without opening it. He knew it contained partial payment for the job and if he dared to check it for accuracy, he knew it would be his final act. Romonov watched the monitor fade to black and he turned without another word and retraced his steps to the car waiting for him. He placed the package in the trunk, covered it with a blanket, and locked the trunk. He sat in the driver's seat, exhaled deeply, and jabbed one fist into the other. "Yes!" he exclaimed.

Chapter 10

The men moved through the woods as silently as they could do so. Some were in Jeeps; some were on horseback; and others were on foot. It was slow going, as they wanted to be sure they overlooked no hiding place. After a couple of hours, Lander and Kent approached the area where they thought the getaway car was possibly hidden. McKenzie joined them, riding up close and saying, "If the men escaped in the helicopter, they would have had to leave their car someplace. How far from here do you think the helo was when it extracted them?"

Lander reined his horse to a stop and peered around. "I think we are less than a quarter of a mile from the pickup spot. We need to look for three places. The first is the spot where the car was left. It will probably be hidden a short distance off the road and covered with either brush or a camo tarp. For that reason, the search needs to be centered on the fire trail with searchers on both sides of the path."

Lander paused while the ranger gave directions over his radio. When he had finished, McKenzie asked, "What is the second spot?"

Lander replied, "The extraction point. It will be a clearing, not necessarily large enough for a helo to land, but clear enough that a pilot could drop a cable and pick the men up. Those two spots are the first ones we need to identify."

I looked at Lander and thought a minute before saying, "And the third spot would be where the men spent last night—right?"

"Yes, you *are* learning, aren't you? There may be hope for you after all," he said with a smile. "Where would you hide for the night if you didn't want to be seen?"

I considered the question before answering. "The most obvious place to sleep would be in the vehicle. If it were concealed enough, it could be safe to sleep in, but . . ." I paused, deep in thought.

"But . . . what?" asked Lander.

"I would want to get away from the car. A vehicle is much easier to track than a man on foot. As thick as the trees are here, a car would not be able to stray too far away from the trail. I would hide it and hike a distance away to spend the night."

"Then what would be your options?" continued Lander.

"They could have pitched a tent . . . or built a lean-to if they had no tent. Either one could be done quickly in relatively dense forest. Or, for that matter, I guess they could have just slept on the ground with blankets or sleeping bags."

McKenzie watched and listened to our banter with interest. It served not only as a teaching session, but it also was free-flow Q & A that made us consider all the options. I knew that there would be other follow-up questions.

"We'll consider those options, but first, let's see if we can find their vehicle. If we are on the right trail, it shouldn't be too far away from here."

About thirty minutes later, our radios squawked to life. "I have a car spotted off the right side of the road." We listened as he added the GPS coordinates. We set those in our phones and moved quickly toward the spot. We were almost on the car before we could see it. The camouflage covering was so good that it would never have been spotted from the air. No one had yet approached the car—they were waiting for directions from McKenzie or Spencer. McKenzie was with us and in just a moment, Spencer rode up and dismounted. They pulled their weapons and slowly moved to the vehicle. Spencer loosened the bungee cords at the rear and they gently tugged the covering to the front of the car. As they did, other rangers rushed in to cover the interior of the car in case someone was there.

"No one is here!" shouted Spencer. It was a statement that surprised no one. "Get the forensics team here ASAP." He put on a pair of gloves and tried the doors. "It's locked up tightly; no one touches anything."

I noticed Lander access his phone and confirm the coordinates for the spot, so I did the same. We grouped in the middle of the trail and circled around McKenzie and Spencer.

It was McKenzie who spoke first. "Good job, Men! There is no doubt that this is the getaway vehicle; it matches the description that Dr. Yates provided. Our next task is to track the men and. . . ."

Spencer interrupted him. "If the helicopter extracted them, maybe we need to search for that spot. It should be fairly easy to find a clearing that would allow that. McKenzie, do you have an updated topo map with you?"

"Yes, I do. It should identify cleared areas. Great idea, Sheriff." He reached into a pocket of his cargo pants and pulled out a map.

I suddenly remembered the map I had downloaded to my phone. "I have one—updated as of four days ago. I clicked the power button, waited while the phone booted, and then clicked the app." Lander gave me a thumbs-up.

The iPhone marked the spot where we were standing and I zoomed in to show the surrounding area. I handed the phone to McKenzie and said, "Here! You are more familiar with the region than I am."

He studied the map for a couple of minutes, dragging the map around to show adjacent areas.

Finally, he said, "It looks like there are about four spots within a two-mile radius that could allow a helicopter to either land or get close enough to winch a person aboard." He pointed them out to Spencer, who nodded agreement. "We'll split up and a team will take each one. Keep your radios on and stay alert. We're not one hundred percent sure that they have already gone. If you see any sign or hear anything at all, let us all know."

The next five minutes were spent dividing up into teams. The sheriff and his chief deputy took one each while McKenzie and another ranger each led another. The other members were chosen based on their mode of transportation, with the ones in vehicles assigned the furthest spot and the men on foot the closest location. Lander and I found ourselves with McKenzie again. Teams set out with another warning to be careful and to stay in communication.

Chapter 11

Our search team followed McKenzie on horseback. We had been assigned the far-western clearing to check out because it had no road or trail access to it; this was good because it was the spot that most closely approximated the area where we had heard the helicopter. The coordinates were marked on our phones and we negotiated our way through the trees in a slow but consistent manner, always on alert for sudden danger. According to the topo map, we had to move up and over three ridges and cross two streams to get to the possible extraction point.

After an hour of riding with no incidents, we paused on the top of the last ridge and looked down at the clearing. We still couldn't see anything helpful from this distance so we picked our way down the hill and rode up to the spot. We stopped, dismounted, and tied our horses to the trees that outlined the clearing. Seeing no one around, we entered the area. After a minute, Lander held his hand up in the universal stop signal and said, "Someone was here recently and left some nice footprints behind."

We all looked at where he pointed and saw the faint outline of boot prints. Peering closer, I said, "Why do I see only one set of prints? Shouldn't there be two?"

"Good question. We know there were two men involved in the attack." Lander followed this with another question, "What are the possible scenarios that would fit this clue?"

McKenzie said, "Maybe they had split up and approached the extraction from different points. Let's do a circle of the area. Maybe we'll find the other set."

Lander replied, "Good idea. But keep your eyes open. It's possible that the second man failed to make the pickup and is still hiding in the area." We pulled our weapons and made sure they were ready; then we began the walk around the clearing, staying at the edge of the trees. We returned to our starting point without seeing any additional tracks.

"Let's follow the tracks," Lander said. "They will go to the center of the clearing and then disappear."

McKenzie spoke to the other ranger, "Rick, stay here and cover us. We'll be out in the open and we still don't know where the other man is."

We followed the prints, looking for any other clue. Just as Lander had predicted, the prints ended at about the center of the clearing. We paused there and looked around. Lander said, "This is the extraction point. If you look carefully, you can see the grass lying over from the rotor blade wash of the helicopter." We looked at the area to which he was pointing.

"Only one man made the pickup," Lander said. Looking at me, he continued, "Why would only one of the two men be here?"

I stood still a minute, thinking while the other men watched me. "Well, it could be a number of things. Maybe he was supposed to hide out until the search was over and then retrieve their car. What about that?"

"If this were the act of an impulsive robbery attempt, then I could buy that," said Lander.

"What do you mean?" asked McKenzie.

"This whole operation has the earmarks of a well-planned project. It wasn't just a coincidence that those men happened on a chance to commit a robbery. Phil, what are the clues that point to a planned attack?"

Lander was determined to get me to thinking like a SEAL and, for that, I was thankful. "For one thing, the perps"—(yeah, I actually said perps)—"knew where the site was and they also knew that Yates was in charge and had information on her computer."

Lander smiled and said, "That's two, but go on."

"They evidently were after one item and used a saw to get what they needed. I think they knew exactly where they wanted to go after the attack and came prepared to hide their car with a camouflage tarp."

"Go on," said Lander. You're not through yet."

"Well, I guess the biggie is that there was a helicopter standing by to get them out."

"And? What does all that tell us?" pressed Lander.

"That this is the work of more than the two men that attacked the camp," said McKenzie.

I looked at Lander. "You think this is a major operation, don't you? Someone with the means to have the men extracted by helicopter has to be behind it." I suddenly remembered something else. "This is the second attack within the week. Yates told us about the other one. Maybe they *are* related."

Lander replied, "Yes, I think we're on to something here. There's one more item that points to a coordinated attack . . . and, if we're right, there will probably be more."

McKenzie asked, "What is that? Have I missed something else here?"

Lander teased us, "How did they know where to come?"

Suddenly it hit me. "You believe someone is providing inside information. Who do you think it is? That Dr. Pasternak?"

Lander replied, "I don't know. I don't want to accuse anyone yet. But we'll have to run a check on everyone involved."

We all considered the implications of our conversation for a minute. Finally, McKenzie asked, "What is our next step then?"

Lander answered, "We look for the place the men holed up last night. When we find it, we may just find the other man. Let's look at your map, Kent."

I accessed my phone and clicked the maps app. Lander said, "Mark this spot." When I had done so, he continued, "We are here and this is the spot where we found their car." He pointed at another arrow on the map. "We need to locate an area within easy reach to both locations." He gazed at the map, and then fingered an area in it. "Somewhere in here. There is a ridge here. I think we need to check it out."

The other ranger joined them in the clearing. "Have you told the other search teams that we found the extraction point?"

McKenzie looked appalled. "No, I have not. Thanks for reminding me," he said as he reached for his radio.

Chapter 12

After riding for half an hour, we turned our horses up the last ridge, the one that Lander had pointed out that could be the likely hiding spot. As we neared the top, Lander held his hand up and said, "We need to tie our horses here and walk the rest of the way. Look for signs of recent activity and any type of unusual sight or sound. Let's spread out just in case, so that if there is any shooting, we won't be taken down together. Move one at a time and try to stay behind some cover as we make our way to the top."

I can follow directions, especially if there is a possibility that not following them increases the likelihood that I could suddenly be carrying an extra bullet.

It took about thirty minutes before we stood at the crest of the hill. We had seen nothing as we ascended the slope and there seemed to be nothing out of place on the top. "Nothing," McKenzie said. "I don't believe anyone has been here. Maybe one of the other groups has found something. I'll check in with them."

I watched Lander, who seemed to be paying no attention to McKenzie's speech. He walked over the short flat summit and peered over the far edge. "Come here, Kent. Let's have a look at the path down this side."

I followed him down the worn path. It was steep and I slipped a couple of times, sending small rocks skittering down the hill. About a third of the way down, Lander paused, stepped carefully to the side of the trail, and motioned me to follow. When I joined him, he reached his hand out and tugged at a dense limb lying against the rocky ledge. "A cave opening!" I cried. "How did you know?"

Lander just grinned and said, "If I told you, I would have to kill you." That's not the first time I have heard that from him and I—for once—did not try to match his wit. "Let's go back to our horses and get some gear." We made our way back to the top where the two rangers were waiting on us. Lander told them what we had found and then we hurried to our horses. When we were standing beside them, Lander said, "We can take the horses back to the top this time; we'll be safe."

I didn't even ask him how he knew that; I just took his word for it. We mounted and let the horses pick their way up the slope. At the top, we tied them to a tree. Lander hopped down and said, "Get your flashlight and rope. I know we'll need the light and we'll probably have to have some rope. Oh, and bring some hardware," he continued as he looked at me.

I got my supplies and we fell in line behind Lander as he again descended the cliff. He ducked into the opening, turned his light on, and said, "Come on in, but watch out for the sharp rocks overhead." Once in the cave, we were able to stand up; we pointed our lights around the room and saw nothing alive.

There was the scent of burnt wood and my light stopped on a charred circle of wood. "Uh oh, I believe you are right. Someone's been here . . . and recently. That wood is still smoking."

"Over here are some food wrappers," McKenzie said as he stooped and picked up some paper. "Cheese crackers and Snickers."

I thought, *Can't beat that for a meal in the wild,* but didn't say it. I watched Lander move around a large rock that seemed to block the back of the cave and quickly moved to go after him. "Did you find something else?" I asked. I pulled up beside him and we peered down the open shaft.

"If anyone were here, I don't think they went down there; I don't see any steps or ladder anywhere," I said, shining my light all around."

"Oh, there was someone here, and I think he is down there."

"And you know that how?" I know that Lander is a former SEAL and has had a lot of training, but sometimes I think he goes way beyond that in being able to read a scene. At times, it's just plain eerie, but I've learned by now not to doubt it.

He looked at me and said, "You should know that, too. You've got to be more observant. See the spots at the edge."

I looked closely at the copper-colored spots. "Blood!" I said. "You think the second man is down there." He just nodded and I continued, "And I guess you are going down there to see."

"No, you're wrong; *I'm* not going down there. *We* are going down there. Your next lesson in rock climbing is about to happen." As we spoke, the two rangers joined us.

In five minutes, we had the ropes anchored to the large boulder. We tested the knots for stability and dropped our lines over the side. We leaned back and walked our way down the side. I have to admit it was a little scary walking backwards down the drop-off in the dark. After about thirty-five feet, I heard Lander's boots hit the surface and one step later, I joined him on the floor. We both clicked our lights on and looked around. We saw all sorts of items that had been tossed down there through the years, but the one that got our attention was the body. It was obvious that he was dead; his head was caved in and lying at a right angle to his shoulders. There was a pool of blood around him, not yet completely dry. Lander took his phone out and snapped several pictures of the man, then moved to the side and carefully picked up a mask. He removed a clear, plastic bag from his pocket and slid the mask inside before holding it up. "Maybe we can get some information from this. The plot thickens," he said. "Both men that Smith saw are down here, but one has left only his face. We may no longer be looking for a Japanese."

Chapter 13

Lander and I rode into the excavation site and stepped down from our horses. I bent at the waist and stretched my back. Lander smiled and said, "What's wrong, Ole Boy? Getting too old for a little adventure?"

"No way! If I am, then you are, too. I just haven't been on a horse in a while . . . and my bottom will attest to that," I said, as I ran my hands along my thighs and backside. I looked around. "I wonder where Dr. Yates is?"

"Well, she was standing behind that tree over there with a rifle trained on us as we rode in." As he spoke, she stepped out in the open and walked toward us, carrying the gun barrel pointing down.

"Hi; welcome back. Did you find the men?"

"We'll tell you about it, but first, how about some coffee?"

Sipping our drinks, we relayed the information. Yates listened without interruption. When we finished, she said, "So you think one of the two men is dead and the other may not have been

Japanese after all. I guess we have nothing to go on now."

Lander spoke up, "I wouldn't say *nothing*. Forensics will go over the car with a fine-tooth comb and then we have the mask; they should be able to get something from it."

I added, "And hopefully, they will be able to identify the dead man. It will just take some time. Where's Kim? I thought she was here with you."

"I sent her to go to the hospital to check on Dr. Smith and Shannon. I didn't think she would be much use here. I talked to Dr. Pasternak about the situation. We agreed that we would close the site for a couple of days until we see how Dr. Smith and Shannon recover. I think he will be fine in a day or two; Shannon, I am not sure about. While you all were gone, I secured everything I could and I am going to stay in town so I can be at the hospital with them. What are your plans?"

I looked at Lander before replying. "I don't think we can do anything else here right now so we are going to Durango. We're supposed to meet my wife there tomorrow afternoon; we're going to do a little sightseeing and exploring in that area. Before we leave in the morning, we'll stop by and talk with Ranger McKenzie. He probably will not have anything new yet, but we'll still check in with him. You have our numbers; let us know when you find anything. When are you leaving camp?"

"I'm just about ready; I'll leave within the hour."

"We'll stay until you leave. That'll give us enough time to pack our gear and then hopefully get back to the ranch before late tonight." Lander grinned and said, "I think Kent is chaffing to get back in the saddle, anyway."

I grimaced and said, "I'm chaffing, all right, but it's from being in the saddle already."

Chapter 14

We pulled our Wrangler into the parking lot of the ranger station. We had ridden hard yesterday afternoon and gotten back to the ranch a little after dark. After what seemed a short night's rest, we had eaten a hearty ranch breakfast of eggs, sausage, ham, fried potatoes, and gravy and biscuits. The gravy and biscuits were a surprise to us, as we didn't expect to find that southern staple this far west. It's a good thing that we were able to get into the Jeep instead of having to crawl back on a horse after such a meal.

McKenzie saw us from the window and motioned us inside. We entered his office and saw that Sheriff Spencer was there, also. McKenzie said, "We were just discussing the case. Sit down and join us."

"Did forensics come up with anything yet?" I asked.

"They didn't find much in the car. It had been wiped down and was spotless inside."

"And the body in the cave?"

"No ID on him. We'll try to get DNA or fingerprints, but it will take a couple of days to get someone there to retrieve the body."

Lander asked, "What about the mask; was there anything useful there? That's the man we really need to focus on."

"A lot of oil but not much else. A couple of hairs, but that won't tell us much unless we can match DNA."

Lander replied, "It might tell us something. There's a test that can identify the ethnicity and race from hair."

"I've not heard about that test," Spencer said.

"It's relatively new but I understand that it's pretty reliable. It can detect the ethnicity and gender of someone using nothing but a single hair, and in less than two minutes. Have your analysts to check it out. It may help us to determine who this person is—or at least whether or not he really is Japanese."

After a few more minutes of talk and assurances that we would keep in touch, we left. We traveled a few small, secondary roads before we finally turned onto Highway 550 toward Durango. I thought we would discuss the case as I drove, but Lander had other ideas. Within two minutes after hitting the highway, he was sleeping. And Cyndi thinks I can fall asleep quickly! But then he's faster than me on just about everything. I've learned to suck up my pride and accept that fact.

But since Lander is exceptional at whatever he does, I feel honored to even be able to keep up.

I pulled into the Strater Hotel and parked. I looked at Lander and he opened his eyes. "Good job driving, Kent," he said.

"Yeah, like you'd know. You snored all the way here."

"Just making some noise to keep you awake," he said.

The Strater Hotel is a distinguished-looking structure built in 1887 and may be the most prominent landmark in downtown Durango. It has been operated by three generations of the Barker family and is filled with antiques. When Cyndi found out we were coming to Durango, it didn't take her long to tell me where we were going to stay. I didn't argue with her because, truth be known, it was exactly the place I would have chosen on my own. We checked in and deposited our gear, then met in front of the hotel. We had a couple of hours before Cyndi's plane was scheduled to arrive, so we went for a five-mile training run. This was our first run in the mountains, so we ran easy, not pushing ourselves in the lower-oxygen atmosphere. Boy, I could tell we were at altitude; after a half-mile, we were both gasping before we adapted to the oxygen level. I watched my iPhone App and when we reached two and a half miles, we turned back. When we finished, we agreed that the five-miler felt like a fifteen-miler at home. A quick shower and we met back at the car.

We made a circle once around town and then headed for the airport, which was about twenty minutes south of Durango. We found US 550 and drove south on it for almost five miles; we turned east onto Highway 160 until it intersected with Highway 172, where we turned right and continued to Airport Road. We parked and made our way into the airport. We waited about fifteen minutes and the flight from Denver arrived on time, which is always a nice surprise these days. Cyndi waved as soon as she spotted us and then gave us each an enthusiastic bear hug before we went to retrieve her luggage. In about forty-five minutes we were back at the hotel. Lander's room was adjoining ours, but we all went to our room for a while.

Lander said to Cyndi, "Has Phil brought you up to date on what he has gotten us into?"

She replied, "Just that something had happened, but no details yet. Why am I not surprised that you all found 'an incident'?"

We spent the next half hour telling her the story and answering questions. When we were through, she asked, "Have you heard anything new today?"

Lander said, "No, we haven't. I told Ranger McKenzie that we would check in with him tonight."

Cyndi said, "Ranger McKenzie? What's his first name?"

I answered, "Tyler. Ranger Tyler McKenzie. Why? Do you know him?"

She said, "I don't know; the name sounds awfully familiar."

I said, "We have tickets for the train ride through the mountains for tomorrow. You'll enjoy that."

Cyndi said, "The one up to Silverton? You rode that on an earlier trip here, didn't you?"

"Yep! It's a beautiful trip through the mountains. The weather is supposed to be nice tomorrow, so I bought tickets for the gondolas or open-air cars. It'll be a little cooler, but we'll be able to see better and also get to experience the fresh air."

Lander had to add his two-cents worth. "Yeah, fresh air with all the allergens and the flying cinder dust; it's a coal-burning engine, so there'll be a lot of black smoke and ash. Better take some sunglasses to keep it out of your eyes." He smiled and said, "The whole trip down here, I tried to talk Phil into getting tickets for the closed cars so you wouldn't be exposed to all that trash, but, no, he wouldn't have any of that! He said you needed to experience the real feel of the old-west railroad."

I looked at him and asked, "Hey, Lander. What's wrong with your face? Have you seen it?"

He put his hand to his face. "Where? I don't feel anything."

"Right in the middle; it looks like your nose is growing!"

We all laughed at that and then I admitted, "Okay, I'm not fooling anyone—I wanted the fresh air ride, but, really, doesn't every man want to be a cowboy?"

We then decided we were hungry. I called McKenzie before we went to eat. "Hey, McKenzie. This is Phil Kent. Anything new up that way?"

"No, not yet. I haven't heard from forensics yet. They said it would take a couple of days to get anything. We were able to retrieve the body from the cave today. Too bad you weren't still here; you could have helped there. How long are you going to be in the Durango area? Did your wife get there yet?"

"Yes, she flew in this afternoon and we're settled in the Strater Hotel. Beautiful place! Tomorrow we're going to ride the train from here up to Silverton. Have you ridden it?"

"No, I haven't. I was just assigned out here a few months ago and haven't got to do much sightseeing yet."

"Where are you from?" I asked.

"Originally from Tennessee. I began my ranger career in the Smokies and after two years there, was assigned out here. I really like this area."

"The train's pulled by an old steam engine and is a beautiful ride through the mountains. It's forty-five miles to Silverton and takes about three and a half hours one way; we'll have about a two-hour layover in Silverton, so we'll be gone most of the day. The next two or three days we're planning to explore some of the surrounding area, beginning with Mesa Verde. The cliff dwellings are fascinating. But, if you hear anything, please let me know; I'll have my cell at all times. If you can't get me, call Lander. You've got his sat number. If we can help you in any way, just ask; we're pretty flexible right now."

"Okay, I will. Have a good time. The weather should be good for a couple of days. Talk to you later."

"Bye, McKenzie."

We left the hotel and walked down the street. Cyndi was thrilled with all the shops. I told her that before we left Durango we would spend some time shopping. I'm smart enough to know that would make her happy and it did. If she's happy, I'm happy. I think there's an old saying that illustrates that, but you know it, so I won't tell you. Making a quick tour of the main street, I saw Cyndi eyeball a Starbucks—I swear her eyes changed to a brighter brown; I knew where we would be in the morning. We circled back and entered the Mahogany Grille, a West Mex steakhouse located in the Strater Hotel. Lander ordered an elk steak while Cyndi and I stayed with the beef and got the flatiron steak. We all agreed that the meals and service were excellent, the perfect ending to a long day. Cyndi and I read for a while, and then turned in early. We both were looking forward to tomorrow.

Chapter 15

Two days after Romonov talked with The Man, he was within fifty miles of his destination. Ever since he had gone through Houston, he had become increasingly anxious to get there. During the trip from the Denver area, he had met three contacts and picked up packages from each of them. The first had been just east of Durango. His contact there had questioned him about why he was stealing the bones. Romonov smiled as he remembered his answer, one that would ensure the contact's silence forever. After that, he had driven over three hundred miles south to meet his next contact. According to The Man, this sample was one of the two most important Romonov would obtain, the other being the one that Romonov himself had secured. Romonov had met the contact in an isolated section between Flagstaff and Phoenix. He knew the man would never talk about the exchange; in fact, his body in the canyon may never be found until it became just bones and teeth. Romonov thought that scenario just might be fitting. The last item he obtained was east of Phoenix, in the foothills of Superstition Mountains. Another two hundred miles, he made the trip in about three hours. Although his car would travel much faster, he was careful to stay within all speed limits as he definitely did not want to be pulled over for a traffic violation and his car searched. The man he met there would be just one more unsolved disappearance in the area.

After he had talked with The Man, he had divided the bones into four identical packages instead of the three that The Man had ordered. The extra package would make him more than the other three combined. After a few minutes, he began seeing signs for Beaumont. He had chosen the Port of Beaumont for shipping one of the packages for a couple of reasons. Although it is about forty miles inland from the Gulf of Mexico, it is one of the major seaports in the U.S. for shipping to the Middle East and Asia. The military uses it for transporting war supplies and equipment to overseas bases and troops. In fact, to save money, the military now uses commercial vessels to send many of its shipments. It is this fact that is important to Romonov. The other reason to choose Beaumont is that it is not as heavily secured as the more known ports of New Orleans, Miami, New York, or others from major coastal cities. It would be easier to sneak the package in among all the others. He had a friend who worked there and had agreed to hide his package among a shipment of supplies to Hong Kong. Once there, it would be picked up by another contact. He had to be careful to make sure that The Man never found about this shipment. It was a great risk, but he was earning a huge fee.

He left I-10 at Exit 851 toward US-90 and then turned onto College Street. Romonov turned down several streets, following his navigation system directions until he turned onto Port Street. In less than a mile, he arrived at his destination. He looked around and found a deserted parking spot. Accessing his contact list, he clicked on a name. Although it was not the real name of the person he wanted, he knew it would call a throw-down cell phone. After two rings, a man answered. "I'm here," Romonov said. The man said nothing and then there was the silence as the call was disconnected. Although there had been no reply, Romonov knew the man would be there in mere minutes.

In six minutes, a man slowly pulled into the deserted lot and parked his SUV facing Romonov's car; the driver flashed his lights two times and Romonov did the same, flashing his two times, then paused, then flashing them three times. Only then did the man exit his car. Romonov pulled his tired body out of the car and went to his trunk. Looking around once more and seeing no one else, he then pulled the cover for the spare tire up and revealed the four packages. He removed one and handed it to his friend. "Guard this with your life. When will it go out?"

His friend replied, "I have a shipment to Hong Kong loading tomorrow and will depart in two days." He held the container up and said, "This is waterproof, isn't it?"

Romonov replied, "Yes, it is sealed; no water or air can get to it. Still, you must treat it very carefully." He reached into the inner pocket of his sport coat and removed an envelope. "Here is the first half of your payment. The rest will be sent to you when the shipment has been safely delivered."

The man took the envelope and placed it in his pocket. He knew the amount was correct because he had shipped various items for Romonov in the past. He turned and placed the package in his car. Looking back at Romonov, he said, "It will be done—as always. Thank you for your business, my friend." He quickly entered his car and sped away.

Romonov watched him depart and breathed a sigh of relief. "I'm glad that part is done," he thought. He slowly got back in his car and set his GPS for his next delivery. He looked at the overview and groaned, "Fifteen hundred and fifty miles!"

He could take a flight to New York, but The Man felt the package would be more secure in the car. So Romonov had agreed with him . . . as if he had a choice. "Oh, well," he thought. "I'm getting well paid to be a courier. If I weren't here, I'd have to be somewhere else." And, if the truth be known, Romonov really didn't mind driving long distances. He had developed the skill of being able to pull into a rest stop, sleep an hour, and then wake ready to drive another eight hours. Quick stops for food and to use the bathroom and he could drive indefinitely—as long as he had a supply of coffee. At one time, he had listened to music all the time he drove, but recently he had begun to listen to audio books. He felt himself a professional and listened carefully to the thriller stories to try to pick up tips for helping him succeed in his escapades. Many of those writers were clever and he had already picked up some ideas that had paid off for him.

Continuing east on I-10, then I-12, he turned north on I-59 toward Hattiesburg. Finally finding a rest stop on I-59, he pulled his car in, went into the rest area to use the bathroom and to be sure there were no potential problems at the stop. Although there were employees on duty, they seemed content to just wait for questions from travelers. Romonov went back to his car, cracked his windows to let in a little fresh air, reclined his seat, and, within three minutes, was fast asleep. Right on cue, he awoke after an hour. Looking around, he exited the car, stretched, and walked back to the vending machines, where he bought a Coke and a Snickers bar. He walked around his car, looking at his tires and surreptitiously checking to see if there were any suspicious people interested in him. Seeing no one, he sat back in his driver's seat and merged back onto the interstate traffic.

After several hours of driving, he decided to stop for the night. Finding a Holiday Inn Express at Exit 27 in Cleveland, he pulled under the covered parking area. "Whew, I didn't even realize I had entered Tennessee," he thought. "This is a good place to get a good night's rest." He went in and paid cash for a room for the night. Before he went to his room, he drove the two hundred yards to a Longhorn Steak Restaurant and went in. After a meal of salad, New York Strip, and baked potato, he drove back to his room. Backing his car into the spot in front of his room, he carried his travel bag and the container into his room. After securing the extra latches, he took a long, hot shower and then lay down on the firm mattress. The next thing he knew, it was six o'clock in the morning. He locked his things in his trunk and then went to the included breakfast off the lobby area. He had a meal of scrambled eggs, sausage, and toast, and, of course, coffee. Feeling full, he checked out and drove his car up the nearby ramp to I-75 north to continue his trip. Looking at his navigation display, he said to himself, "Only seven hundred eighty-nine more miles."

Romonov worked his way through Tennessee and entered Virginia just past Kingsport on I-81. He stopped somewhere near Blacksburg for lunch and a quick nap, and then continued into

Pennsylvania. He almost was unaware of the passing hours: just drive, eat, relieve himself, nap—and then repeat. Only when he saw the exits for Newark did he realize he was close to New York City. He looked at his watch and saw the day and time: Wednesday, five o'clock in the afternoon. His meeting was set for six-thirty tomorrow, a little over twenty-four hours away. "I can find a room for tonight," he thought. A short time later, he took an exit that advertised several motels and dining options. Choosing a Doubletree by Hilton, he checked in and then found a nearby restaurant. Satisfied, he went back to his room, showered, and made himself comfortable. Laying the container and his handgun next to him on the bed, he watched television for a while, and then went soundly asleep. His last thought before he slept was, "Tomorrow this time, it will be finished."

Romonov awoke to a cloudy, foggy morning. He showered and then took his items to lock in the trunk of his car. He went back inside to eat breakfast. Feeling his phone vibrate, he checked the message. It was the one he was waiting for to give him directions to meet his contact from New York. He read, "Use I-78 to cross Newark Bay. Exit to 440 and follow it north along the waterfront of the Bay. After you go back under I-78, look for a vacant lot on the right with a black SUV facing the highway; it will have a red flag sticker on the front bumper. Be there at two-thirty and don't be late.

Be sure you are not followed. Text back that you understand."

Romonov read the message two times and then thumb-typed, "Understood." He clicked **Send** heard the swish, and closed his phone.

At two-thirty, Romonov slowed his car and looked at the black SUV; it had a small, red flag on the front bumper. He had already driven around many blocks and backtracked several times to be sure no one had followed him, but he looked carefully all around to confirm that he was still alone. Easing his car behind the SUV, Romonov exited the car and stood with his hands out in front of him to show the contact that he had no weapon drawn. After a minute, the door opened and a tall, dark-skinned man stepped out of the SUV. He approached Romonov and asked him, "Are you lost? What are you looking for?"

Romonov thought a minute and replied, "I'm looking for Lincoln Park. Am I on the right road?"

The man said, "You are correct. Are you by yourself?"

Romonov replied again, "Yes, I am by myself. I know that no one is behind me."

With the code phrases correctly uttered, the man said, "Hurry, give me the package."

Romonov quickly went to the trunk of his car and removed one of the packages. It was wrapped in nondescript brown paper and as he handed it to the man, he said, "Please be careful with this;

don't let it out of your sight until you hand it over to your contact."

The man took the package, cocked his head, and said, "Is this all?"

Romonov reached into his breast pocket and removed the fat envelope. Handing it to the man, he said, "This is half; you will get the rest when you deliver the package. That is our agreement."

"Yes, that is our agreement," said the man. He pocketed the envelope, placed the container under a mat in the back of his SUV, and sat behind the wheel of his car. He saluted Romonov and said, "Thank you. I will see you again." He quickly accelerated onto the highway and smiled. He enjoyed these extra deliveries and this one was worth a cool half a million dollars. His assignment to the U.S. was really paying off; another two years here and he may be able to retire. "Yes, life is good!" he thought.

Chapter 16

After a breakfast at Starbucks, we boarded the train in Durango the next morning under a blue sky. In June, there are three departure times and we had chosen the middle one, leaving at eight forty-five, putting us in Silverton at fifteen minutes past noon. We enjoyed the gondola coach with its fresh air. Well, I don't think Cyndi liked all the smoke and ash in the air. I wasn't really sure about this until she had told me the fifth time; Lander just happened to hear her all the times and didn't say "I tried to tell you;" he just sat there with that smirk of his. But, I digress. The scenery was beautiful. The railroad followed the river canyon and offered spectacular views of the San Juan Mountains.

Cyndi asked, "How long has the railroad run this route from Durango to Silverton?"

I hesitated to let Lander answer, but mainly because I didn't know.

Finally, he said, "The route was completed in 1882 and was intended to carry both freight and passengers."

Cyndi asked, "What freight did they carry?"

"It was built to carry silver and gold ore; that eventually was phased out, but the passengers realized that the real value of the trip was the scenery, so the trips were continued." Lander looked at me and continued, "Do you know why it's called a narrow-gauge railroad?"

He thought he had me, but I had read that. "It's a narrow-gauge track because the rails are only thirty-six inches apart while most tracks have rails about forty-five inches apart."

Cyndi entered the exchange, "I would guess that the reason is that it is easier to build a narrow track through the mountains."

Lander said, "That's exactly right. When they had to level a roadbed along the edge of the cliffs, it made sense to make them as narrow as possible and still keep them safe. You can see that we have almost no extra room along this side." He pointed as he said this. We could look right out the edge of the gondola straight down the mountainside. On the other side of the car, the edge of the mountain was almost against the side of the train. Although not all sections of the trip were as extreme or scary as this one, one side was always up and the other was always down.

After a trip of three and a half hours, we chugged into Silverton. We all exited the train and looked around the town. Silverton was not nearly as big—or neat—as Durango, but it still was interesting to explore; it had had extensive development since I had been here years ago. We all agreed that we could tell the difference in the oxygen level at that altitude and found ourselves puffing all too quickly. Lander pointed out that Silverton sat at an altitude of over nine thousand feet, so shortness of breath was a common experience for most visitors. I said to Lander, "You ought to come here to do your training runs; maybe then you could keep up with me." I thought he might have said something back, but it was so quiet that I couldn't understand it. I guess that was because Cyndi was with us.

We ate lunch at Handlebars Restaurant & Saloon, which was a recommendation of one of the conductors on the train; we thought about eating at the Rocky Mountain Funnel Cakes, but Cyndi is watching my weight, so we opted for the Handlebars. I had never had an elk burger, but it was actually pretty good and the cowboy fries were a great addition. We all chose the same items. It's a meal I won't get in my hometown in Tennessee, but was a good experience of local cuisine. Before we knew it, the two hours were up and we were boarding the train for the trip back to Durango. The ride was uneventful, but the scenery was still outstanding. Years ago, when I first rode the train, I spotted a white bear on one of the steep slopes. Most people don't believe that, but somewhere I still have a picture of it; although I looked for the bear again, I didn't see it. It was six o'clock when we departed the train. It was a long day, but a good day.

"Are we ready for dinner?" I asked.

Cyndi just looked at me, you know, with that look. "I'm going to take a shower before I go anywhere," she said, as she removed her fedora and shook both it and her hair. I pretended not to see the ash fall from both.

Lander just stood there and smiled. *Smart ass!* I thought.

We made our way back to the Strater Hotel and agreed to meet again in an hour and a half for dinner. That would give Lander and me time for a quick run before our showers. When we entered our room and Cyndi looked in the mirror, I braced myself. She looked at me and said, "It was a good day and I'm glad we rode in the open-air car . . . I think, unless my allergies really begin to act up." After a quick change to my running gear, I met Lander in front of the hotel and we turned left, the opposite way we had run yesterday. We were a little more acclimated to the altitude, so the run today was a little easier than the one yesterday. Even so, we were breathing hard when we returned to the hotel. As usual, I enjoyed the sweating and felt as if I had worked hard enough so I could eat a good meal without feeling as if I was blowing it. Some people like to diet to keep their weight down, but I had rather work out so I can eat and enjoy it.

After showers, we met Lander back in the lobby. "Your choice tonight, Bill," I said. "Where do you want to eat?"

"I don't care. Pick something."

Cyndi said, "We're following you." Lander will argue with me, but not with Cyndi, so he began walking and we stepped right behind him.

He led us down East Second Avenue to Gazpacho Restaurant. He paused at the door and said, "This is supposed to be a great Mexican/American place to eat. We'll see for ourselves."

We went in and were seated in about twenty minutes. Lander got the New Mexican Steak Platter while Cyndi ordered the New Mexican Fajitas; it had sour cream and guacamole, so I knew she would like it. I opted for the Enchilada Trio. And margaritas all around, ice, no salt. During the meal, we talked very little, which was a positive vote on the taste of the food. As we left, I did a quick survey and we all gave fives for the restaurant. "You did well, Bill. We may let you choose again sometime," I said. We worked our way back slowly to the hotel, where we said our "Goodnights" to Bill and I agreed to meet him at eight-thirty in the morning. Sleep is good in the mountains and day broke before it had a right to . . . or at least according to my body.

I met Bill and we began walking to get a coffee. Bill said, "You all like Starbucks, don't you?"

"You ought to know that. How many times did we stop for drinks last year in Nova Scotia?"

He grinned and said, "That's right; we even had to delay some troublemaking so you could get your coffee. Don't get me wrong; I like my Joe, too. It just doesn't have to be designer coffee."

"Hyperbole! It wasn't that bad . . . was it?"

"Ha! Some of your readers seem to think so. I remember one review that said reading your novel with all the coffee breaks kept her awake at night. But enough of this. I talked to Ranger McKenzie last night. He still has no answers. He said he would check back in with us tonight. What's on the agenda for today?"

"We have to decide. We're here two more days; one day is to go explore Mesa Verde and one day for shopping." When I said the latter, Lander lowered his eyes and stared at me. "You don't have to go shopping with us," I said.

He gave a sigh of relief and grinned. "Actually, I do want to go with you. If I go home without a gift for Lisa, she may not let me travel with you anymore." Lisa was Bill's wife and was home working while he was in Colorado.

We ordered our coffees: a skinny hazelnut latte for Cyndi and a vanilla half-caff for me, both extra hot. Bill got a doppio espresso, which is a double shot of espresso. Of course, he didn't know what that was; he just ordered coffee hot and strong. "I'd be climbing the walls if I drank that," I said, pointing at Bill's drink.

We walked back to the hotel and met Cyndi in the lobby. As I handed her drink to her, I asked her, "What do you want to do today? Shop or go to Mesa Verde? We'll do the other tomorrow."

Cyndi thought a minute and then said, "Let's stay here in Durango. I'm still a little tired from our trip yesterday. We can go to Mesa Verde tomorrow."

As she said that, my phone rang. I looked at the caller ID, but did not recognize the number. I clicked "Accept" and listened to the voice on the other end. I spoke with him a minute, then disconnected the call. I looked at Cyndi and Lander and said, "That was Sheriff Spencer. He has some information. He wanted to know if we were still close enough that we could run back over there for a while. He would like to meet with us."

Lander spoke up quickly. "I'll run over there while you all shop today."

Cyndi looked at me and read my mind . . . or maybe my facial expression. "No, both of you go. I'll stay here and shop a little, then go back to the room and read. I'll be fine. Besides, I need some time away from you two."

I looked at her and said, "Already? You just got back with us." I think I said it, but may have just thought it. "Are you sure?"

"Of course; I'm a big girl. I can make it without you for a day." Three months ago, she had her fifth back surgery and, after a month of extreme pain, she was now doing much better; in fact, she is the most mobile she has been in the last fifteen years. "Get gone; I've got my coffee and am ready to go shopping. When I get tired, I'll come back to the room and read."

Bill looked at me and I nodded. I'll get the car," he said, maybe a tad too quickly. I hated to miss the shopping; at least I admitted as much to Cyndi. I kissed her to prove it and, in ten minutes, we were headed out of Durango.

Chapter 17

Romonov **removed his vibrating phone** from his pocket and looked at the display. He shivered as he recognized the number. "Yes?" he answered.

"Where are you?"

"I'm in a hotel room."

"Alone?"

"Yes, of course!"

The man chuckled loudly and said, "Don't pretend that you never—how do you say—participate in utilizing escort services. Do you have the computer?"

"Yes, it is with me now."

"Have you accessed it yet?"

"No."

"Good; get it and turn it on. I'll remain on the phone with you."

Romonov retrieved the case and removed the computer from it. He laid it on the bed and opened it. *A Mac!* he thought. He pushed the button on the upper right side of the keyboard and immediately the computer came to life. He watched the Apple logo post into the middle of the screen and the centerline fill and then pause as he was asked for his username and password. He typed in the information he had been given and watched as the screen filled with the default display. "Yes!" he exclaimed. He lifted the phone and said, "I am at the home screen. I'm not familiar with Macs, so where do I look for the information?"

"At the left bottom of the screen, there should be a two-color face. That's the Finder icon. Click it and we'll look for a folder that has the dig information. Go ahead and click it now."

Romonov clicked it and watched as the screen filled first with a list of folders; then, almost immediately, the screen exploded in what looked like the finale of a great fireworks show. As soon as the colors faded, the only words left on the screen were, "Too bad! You don't get the information!" Then the screen went black. In a panic, he pushed the power button, but got no response at all from the computer."

Romonov swore as he picked up the laptop and threw it across the room. He yelled into the phone, "The bitch booby-trapped the computer; it self-destructed. It will not even power on anymore." Romonov waited for his death sentence.

The Man said, "You know what this means. You have failed me!"

Romonov gasped, "Wait; we can still get the information. You know that Yates has a backup of the files. She would not leave something that important only on her computer."

For a minute, The Man was silent. Finally, he agreed. "You are right. She has to have copies of those files—either in the cloud or, more likely, on a portable hard drive or flash drive. Leave the car and get on the first flight back out there. Get that drive. You also have to deliver the other two samples to our lab in Arizona. Don't disappoint me again. You understand what's at stake here, don't you?"

Romonov nodded his head and said, "Yes, I most certainly do. Don't worry; I will get those files." As soon as he disconnected the call, he gathered his things and was outside in less than ten minutes. Passing a dumpster, he dropped the Mac into it and moved toward his car. *I can be at JFK within an hour,* he thought.

Chapter 18

Lander drove into the parking spot and shut down the engine. We exited the Jeep and walked into the building. The same receptionist pointed to the closed door. "Go on in. They are expecting you." I looked at Lander to see if he had heard "they" also. He shrugged and pushed open the door.

In addition to Sheriff Spencer, there were six other people in the room. Of course, we recognized Ranger McKenzie and Dr. Yates. Spencer said, "Come in, we were just getting ready to start." He pointed to the woman sitting next to Dr. Yates and said, "This is Dr. Pasternak." She nodded at us and then Spencer said, "The man beside Dr. Pasternak is Dr. David Lee. I'll let him tell more later."

We looked at the other two people sitting on the opposite side of the table. Spencer pointed to the one on the left and then the other. "Brett Daniels and Jeff Wilson." I saw Federal Operatives written all over them, but Spencer did not confirm that. I also saw by the look on their faces that they did not welcome us to this meeting.

Spencer said, "Let's get started. I wanted Kent and Lander here, and Dr. Yates insisted that they be invited. They probably know more about what happened than anyone else."

Wilson said, "We usually don't invite civilians to sit in on our meetings."

McKenzie looked steadily at him before replying. "I had them checked out. Lander is a former SEAL who has had more action than you have ever thought of. He, along with Kent—and his wife, I might add—were instrumental in a major crime stop last year in Nova Scotia. I couldn't find out any details, but the highest level in the CIA told my boss in Washington that if these two were available to help in any way not to let them get away." He grinned and continued, "I hope I don't have to arrest them to keep them here. Now, if you want to check with your Director to see if we can include these 'civilians' as you call them, then feel free to go make that call."

Wilson turned red and looked sheepishly at Daniels. "If you can vouch for them and take responsibility if they are injured, then go ahead with the meeting."

I gruffly replied, "I think Mr. Lander and I can take responsibility for our own safety. Don't worry, your butt won't be on the chopping block if we get hurt!" I turned and looked at the others. "Now that we have introductions, can we proceed with the important stuff?"

Spencer cleared his throat and said, "Good idea. Mr. Daniels, do you want to begin? Tell us why the Feds sent you two down here to investigate a robbery."

Daniels lowered his head and seemed to choose his words carefully. "It's complicated," he said. "Let me just say it may be of more importance than a simple robbery. I might add more as we discuss the situation. I'll defer to Dr. Lee for now."

We all looked at Lee, who began, "As you know, I am the Principal Investigator for the dig site northwest of here that was attacked a little over a week ago."

"I thought everyone in that site was killed," Lander said.

"Everyone else was," replied Lee. "The only reason I wasn't was that I was away from the site for a few days. I don't know if the outcome would have been the same if I had been there, but I feel responsible for them. The dig site was attacked just after daybreak. They shot all our crew—actually, executed them with shots to the back of their heads—and then they destroyed all the bones and artifacts. Nothing was left intact."

Lander asked, "Did they take anything?"

Lee replied, "We didn't think so at first until I talked with Dr. Yates here. She told me about the missing piece of bone. I went back and looked more carefully at the bone pieces from our site."

I interjected, "You discovered that some bone had been stolen, didn't you? Maybe a short piece of a femur?"

He looked at me, "Yes, I did. I just don't see what they wanted with a small piece when they could have taken much more and sold it for a small fortune."

Lander asked, "What was discovered at your site? What were the bones? Were they dinosaur like the ones here?"

"No, the bones were from a sabre toothed tiger. Actually, they . . ." He caught the eye of Pasternak and paused before continuing, "Actually, we think they may have been, but we have not yet verified that."

"I wonder what that was about," I thought. I made up my mind to ask Lander about it later; I know he also caught the change in tenor. I wondered if the Feds noticed and I looked at them to see if they showed any emotion, but I couldn't detect any change in expression.

"What about the attack here?" Wilson looked at Yates for an answer.

Yates outlined everything that had happened. "Did I leave anything important out?" she asked, looking at us.

Lander made quick eye contact with Yates and said, "I didn't hear you tell the agents that the robbers had stolen your laptop, the only computer with all your notes and files on it. It's too bad that you failed to make a backup."

I stared at Yates to see if she understood what Lander was saying. She lowered her head and whispered, "Yes, I'm afraid you're right. I had those files on no other computer. I was so busy that I hadn't gotten around to it yet and I just never expected that anything would happen to my computer. I can't believe that I was so careless."

To her credit, Pasternak realized the direction of the conversation and asked, "You didn't save them to our backup server in the cloud?"

"No, I'm afraid of the cloud. I thought too many people know how to hack into it. But from now on, I will use it for backup."

Pasternak feigned irritation. "If there is a next time. In addition to the bones, you have lost valuable information, information we can never duplicate."

Lander gazed at Yates and sadly shook his head. He then looked at Daniels. "You said earlier that these attacks might have been more than a simple theft of rare bones. What did you mean? Do you think the robbers intend to sell the pieces they made off with?"

I gazed around the group. I had the distinct impression that there was more to be said, but no one was volunteering any information. "Were Lander and I the reason for the reticence to discuss the situation?" I wondered.

Wilson replied, "I think it was just a group of grave robbers trying to get some bones to sell; they may also have been vandals, but I doubt that they intended to break up all the other stuff."

I looked at Lander and thought, *Is he this stupid to think we believe that?* I swear Lander read my mind as he nodded.

Wilson continued, "Does anyone have any more information or have any questions?" When no one responded, he said, "If not, we'll go. I would like to ask that you not discuss these attacks with anyone else, especially reporters. We don't need a media feeding frenzy out here. If they get involved, it will delay your getting back to your jobs."

Wilson and Daniels stood to their feet and looked hard at all of us. "Also, if you have any questions, direct them only to one of us." As he said this, he handed Spencer a small stack of business cards. "Would you pass these out?"

They exited the building and we watched them get in their car and drive down the road before anyone said anything. Finally, McKenzie said, "Well, that was enlightening. Those two will be a big help." He grinned as he said that.

I looked around and read the faces. I realized the reluctance to talk had not been because Lander and I were here, but instead was because Wilson and Daniels were present. Everyone seemed much more relaxed now.

Spencer said, "When Feds enter a meeting, things tend to get pretty hush-hush. Those two know a lot more than they shared with us."

Pasternak spoke up, "I think they were here to determine if we thought the attacks were more than robberies? I'm glad no one volunteered any more information."

Lander eyed Yates and said, "I'm impressed that you and Dr. Pasternak picked up on what I was doing. I didn't want those two to know that you had a backup. Good job. Did anyone actually see their IDs?"

Spencer replied, "I did. They showed them to me, rather quickly, I might add. I didn't look too closely at them. The men seemed legitimate."

I spoke up, "We can verify that. Before we go any further, how are Dr. Smith and Shannon doing?"

Yates answered, "Both have made progress. Dr. Smith may be released tomorrow. He has a lot of bruising and soreness, but Lander was right, there were no major organs damaged. He will be moving slowly for a while, but he is eager to get back to the dig. Shannon is lucky. The doctors were afraid she would be paralyzed, but she is conscious now and can wiggle her fingers and toes. It will take some time, but she should recover completely."

"Where is Kim now?" I asked.

"She is back on campus. The University cancelled her assignment to the excavation project for now because Shannon was injured so badly; they said it was too dangerous for Kim to remain here."

Dr. Pasternak said, "I think most of us believe that these attacks were not perpetrated by common thieves. They knew exactly what they wanted."

Lee said, "So you do think the two attacks were related, don't you? We discussed that as a possibility."

"I'm positive they are related." It was Yates who answered. "And I think they wanted the bones for a reason other than to sell. Otherwise, they would have taken as many of them as possible—and why would they destroy what they didn't take?"

Lander had remained quiet to this point, but I knew that he was two steps ahead of the rest of us. He said, "They could have been getting samples for someone's collection of rare bones." He saw Yates shake her head at this. "Why don't you think this is a viable motive?" he asked.

Yates replied, "Again, any collector would want as large a sample as he—or she—could get. It would be difficult to convince anyone that such a small section of bone came from a rare giant dinosaur."

Lander nodded his head. "I agree completely. I just wanted to place that option on the table to consider. I think we can disregard it." He looked at

Lee. "By the way, you wanted to tell us more about your sabre toothed tiger."

Lee said, "The sabre toothed tiger is not really a tiger although it is a member of the cat family. It is more accurate to label it as a Smilodon."

Lander said, "I thought that may be the case."

Lee looked astonished. "You know about the Smilodon?" he asked Lander.

"Not much. I do know that the name means 'Knife-Tooth'. I think there were two types of Smilodons."

Lee said, "You are right about the name. But there are actually three species: S. populator, S. fatalis, and S. gracilis."

"Which did you discover?" asked McKenzie.

"The largest, most ferocious type, the populator. It weighed as much as half a metric ton and had teeth up to twenty-eight centimeters long."

"Haven't they found remains of Smilodon in the La Brea tar pits in California?" asked Lander.

"Yes, they have. But the one we found was in excellent shape and one of the few populators discovered outside the tar pits."

"I have a question," I said. "If their sabre teeth were so long, how did they eat their prey? Wouldn't the teeth be in the way of getting the food in their mouths?"

Lee looked at me. "Good question, Kent. Most felines can open their mouths to about sixty degrees; the populator could open its mouth to a hundred twenty degrees. This allowed its sabre teeth to be clear of the mouth." Lee had become more and more animated as he discussed his passion.

McKenzie said, "So we have thefts of a partial bone from a giant dinosaur and a giant tiger, or cat." He corrected himself. "We don't think it was to sell them or steal them for a collector. Am I right in our thinking?"

I looked around and we all nodded.

"Then what other motive could be so important that the attackers were willing to kill for the bones?" McKenzie asked the question on all our minds.

Chapter 19

Daniels asked, **"What do you think?"**

"I think we are safe to leave. They don't have a clue about what is really happening. We can let the redneck ranger and the local yokel sheriff look for robbers."

"What about the others?"

"The scientists believe that the intruders were after bones to sell. They are smart in their areas of expertise, but have no inkling about anything else."

"Book smart, but no common sense is what you are saying," said Daniels.

"They bought that we were federal agents, didn't they? Our fake IDs worked like a charm. We need to check in with Romonov; he's on his way back here."

"Why is he coming back here?" asked Daniels.

"The Man thinks they have a backup stashed somewhere. The lady scientist rigged her computer to erase all her files when it was logged on."

"You mean like the show that used to say something like 'this disc will self-destruct in ten seconds'?"

"Yeah, but it was five seconds, not ten. Anyway, Romonov is coming back to see if there really is a backup somewhere. I need to tell him. We're federal agents and this group wouldn't dare to lie to us." He exploded in a loud horselaugh.

After he was able to control his laughter, Wilson clicked his phone on and dialed the number.

Romonov looked at his vibrating phone. Although he recognized the number, he was still irritated that his comrade would call him. He had given him orders to never call unless it was an emergency. He connected and growled, "Why are you calling?"

Wilson could tell Romonov was angry, but he really didn't care. "I called with an update. We met with the group in Colorado. They don't understand what is happening; they think young hoods trying to make a buck carried out the robberies. And, oh yeah, the Yates lady has no backup."

"How do you know that?"

"She told us herself."

"And you believe her?"

"Yes, I do. They wouldn't lie to federal agents. That worked just like you said it would; they believed our IDs were the real thing."

"They ought to. It cost me plenty to get them made. They may have no backup, but The Man has instructed me to return there to confirm that. Who knows, I may just convince the lady to remember all she put in the files. That would be fun. I'm not sure she would enjoy it, but I sure would."

"Do you want us to meet you here?"

"No, but stay close to your phone in case I decide to bring you back."

Chapter 20

The next morning was clear under a crystal blue sky. Although it was cool at seven-thirty, the forecast called for a perfect day with temperatures in the afternoon getting to seventy-three degrees. After a quick breakfast at the hotel and then our customary stop at Starbucks, we were in the car heading for Mesa Verde. The site was designated a World Heritage Site and we looked forward to seeing it. Lander and I had gotten back to the hotel late last night, so we had not brought Cyndi up to date on the happenings.

"How did your meeting go with the sheriff?" she asked.

Lander and I looked at each other and I nodded to him. He said, "It evolved into a group meeting."

"What do you mean?" asked Cyndi.

I said, "The sheriff was there; we knew he would be. Also, Ranger McKenzie and Dr. Yates were present."

Lander added, "Then there were Dr. Pasternak and Dr. Lee."

Cyndi interrupted. "Dr. Pasternak is the one from Washington in charge of the excavations, isn't she? Who is Dr. Lee?"

I answered her first question, "Yes, Dr. Pasternak is from Washington and is in charge of the NSF projects relating to fossils. Lee is the project director of the other site that was attacked last week."

"Didn't you say everyone there was killed, executed, you said?"

"That's what they thought. But Lee had been on a fishing trip and showed back up a few days later; he had not even heard anything about it."

I pointed at Lander, who was driving. "Tell her who else was there."

Lander laughed. "There were two federal agents that showed up."

"Two federal agents? What were they doing there?"

I said, "No one knows; they didn't say why they were at the meeting. They just showed up, flashed some credentials, and sat in on our meeting."

Cyndi asked, "Who invited them . . . or, at least, how did they find out about the meeting?"

"I don't know how they were aware of the meeting? No one invited them. If I can read Lander right, he thinks they were imposters." We hadn't discussed the meeting last night on the way back to Durango. I drove while Lander slept. He claims I drive better when he's asleep. "Anyway, we didn't volunteer much information or discuss the cases until the agents left. In fact, Lander lied to them."

"No, I did not! I just didn't tell them all the truth. I led them to think something that I really didn't say." He explained how he, along with Yates and Pasternak, convinced the two that Yates had no backup.

We filled her in on the rest of the trip, the real meeting after the agents had gone. She asked, "Could the two agents be the two attackers?"

Lander replied, "No, I don't think so. In fact, I know they weren't. Remember, one of the attackers was pulled dead from the cave."

"Oh, that's right; I forgot that. But there's got to be someone on the inside providing information. Otherwise, they wouldn't have known about the meeting."

"You're right. I'm just not sure right now who that is. I thought for a while that it might be Dr. Pasternak, but now I'm not so sure."

I said, "I agree with you, Bill. I initially thought it was Pasternak, too. But, after the meeting, I don't think so. Right now, I am at a loss."

Thirty-six miles west of Durango on U.S. 160, we took the entrance to Mesa Verde, a two-lane paved road winding upward two thousand feet through piñon-juniper forests and canyons. We stopped at Park Point to enjoy the panoramic view. We continued to discuss the possibilities until Lander slowed the car and we pulled into the parking lot for the main visitor center. We checked in there and got some literature, then got back in the car and drove on. Mesa Verde covered an area of over fifty-two thousand acres. We did the self-guided Spruce Tree House tour and saw some spectacular cliff dwellings. Spruce Tree House is the third-largest cliff dwelling with over one hundred twenty-five rooms and eight kivas. Doing the tour on our own was free—always a good thing. Then we retrieved the car and drove along Mesa Top and stopped at the various viewpoints. From the stops, we could see many of the other places that charged to visit. Looking at them, we were glad we chose the self-tours because all the spots we could see had long lines waiting to get close.

As we stood gazing in wonder at one of the dwellings, Cyndi said, "This place is amazing. Can you imagine the work it took those natives to build these structures on the sides of the cliffs?"

I agreed with her and said, "And then, after all that work, to just abandon them suddenly."

She said, "Did they choose to leave or was there a catastrophe that wiped them out?"

I looked at Lander and said, "I'm sure Mr. North America here can fill us in on all the facts."

He laughed heartily at that before speaking. "The Anasazi Indians were in this area long ago. The dwellings were built at various times between the sixth century and the twelfth century."

Ah ha! I had caught him with that statement. "I thought the Pueblo Indians were the architects of the buildings." I smiled at him.

He gave me that look. "As I was saying before I was rudely interrupted, the Anasazi were originally in this area; they constructed their shelters mostly on the plateau. From about seven hundred fifty A.D., larger valley villages were built. Over the years, the Anasazi disappeared and their descendants, the Pueblo stayed and continued to build. During their classic period, there was a population of several thousand. From about eleven hundred to thirteen hundred, the greatest of the cliff dwellings were built. They include the Cliff Palace and Long House, which has one hundred eighty-one rooms and fifteen kivas."

"What's a kiva?" asked Cyndi.

Lander continued. "You saw some of them when we went through Spruce Tree House. A kiva is an area set aside for religious or ritualistic ceremonies. In some tribes, they were square, but, for the Pueblo Peoples, they were round and usually sunken or underground. Although most were fairly small—maybe twelve feet by nine feet—some kivas were built as meeting places for large numbers; some of those were as big as fifty feet across and nine feet deep. Kivas even had a hole in the floor—called a sipapu—to allow Anasazi spirits to move between the underworld and the surface of the world. One of the souls was

Katchina, a spirit who came and went through the sipapu to bless the Anasazi on ritualistic occasions."

"Why didn't they just build teepees and why did they build their houses in the cliffs?"

"Native Americans who lived in teepees were hunters and gatherers, so they had to be able to pack up and follow their food sources. The ancient Puebloans, another name for the Anasazi, were farmers. They stayed in one place to plant, cultivate, and harvest their food; they raised corn, beans, and squash. Archaeologists are not sure why they built their homes in the cliffs. It likely was for protection. During that time, there were droughts and they probably did that for protection from other tribes who wanted their food."

Cyndi said, "Okay, thanks. Is that why the Indians suddenly evacuated the dwellings?"

"There are different theories explaining why they left. The most common and believable is that there was a prolonged drought during the late thirteenth century that forced them to relocate. Other people believe that they had a major change in their culture and there is some evidence to suggest that they resorted to cannibalism."

Although I tried not to sound sarcastic, I may have failed when I asked, "What other interesting facts do you know about the Anasazi?" It really was fascinating to me.

"Well, some structures are aligned with heavenly bodies and they built astronomical observatories; this shows us that they had some knowledge of the planets and stars. In another area, there is a four-hundred-mile network of roads built in completely straight lines across deserts and canyons. Some of the roads are as wide as thirty feet."

"I'm surprised that the structures have survived as well as they have, particularly considering how many people have walked through them," I said.

"Some dwellings take little maintenance now, the ones that are sheltered by overhanging cliffs. That was where the Puebloans built when they could. Some of the others require constant work. Many pueblos were constructed out of sandstone rocks covered with adobe. They shaped the sandstone into rectangular blocks about the size of a loaf of bread and then used mortar made of mud and water. For their daily work, women made pottery; the men made various tools or weapons— items such as knives, axes, awls, and scrapers out of stone or bone. They were even traders, bartering their baskets or pottery to others in the community or even to people outside their tribe. When the dwellings were first discovered in the late eighteen-hundreds, there were a lot of artifacts, pottery especially, in the dwellings. Many were stolen or even sold off in pottery sales. After they became a protected treasure, then most of the looting was stopped."

Cyndi asked, "What type clothing did they wear?"

Lander replied, "In the summer, the adults wore mostly simple loincloths and sandals; in the winter, they wore clothes made of hides and skins. They also used blankets made of turkey feathers and wore robes made of rabbit fur."

I had to add to the conversation, "They probably didn't carry purses." I'm sure that Lander smiled but Cyndi didn't.

We continued our tour and about four-thirty, we decided to call it a day. We had been so engaged in the exploring that none of us had even thought about lunch. The ranger in the visitor center had suggested that we eat at the Metate Room and we were glad that we took his advice. Cyndi tried the Poland Rellano and said it was the best she had ever had. Lander ordered the Far View Pasta and I had the Elk Sheppard Pie, both excellent! After the great meal and fantastic scenery, we headed back to Durango.

I said to Cyndi, "On our trip over here, we talked about our day yesterday. What about you? Did you find any good stuff shopping? Did you find me a good souvenir?"

I felt bad when she said, "I thought you were never going to ask." I really did feel bad and I looked at Lander; his face was red. It could have been sunburn from the day outside or it could have been embarrassment that we had not let Cyndi tell us what she did yesterday.

Cyndi laughed. "I spent the morning shopping; there are a lot of neat shops in Durango. It would take a week or more to go through all the ones I would like to visit. I was getting tired so I ate lunch at one of the delis and then went back to the room."

"What did you read? I know that you didn't take a nap."

"I took a shower and cooled off. After that I got my iPad and piddled a little bit. I started thinking about the attacks and thefts of the bones, so I began looking for information related to them. Someone has a pretty good lid on both incidents, although I did find one news report about the first attack, the one where several people were killed."

"It doesn't surprise me that you were not able to find much," I said.

Cyndi lit up with one of those smiles, you know, the ones that look like the 'cat ate the canary'. She obviously wanted to say more.

"Okay, out with it. I know you have something else," I said.

"What if I told you that these two attacks were not the only ones in the last two weeks?" she said.

Chapter 21

The tall dark man stepped out of his car while his driver held the door for him. He picked up his attaché case and his overnight bag. He walked into the airport and turned left to avoid the check-in lines. He hurried past the guards and went to the front of the line to board. As he entered the first-class section, the hostess said, "How are you, Mr. Ambassador? Have a great flight."

He nodded to her and replied, "Thank you, Mary. I will." He thought to himself, "Diplomatic Status is good!"

He sat down in an aisle by himself, placing the overnight bag under his seat. He smiled and pulled a document from his case and reviewed the contents until the plane was in the air. At that time, he wrapped the carrying strap of his overnight case around his ankles, reclined his seat, and closed his eyes. The non-stop flight to Ankara was about ten hours and he slept a good part of that time.

After the plane landed and taxied to the gate, Adem Serhat carried his bags close to him. He walked quickly through the concourse and stepped out to the sidewalk. Looking around, he spied a man holding a sign with his name on it. He followed the man to a car and sat in the passenger seat. He looked at the two men sitting in the back and nodded. No one spoke a word, but the Ambassador from Turkey knew the men in the car were there to protect him.

The driver maneuvered the car through the airport traffic and left the city lights of Ankara behind. He drove north on O-4 toward Gerede; shortly before they got to Gerede, he turned east on D-100. Close to three hours later, the car exited toward Samsun, taking D-795 to the city. Working his way through 19 Mayis Bulvan and turning left on Fuar Caddesi, the driver zigzagged and backtracked through several blocks before stopping his car at a private dock on the Black Sea. The Ambassador recognized the man walking toward him; standing about five feet eleven inches tall, he was stocky and weighed north of two hundred fifty pounds. His square face was wrinkled from the sun and showed the scars from three knife wounds. Although he walked with a slight limp, Serhat knew that Anatoly Ivanov was extremely agile and could be deadly in hand-to-hand combat. The Ambassador instructed his guards to stay in the car and walked to meet the man.

Ivanov met him and greeted him with a firm handshake. "How are you, my friend?" asked the Russian.

"Well. And you and your family?"

"Doing well. Is that the package?"

"Yes," said Serhat. "Please see that it arrives safely."

"This is for your trouble." Ivanov handed him an envelope that Serhat promptly placed in the breast pocket of his jacket. With a nod, Ivanov turned and walked back to the idling boat waiting at the dock. He jumped to the deck and with a roar, the boat sped away. Serhat watched the craft head for Sochi. He knew it would take Ivanov a good four hours to cross the Black Sea, but this was the safest way to get the package into Russia.

Serhat did not know what was in the package nor did he know the final destination; he didn't care. His periodic courier services were very lucrative. He dialed Romonov and said, "Package handed off."

Chapter 22

Lander and I both looked at Cyndi incredulously. I asked, "What did you say?"

She repeated what she had said, "What if I told you that these two attacks were not the only ones in the last two weeks?"

"I knew you wouldn't shop and read all day yesterday. What did you find out?" I asked. "You can't stand not to be involved in the case, can you?"

"What? You don't expect me not to get involved in what you two are doing? Somebody has to keep you all straight."

Lander said, "And I can't think of anyone whom I would rather be helping us."

"Okay, enough of this. What did you find out?"

Cyndi looked at us a minute; I know she was just building up the suspense. She's pretty good at that. Finally, she said, "There have been more attacks than the two that you know about. At least two more have happened and are probably connected to these two."

I asked, "And the other two incidents have also had bones stolen—or at least a portion of a bone?"

"Yes, same M.O. as the others. A surprise attack on the site; most bones and artifacts destroyed, but a small portion of a major bone was taken."

Lander said, "You and your iPad. Were the bones those of a dinosaur?"

Cyndi replied, "No. One was from a skeleton of a bear and the other was from a partial skeleton of a giant."

I looked expectantly at her. "A giant what?"

She just repeated, "A giant."

Lander asked, "Do you mean a giant person?"

Cyndi shook her head, "Yes, a giant person. What we would call a giant."

I said, "Okay, a giant. But let's talk about the bear first. A bear is not an extinct animal. Why would the robbery of the bones of a bear be a connection to thefts of extinct animals?"

Cyndi looked pleased and said, "I'll explain it to you. The bear in question is not your every-day bear. It is a short-faced bear."

I laughed and said, "A short-faced bear? What kind of bear has—or had—a short face?"

Lander interrupted. "Don't laugh so quickly here. I seem to remember a bear that was called a short-faced bear . . . and it is extinct."

Feeling properly reprimanded, I said to Cyndi. "I'm sorry I laughed; the way you said it just sounded funny. Okay, tell us. What is a short-faced bear and where did the robbery take place?"

"If we could look at the bear, it would appear to us to have a shorter snout than most other bears; that, of course, is why it became known as a short-faced bear. However, that was an illusion caused by their deep snouts and short nasal regions. There are two recognized species: Arctodus pristinus and Arctodus simus. The Arctodus simus is considered to be one of the largest known mammalian carnivores."

"How big did they get?" I asked, now completely intrigued by the information.

"A normal size one stood eight to ten feet tall on its hind legs. Larger ones are estimated to have been eleven to twelve feet tall with a fourteen-foot vertical arm reach. One site in Missouri has a series of claw marks up to fifteen feet high, indicating bears taller than the twelve-foot range. It is estimated that a giant short-faced bear could have weighed over two thousand pounds."

Lander said, "I wouldn't want to meet one of those in a dark alley—or anywhere else. Have there been many skeletons of these bears found?"

"According to what I have found, only one short-faced bear has ever been found and its original bones are in the Field Museum in Chicago. Replicas of the bones have been cast and are displayed in a few other sites."

"Then the theft was in the museum in Chicago?" I asked.

"No, it wasn't," said Cyndi. "It happened on the southeastern side of Colorado."

"So, they have discovered another site with the bones," I said. "Where did you find out about it?"

"Well, the article I read did not identify the bones as being those of the short-faced bear; it just reported that a new dig site had been attacked. It implied that everything there was destroyed."

"I'm thoroughly confused now. What makes you think that the bones there were those of a short-faced bear?"

"The person that the reporter interviewed let slip that the site was an exciting find and had bones from an extinct bear, a bear for which authentic bones had only been found once before. From that article, I searched for extinct bears that met that condition. Ergo, the short-faced bear!"

I said, "So, the bones were never identified as being from a short-faced bear, or even a long-faced bear?" I smiled at my response.

Cyndi did not smile; I looked at Lander and even he did not smile, so I quickly wiped the expression from my face. She said, "No, nothing official, but I know that was what the skeleton was."

"Okay, I'll agree with you for now. Tell us about the giant." I thought about saying giant giant, but decided it was not a good idea.

Cyndi gazed into space a minute before continuing. "As you both know, there have been reports of the skeletons and fossils of giants in North America for hundreds of years. Supposedly, there were numerous bones that were presented to the Smithsonian Institute's Natural Museum of History in Washington. However, there is now no record of what happened to them."

"So where did the theft of the giant's bones happen?" asked Lander.

"Well, I found an obscure news release about an attack at a new excavation in the Grand Canyon. As you may or may not know, the Grand Canyon is perhaps the site where the most famous giant was discovered."

"When was this discovery?" I asked.

"The late 1800s," Cyndi replied. "Footprints as large as twenty inches were discovered, with stride lengths about five feet."

"Was this verified? How was it reported?" asked Lander.

"The L.A. Times is supposed to have printed an article about the discovery in 1896."

I asked, "Were footprints the only evidence found?"

"No, it is reputed that a petrified body of a giant was found, also in the same area; this body was estimated that his—and it was a man—height was eighteen to twenty feet."

"Okay," I said, "over a hundred years ago, there was a report of a giant found. What does that have to do with the recent theft?"

"The news report stated that—and I quote—'a piece of a giant femur bone was taken and the rest of his skeleton was destroyed'."

"Are you sure it wasn't another bear?" I asked. Or maybe I just thought it because it got no response.

We were interrupted when Lander's phone chirped. He answered, listened a minute, and clicked it off. "I think we need to have another talk with Dr. Yates," he said, "and the quicker the better."

Chapter 23

Romonov's plane landed at Phoenix Sky Harbor International Airport at four-thirty in the afternoon. It had been a smooth Delta flight. Although PHX was a busy center he was not held up. He was traveling light, so he had only the carry-on bag. Entering the gate area, he was pointed to his connecting flight, where he had only minutes to make the U.S. Airways Express flight, a regional service of American Airlines. On the flight, he closed his eyes and napped for a few minutes, waking shortly before the one-and-a-half-hour flight began its landing procedures. Quickly exiting the airport terminal, he entered the shuttle for the car rental lots. In twenty minutes, he had rented an SUV from Alamo; of course, he had provided a false identity and encountered no problems in securing the vehicle.

Following the directions to Durango, he pulled into the first motel he came to. After he checked in and paid with cash, he backed his car into the parking spot directly in front of his room. He spied a Subway across the road and walked over to it.

He ordered an Italian BMT to go, grabbed some chips and a Coke, and walked back to his room. He locked the door, closed the blinds and curtains, turned on the TV, and settled down to eat.

At ten o'clock, he heard a knock. He moved to the door and looked through the peephole, recognized the two men standing there, and let them in. They quickly moved into the room and sat on the bed.

Romonov asked, "Did you get everything we need?"

The man known as Alex answered, "Yes, we have it all; it's in the van."

"What about the weapons? Did you secure untraceable ones?"

"Of course. And we have already test-fired them and set the sights." Kronov pulled a handgun from his jacket and handed it to Romonov.

Romonov took the gun and looked at it carefully. "A Glock—very good." He released the magazine, cleared the firing chamber, and dry-fired it. "This will do," he said. He reinserted the magazine and pulled the slide, readying the gun to fire. "Where is the van? You didn't park it outside the room, did you?"

"It's across the street, in the parking lot of the Subway."

Romonov nodded. "I don't want to be seen leaving with you. I'll meet you at the airport in two hours." The men shook their heads and left.

As soon as they had gone, Romonov opened his bag and removed some clothes. He put on black cargo pants and a black long-sleeved hoodie. He pulled his black hiking boots on over calf-high athletic socks. Standing up, he pushed his black toboggan into one of his pockets, stuck the Glock into his back waistband, and slid the serrated Ranger knife into an ankle sheath. The last item he pocketed was a fifty-foot roll of paracord. Checking one last time to be sure nothing was left, he took the pre-moistened cloth and wiped down everything in the room. Satisfied, he grabbed his bag, opened the door, and looked around. Seeing no one, he quickly closed the door and entered his SUV. Driving around the town with several random stops and starts, he made sure no one was tailing him. Only then did he head toward the airport. He entered the short-term parking lot and eased into a spot beside the white van. He wiped the car carefully and locked it before getting into the front passenger seat of the van.

"Run by the Alamo car rental," he said to Kronov, who was driving.

Kronov steered the van out of the parking lot and followed Romonov's directions to Alamo. "Pull over here a minute," Romonov said. He took the keys and rubber-banded to them a note he already had written. He dropped them into the lockbox at the front entrance. Getting back into the van, he said, "There. They will think that I have taken a flight out and just left the car for them to pick up." He looked at Kronov and said, "Head north. You know where we are going."

Chapter 24

Lander clicked the phone number for Dr. Yates and placed his phone on speaker. "Hello, Mr. Lander," came the response. "How are you?"

Lander said, "I'm good. I've got you on speakerphone. Kent and his wife are here with me. Where are you now? Or, rather, where will you be tomorrow?"

"I'm in the hotel now, but will be going out to the excavation site in the morning. What can I do for you?"

"We need to talk with you about some new information that I have. Can we meet you at the site about ten-thirty in the morning?"

"Yes, of course. What kind of new information are you talking about?"

"I would rather not discuss it over the phone. Cell phones are not very secure."

"Okay, I will meet you at ten-thirty."

"We'll be there. Oh, and it would be better if we meet with you by yourself. Will Dr. Smith or Kim be at the site?"

"No, no one else will be here. Dr. Smith is supposed to be released back to work in two more days, so I want to get the site ready for us to work again. Dr. Pasternak is coming here at noon, so we'll have an hour and a half to meet before she gets here."

"We'll see you in the morning," said Lander and he ended the call.

"What is this all about?" I asked.

Lander answered, "It's bedtime now. Let me think it through tonight and we'll discuss it during the trip over there tomorrow." He looked at us and continued. "I guess I need to ask you both if you want to ride over there with me? I guess I took it for granted that you would want to do so."

Cyndi answered for both of us. "Of course, we want to go with you; we're like the Three Musketeers—all for one and one for all. This is not just your adventure!"

The next morning, we ate breakfast at the hotel. I went to get the car and drove to the front to pick up Cyndi and Lander. I turned left and headed Highway 550 north. After a couple of blocks, Cyndi cleared her throat and said, "Aren't you forgetting something?"

Although I knew exactly what she was referring to, I played dumb. "What do you mean? We haven't forgotten anything."

She glared at me and I dutifully did a U-turn and drove back to the Starbucks I had just passed. Lander got his strong coffee and Cyndi and I ordered our usual lattes . . . and all was right with the world. Then I found the highway north.

As we settled in for the drive, Cyndi pointed her finger at Lander and said, "Okay, out with it. Who called you last night and what else have you discovered?"

Lander smiled and replied, "The plot thickens! The call was from Director Frazier." Cyndi and I looked at Lander in surprise. Frazier was the Director of the CIA in Langley, Virginia. Lander and he had been in Special Forces together and we had worked with him on a terrorist threat we had stumbled upon last year in Nova Scotia.

I said, "Okay, what does the CIA have to do with what is going on here?"

Lander answered. "I contacted the Director. Remember, I told you that I would run background checks on Dr. Pasternak. Well, I actually requested that he provide background on all the players in this case: Pasternak, Yates, Smith, Lee, and both interns, Kim and Shannon. He gave me some key facts on the phone yesterday and then sent me a secure fax on my SAT phone last night. What he told me led me to request an additional meeting with Dr. Yates."

"Do you think Dr. Yates is a part of the criminal element here?" Cyndi asked.

"No, I don't think she has anything to do with the crimes. She is really a victim."

I was becoming agitated at the cryptic answers Lander was giving. "Come on, quit beating around the bush; give us the whole scoop," I grumbled. Lander loved to play cat and mouse with me, alternating between making me guess and making me beg.

He smiled, knowing that he was leading me on. "No, Yates is innocent, but it does seem that she is holding back information on us. She is really a paleontologist, but I think she is involved in a project that is much more critical than just collecting ancient artifacts and bones from extinct animals."

I asked the next question. "What about Dr. Smith? Is he working with her on this secret project?"

"Smith probably does not know the true nature of Yates' research. The inclusion of him in the excavation lends credibility to the activities being normal excavations."

"Did everybody else check out? There has to be a mole inside the operation furnishing information to the group that attacked the site."

"Pasternak was the obvious insider, but she seems clean according to the deep background checks. Smith is spotless, also; he has nothing in his background that is suspect. He's squeaky clean."

I thought a minute before replying. "That leaves the other project director, Lee."

Cyndi added, "And the two interns."

Lander said, "The girls are probably okay, especially Shannon. I'm not so sure about Kim. Lee may be a different matter."

I said, "He was conveniently gone when the attack occurred at his camp. And he seemed awfully interested in the direction of the investigation."

"You're right. He is the most likely inside man, although I'm not one hundred percent convinced of it yet. We definitely need to keep our eyes on him. And, don't rule out Kim yet, but she can't be the real source; she doesn't have the access to restricted information."

"All right, Mr. Lander. We've discussed all the players. Now tell us what the secret project is that Dr. Yates is involved in."

"Let's leave it at this for now. I want to see if you come to the same conclusion that I made. Listen to our discussion with Yates and see where it leads you."

I sighed. "I know; it's part of the training."

Chapter 25

Yates **parked her car and stepped out.** She was heart-broken at the devastation she saw. All her work was reduced to rubble; bones shattered that would never be seen again; pristine excavation that would never be the same. She shook her head sadly and said to herself, "Snap out of it; at least you still have your files and notes. Get busy and prepare the site for the project to continue." With her head hanging, she slowly entered the main tent and began preparations to reopen the site. She was so absorbed in what she was doing that she failed to hear the vehicle as it eased to a spot next to her Jeep.

The sudden voice startled her. "Good morning, Dr. Yates. We're glad you have returned."

When Yates reached for her waistband, Romonov warned, "Don't do it! Don't give me a reason to pull this trigger. Now, move over to the chair, slowly."

"What do you want? You've already destroyed the excavation site."

"You know what I want . . . what I need. Hand it over."

Yates smiled warily at this. "I don't know what you are after. There are no bones left."

"You sabotaged your computer. I know you have a backup somewhere. Where is it?"

"You're out of luck. Even if I had a backup, it wouldn't be here on the site. That wouldn't be very smart, would it?"

"You're probably right. A smart lady like you wouldn't be stupid enough to have it here, especially after what has happened." He looked at his companions and said, "Tie her up. We'll just take her with us. I have a feeling she will want to help us."

As the two men moved toward her, she laughed, "You have a feeling that I will want to help you? You're out of your mind. You'll have to kill me first."

"Oh, I think you will be glad to help us," Romonov said with a loud chuckle. "You may not care about saving your own life, but what about your family? Are you prepared to sacrifice them?"

Yates jerked her head up and glared at him. "I have no kids. What are you talking about?"

"You have a husband . . . and you have a sister with three kids. It would be a shame if something happened to them."

Yates tried to rush at Romonov. The men grabbed her and, although she kicked at them and tried to claw them, they were finally able to subdue her. Gradually, Yates gave up her attack and decided to try to run, but was unable to escape their grip. "Get her tied up and let's get out of here," directed Romonov. The men secured her hands behind her back, using zip ties tightly wound around her wrists; she gagged when a dirty handkerchief was stuffed into her mouth. They then steered her out the door and toward their vehicle. Before they roughly pushed her into the van, they blindfolded her. Lying on her side, she heard the van doors close and she rolled from side to side as the van sped away.

Chapter 26

Ivanov spent the time crossing the Black Sea by reading. His choice of books came from the genre of Mystery, Suspense, and Thriller. There were a few good Russian authors, but he had finished the books of those writers long ago. He now read mostly American authors, although there were a few British, Canadian, and Australian writers he enjoyed. He placed the book into his bag; while he had it opened, he looked at the package again. His curiosity was compelling, but he resisted the impulse, knowing that if he opened it, The Man would make him pay dearly for it, perhaps even with his life. He would do exactly as he was instructed to do . . . collect the package, hand it off, and collect his payment, just as always. He had made a good living by being a reliable courier and contact between the Ambassador and The Man. He would continue to do so. He closed the bag and stood, looking out at the darkened shoreline sneaking up on the boat.

The boat eased to a stop at the deserted dock in Sochi. Most people in the West had never heard of Sochi before the Olympics; it had been a playground for the Russian elite. Ivanov had vacationed there many times as a boy. Not because his parents had money, but because he worked hard and excelled in academics and athletics, the privileged kids always wanted to include him. Athletics is a great equalizer; everyone loves a winner, even a poor one. But now, because of the publicity, it had a constant flow of common visitors. Ivanov liked it the way it was in the past.

He jumped from the boat and made his way to the dark soccer complex. Staying in the adjacent woods, he emerged only when he heard the helicopter slowly descend. As soon as it was near the ground, he used the attached skid to enable him to enter the passenger cabin. As soon as he stepped inside, the pilot increased the rotation of the blades and the craft lifted into the sky.

The Man had been in the Russian KGB and still maintained his contacts in the military. That was the reason he was able to provide transportation for Ivanov. The helicopter was a Ka 52, an Alligator Attack Helicopter, and could carry two people up front. The Russians claim it is the fastest and deadliest attack helicopter in the world, able to carry an array of deadly missiles. But tonight, there was no ordnance on the wings; it was a simple person transport. It had a range of twelve hundred kilometers with maximum fuel and could cruise at a speed of three hundred kilometers per hour. It would take one refueling and about five and a half hours to cover the distance to Moscow. The pilot said nothing to Ivanov; for this, Ivanov was glad and he settled back into his seat and let the twin-rotors lull him to sleep. He awoke for the refueling and dozed again for the second leg of the trip. When the helicopter settled to the ground, he exited and was met immediately by a man who directed him to the waiting Mercedes Benz.

Ivanov settled into the back seat. The driver checked to be sure he was secure and then he was taken to a deserted building where he made a necessary pit stop. From there, the man drove across two lanes of runway, slowed, and Ivanov stared at the idling plane, a Mig 31 Foxhound. According to the Russian propaganda machine, it was the fastest plane in the world. Ivanov was directed to the lowered steps and entered the airplane. The pilot shook his hand and pointed to the right. "Please make yourself comfortable. There are drinks and food in the cooler. I'm sure you are hungry."

"Thank you. Yes, I am hungry and thirsty." He opened the cooler and removed a wrapped sandwich and selected bottled water. Making his way to his seat, he flopped into the co-captain's chair. Although he had slept some, he was tired of traveling; however, he knew the longest leg of his journey lay ahead; Chersky was over eleven thousand kilometers away. Thankfully, the distance would be made easier by flying in the modern fighter jet.

Chersky was the closest city to his final destination. Normally, he would not look forward to going to northeastern Siberia, as it was usually where someone is sent to be punished or simply forgotten. It is a hard place to live. But this time he was excited about going there because he was finally going to visit the remote facility that was the setting for the project that would propel Russia back into a world-leadership position. Although he didn't know exactly what the project was, he somehow knew that the package he was delivering was a crucial piece of the puzzle. From his conversations, he had inferred that it was an unprecedented power play and was critical to the future of the Motherland. Ivanov relaxed and slept for several hours, but then sat up wide-awake. He was increasingly anxious as the destination became closer. By the time they landed, he was so wired he couldn't relax. He carried the package down the air steps and looked for his ride. A man standing beside a Mercedes waved to him and Ivanov hurried to meet him.

"You have the package?" said the man. Although he was in his fifties, he looked like a thirty-year-old body builder; the light jacket he wore did nothing to conceal the bulging muscles. And Ivanov didn't need to look; he knew the man was armed and extremely dangerous.

"Yes, it is here," replied Ivanov, holding it out for the man to see.

"I will take it now."

Ivanov considered his words carefully before replying. "No, I am to personally hand it to The Man. No disrespect meant."

The man laughed. "Good answer! I was testing your resolve to follow directions. If you won't hand it to me, I doubt you would give it to anyone." He flexed his arms as he spoke those words.

Ivanov gave a silent sigh of relief. He would have been no match for the muscle he was staring at. He smiled and sat in the passenger seat. As the driver closed his door, Ivanov said, "Call me Ivanov. What is your name?"

"I know who you are. It is not necessary for you to know my name."

They followed the Kolyma River southeast until a tall fence came into view. There were no signs announcing the site, which rested in the midst of some of the coldest, most desolate area in the entire world. Even with the chilling cold and travel fatigue, Ivanov eagerly took in every aspect of the approach. As they stopped at a locked gate, he glanced at his driver, who seemed not in the least interested in the place. The driver spoke into a mic on his wrist and shortly afterward, the gate opened. Ivanov looked with amazement at the landscape opening up to him.

Chapter 27

After a late-night storm, it was another beautiful Colorado morning. I parked the car in the excavation site beside Yates' Jeep. "It seems eerily quiet; where are we supposed to meet Dr. Yates?" asked Cyndi. "I don't remember her saying."

I replied, "She didn't say; she is probably in the main tent. I think I remember her saying that she was going to get an early start on getting the site ready to start working again."

Lander didn't say anything at first. I noticed that he was intently looking at the ground around the cars. Suddenly, he said, "You all stay here. I'll be right back." He pulled his weapon and eased out of the car, closing the door quietly behind him.

Cyndi looked at me. "What is that all about?"

"I'm not sure. He obviously saw something he didn't like. He'll tell us when he gets back." I watched Lander go from tent to tent. In about five minutes, he returned to the car.

"What's going on?" I asked.

Lander pointed at the ground. "What do you see?"

I looked to where he was pointing. After a minute, I said, "Fresh tire prints . . . and shoe prints. It looks like there were three of them. Someone else has been here. Yates said Pasternak would be here about noon. She expected no one else this morning."

Lander nodded and said. "You're right. Whoever was here has gone now—and I suspect that they have taken Dr. Yates with them."

Cyndi asked, "Why would they want to come back for her? They obviously got the bones they wanted."

"I'll tell you what I think. But first, we have to report Yates' kidnapping." Lander pulled his phone from his pocket and accessed McKenzie's number. When he connected, he said, "Ranger McKenzie, Lander here. We are at the excavation site where we were supposed to meet Dr. Yates. I think she has been kidnapped. Her car is still parked on the far side of the tents, but there is no sign of her. There are fresh tracks that shows another vehicle with three people was here this morning."

"Don't touch anything. I'll call the sheriff and we'll be right out."

Lander closed the connection and put his phone away. "Let's look around the site." He looked at me and said, "You go left and I'll go right. Yell if you see anything. Cyndi, why don't you look in the tents again; I was in a hurry, so I didn't look closely; I do know that no one is in the tents, so you will be safe." He included both of us in the next statement. "McKenzie said not to touch anything. If you see any more shoe prints, stay away from them."

Cyndi asked, "What am I looking for?"

"Anything that doesn't look right. If you get a feeling about something, don't ignore it. Call it to my attention."

I began slowly walking to the left, staring intently at the ground in front of and beside me. Suddenly I stopped and then walked a couple of yards to my left. I bent and carefully moved a broken twig to the side. I had been right; there was a print in the grass and mud. Looking carefully, I sighed. "It's only an animal print," I thought. Standing back up, I continued the circle, finding nothing else that seemed suspicious. In fifteen minutes, we met back at our car. "Nothing," I said.

Cyndi and Lander echoed my finding. Lander said, "Nothing except these prints. Not even a sign of a struggle. If those perps were good enough to take Yates without a fight, they are professionals."

"What now?" I asked.

"We wait for McKenzie and Spencer," Lander said. "After that, we are going to have a long talk with Pasternak. She is supposed to be here in an hour or so."

About ten minutes later, McKenzie's car came roaring into the site. Lander pointed to the left of my car and McKenzie skidded to a stop next to us. Both McKenzie and Spencer had their doors open before the car came to a complete stop.

"This just keeps getting deeper and deeper," said McKenzie. "What have you found?"

"Not a thing except fresh tire prints on the other side of our car. It looks as if there were three people in the car. That's why I directed you to park here." Lander moved around our car and we all followed him. He pointed at the soft ground. "It rained here last night so the prints are pretty clear."

Sheriff Spencer nodded. "We can get a good cast of those prints. Lab people are on the way now." He looked closely at us and said, "You all seem always to be in the location where something bad happens. Now why do you think that is?"

Lander just shrugged. I started to say, "It's just coincidental," but I didn't. I don't believe much in coincidence, so I replied, "I guess we are just like John Wayne. He always seemed to be in the right place at the right time. I'm sure you understand that."

Spencer finally smiled and said, "I guess I do. If you're anything like The Duke, then you're all right."

Lander spoke up. "We looked around, but didn't find anything other than the tire tracks.

Yates is pretty alert to danger, so whoever took her is professional."

McKenzie said, "We all agree that this is still a part of the earlier attack, don't we?"

We all nodded in agreement. "They are still looking for something," said Lander.

"Do you think they came back after more bones and Yates just happened to be here? If so, then she wasn't a target, but a victim of opportunity."

Lander looked at Spencer a minute before answering. "No, I think that they came here specifically to target Yates. She has what they are after."

"You mean the flash drive backup, don't you?" Spencer said and Lander nodded his head. Spencer continued, "That makes sense. But we don't know what is in those files and, according to Kim, Yates is the only one who does know. Even Dr. Smith doesn't know; he is working on a completely different research objective."

While McKenzie and Spencer were looking around the scene, the lab personnel arrived and we pointed them to the prints. The technician said, "It's a good thing it rained last night; we've got some good prints."

Another car came up the road, slowed, and turned into the site. Cyndi said, "For a supposedly secret excavation, there sure is a lot of traffic here."

I said, "That should be Dr. Pasternak." I looked at my watch. "Right on time; she is supposed to be here at twelve o'clock."

McKenzie and Spencer exited the tent and moved toward us. Pasternak walked up to us and asked, "What's going on? Has something else happened?"

I looked to see if the Sheriff and Ranger were close enough to hear her question. Spencer stepped closer and said, "It seems that Dr. Yates has been kidnapped."

I watched Pasternak's face closely, but she seemed to register only shock. As Spencer explained what had happened, she appeared deeply concerned and asked all the right questions. When the situation was covered, Spencer turned to McKenzie and said, "Let's get back to town. There's nothing else here and we need to get this investigation moving; we also need to put out information for a search for Dr. Yates. You all be careful. If you see anything at all, give us a call immediately."

Lander said, "We'll be okay. They won't be back here. If we see anything else, we'll let you know." The two officers got in McKenzie's Jeep and left.

Lander stared at Pasternak and said, "Let's go sit down in the tent. We need to talk."

When we all were seated, Lander spoke to Pasternak. "Okay, we know that the bones were not stolen to be sold. We also know that Yates was conducting some type of classified research that the other sites were not doing. We need to know exactly what she was up to."

Pasternak replied, "What makes you think that she was doing some secret research?"

"She kept files related to her work separate from the other information and no one else was privy to it. It is important enough to someone that he or she is willing to kill for it. All the clues point to the perpetrators being highly skilled and having perhaps unlimited resources to pour into their mission. Now, we need to know what her real research is. If you have any hesitation about sharing that information with us, call CIA Director Jarrod Frazier. He will instruct you to provide any information you may have."

The use of the CIA Director's name got her attention. She hung her head a moment before looking at us and saying, "You are right. Dr. Yates was involved in a highly-classified project. What do you know about it?"

Lander replied, "I know what her background is and what her specialty is. I know that this is a legitimate excavation and had an exceptionally well-preserved skeleton of a rare specimen. A find that by itself was important to the paleontology community. Yates was one of only a few that could have led that project."

Pasternak nodded. "Yes, all that is true. But you suspect that there is more to it than the recovery of the skeleton?"

Lander shook his head. "I know that there is more to it than the excavation of a skeleton. Do you want to tell us what that is or do you want me to tell you what I think—or what I am pretty sure—is the reason that it is Dr. Yates who is heading this particular project?"

Cyndi and I looked at Lander with astonishment. I couldn't believe that he had been holding back information from us; however, after the initial shock, I realized that this was his typical pattern. He worked things out in his mind before he shared them—not to keep things secret from us but to be confident that he was on the right track.

Pasternak fixed her eyes on Lander. "Go on. You are doing well."

Chapter 28

Ivanov had expected something different, but the vista that greeted him astonished even him. Inside the fence, no longer was there the abundance of the mossy, forested tundra that dominated this area of Arctic Siberia. Instead, he saw endless grassland. He looked at his driver and asked, "How have they changed this? How could they stop the growth of the trees and high brush?"

The driver scowled at him and refused to answer. Ivanov sat back in his seat and gazed at the passing landscape before him. After a drive of about twelve minutes, the driver turned off the main road and bounced down a rugged side road. Stopping before a building modeled after a Quonset hut, the driver nodded to Ivanov and pointed to the door. Needing no further motivation to leave the car, Ivanov grasped his package and headed for the building. The car turned around and left the way it had come. Looking at the departing car, Ivanov wondered, *How am I going to get out of here?*

Before Ivanov reached the door, it opened and a large man stepped outside. "Welcome, Mr. Ivanov." He held his hand out to Ivanov and smiled. "I am Aleksey Leonid."

Ivanov shook his hand and felt some relief at meeting someone who appeared friendly.

"Please, follow me." Leonid turned and entered a short hallway. He stopped at a door and pushed a button. They waited for a few seconds and the door slid open. Ivanov followed his host through the door and realized they were in an elevator. Leonid clicked the down button and the cage began to descend quietly and rapidly. After several seconds, the elevator eased to a stop and the door opened. Leonid stepped quickly into the hallway and turned left. Following him, Ivanov noted the gleaming white hallway. On either side were closed doors, all with security locks on them. Coming to an intersecting hallway, Leonid turned left and led Ivanov to the end room. He pressed his thumb to a sensor pad and looked at the camera. The door opened with a slight swish and they entered the room.

Ivanov almost felt the voice as much as he heard it; it was the deepest bass he had ever heard. He swore that the room almost shook when the man spoke. "Welcome to our lab, Mr. Ivanov. You have the package, I see. Well done! Please hand it over to Aleksey."

Ivanov started to comply, then paused. "May I ask your name?"

"I am The Man. You have talked with me on the phone."

"But your voice sounds different. It is much deeper than the man with whom I have spoken."

"You are right. When I speak on the phone, I use a voice-changing module. I can't take chances that someone will eavesdrop and produce a voice imprint." He held up a device attached to the phone on his desk. "To confirm that it is I with whom you have spoken, please call the number that you last talked with me."

Ivanov pulled his phone from his jacket and powered it on. He accessed his recent calls and pushed a number. When the phone on the desk buzzed, The Man lifted the receiver and spoke into it. Ivanov recognized the voice and smiled. He terminated the call and handed the package to Leonid, who turned and left the two men alone.

The Man offered his hand to Ivanov who shook it. "I am pleased to finally meet you face to face," The Man said. "Please have a seat. May I offer you a drink?" He pointed at a bottle of vodka, and then said, "Or perhaps you would prefer coffee?"

"Coffee would be good."

His host raised his hand briefly and said, "It will be here shortly. I hope you don't mind if I choose this." He picked up the bottle and said, "This is Sibirskaya Strong, the best vodka in Russia."

By the time he had poured his drink, the door opened and a beautiful young Russian woman entered, carrying a mug and a carafe. She paused in front of Ivanov and filled his cup with steaming hot coffee. She looked demurely at Ivanov and asked, "Cream or sugar?"

"No. Black is fine." She handed the mug to him, sat the carafe on the desk, and left as silently as she had entered.

The Man raised his stein and said, "To a successful project."

Ivanov lifted his mug and repeated, "To a successful project." They both drank; then Ivanov said, "What is the project?"

The Man laughed heartily at that. "What do you think?"

"Well, it has something to do with the change in the landscape I saw coming here. All the trees and large brush are gone. There's nothing but grass growing inside the fence now. What's happening here?"

The Man took one more sip from his stein and then said, "There's a lot happening here. Let's go; I want to show you what we are doing. He walked to the far wall and pushed a button. The wall separated down the middle and each side slid away from the other. Ivanov saw a small room with one wall completely covered with monitors. He followed The Man into the room and the entrance closed behind him. The Man approached a desk with a computer on it. With a tap of a key, all the monitors came to life. Ivanov stared with amazement at the scenes.

Chapter 29

Yates raised her head at the sound of the door opening. Three people approached her chair. Since she had been left shackled in the windowless room two days ago, she had had but a single visitor, a young man that had brought her food and water. She had tried several times to engage him in conversation, but he would never respond so she had given up trying. Even though her hands were not restrained, she could do nothing to remove the band around her ankle or the chain that was attached to a steel ring in the concrete floor. The chain was just barely long enough for her to visit the small space a few feet from her bed, an area that contained only a sink and toilet. The only other piece of furniture was the chair where she now sat. It was under a hanging light bulb that produced the only light in the room. It was turned off for several hours at a time; she assumed this was during the nighttime. She had no other reference for the passing of time. No one had spoken to her since she had been left here. She was worried sick about her family. The man had threatened her with harm to them if she refused to help him. Her purse and phone had been taken from her, so she had no possible way to contact help. She was left with no choice but to convince them that she was cooperating with them.

She looked closely at the three men. The first was the person who had been bringing her food and water. One of the other two was the man who had orchestrated her kidnapping and had threatened her. He seemed to be in charge. As he approached, he said, "Good afternoon, Dr. Yates. I have a visitor whom I think you will recognize." As he spoke, he moved to the side so Yates could see the third man.

She stared at him a moment, then gasped. "Dr. Leonid! What are you doing here? Have they kidnapped you, too?" She had not seen him since the conference last year at the Annual Symposium of Vertebrate Paleontology and Comparative Anatomy. They both were featured presenters at the meeting. He had given a research paper on the topic of how the killing of large herbivores had affected the landscape of the grasslands of the Arctic Tundra. He had claimed that was the reason for the climate change. Most noted scientists disagreed, positing that the climate change was the precipitating cause for the disappearance of the grasslands necessary for the sustaining of the large animals. It was a "chicken or the egg" enigma, but she had found herself leaning toward the stance presented by Leonid. They had spent some of their discretionary time at the conference discussing his theory.

"Dr. Yates. I am glad to see you again. I am told that you have agreed to work with me."

"You are a part of my kidnapping? Why is my family being threatened? I demand to be released immediately."

"I'm afraid that will not be possible. The project we will work on is much too important to abandon."

"What project are you talking about?" Yates struggled to contain her anger.

"Why, the project you discussed in your paper. You do remember what it was, don't you? And I know that your current research is related to it."

She stared at the Russian scientist and then it hit her. "You're talking about the Pleistocene Park project, aren't you? You want me to help you with the animals. I thought the project was already being implemented. At least, it is alleged to be factual according to the articles being published."

Leonid laughed. "You're right. But that is only the first phase of the project. The true objective is still not in reach. That is where you can help us. Your knowledge and work with the ancient skeletons can lead us to a quick conclusion, one that will catapult Russia back into the world spotlight. And we have to accelerate our timeline because both China—and, of course, the U.S.—are also working on the same objective. Your presentation proved that you are far ahead of all others. I know that you are struggling with obtaining funding to do what you want to do; it is a slow process in America. On the other hand, we have all the support needed to do whatever we want. You can be a major contributor to the project . . . and we will give you credit in the scientific community for your efforts."

"Even if I wanted to, my organization would not let me work with you."

"Au contraire, mon ami. Your organization wants to be a part of our project."

"What do you mean? Who in my organization wants to collaborate with you?"

"Suffice it to say; it has been signed off on at the highest level."

Yates stared at him with disbelief. She quickly ran down the list of names that could sign such an agreement, but could not identify the one who could do such a thing. Although she knew someone had to be providing inside information, she didn't think it was Dr. Pasternak, even though she was of Russian descent. If not she, then it had to be higher up. She made up her mind. "If I help you, my family will be safe?"

"I assure you they will be safe. We don't wish to harm them; we only want your cooperation. You help us and they will not even know we are close by."

"You have access to a lab here? I'm not going to Russia."

"Now you are making sense. Of course, we have a lab here, a state-of-the-art facility much better than any you have ever worked in. You will enjoy the experience." He looked at Romonov and said, "Release her. She will be safe with me."

Romonov started to protest, but Leonid spoke again, harshly this time. "I said to release her. I see you brought me a package. Leave it here. Then you may leave us. I will escort Dr. Yates to the lab."

Romonov glared at Leonid and then grudgingly pulled the key from his pocket and unlocked the chain. He then laid the package on the floor.

"The ankle bracelet, also; she will not need to be confined like an animal."

The ankle band was removed.

"Now, that's better, isn't it, Dr. Yates?

Romonov said, "Just remember that we have people within minutes of your family and they will not hesitate to carry out any order that I give them. Don't think you could stop them by killing either Leonid or me. If I don't check in with them on a regular schedule, they will assume that something tragic has happened to me and they will proceed to carry out their orders."

Leonid listened to Romonov and then he picked up the package. "Now, let's go check out the lab."

Chapter 30

Cyndi and I watched the exchange of Lander and Pasternak. At last, we were going to find out what Lander had worked out. This was getting interesting and I could see the sparkle in Cyndi's eyes as she leaned forward to listen. Pasternak had told Lander to continue with his analysis of the case and she waited for a response from him.

Lander stood; I recognized the move for what it was. He always stood and paced when he was intensely engaged in a debate, even if it were with himself. "Okay, let me know if I get off track. I'll hit several points, but I think they will all come together at the end."

"First, the hair samples we found in the cave. We had them analyzed with the new process. They proved that the hair was not from a Japanese. They were from a European ethnicity, most likely a Russian."

Pasternak's eyebrows rose slightly at this information. "Go on," she said.

"I had background checks done on everyone associated with the project. There was some interesting information gleaned from those."

"Why do checks on everyone?" asked Pasternak.

"We know that someone has been supplying information about the excavations to the perps. They were too knowledgeable about the sites and timelines not to have inside information."

"Do you think I am the informer?"

"At first, everyone was suspect and, yes, at one time, I considered you to be a high possibility."

"But not now?"

"No. You have reacted in a normal pattern, not like someone who is trying to hide something. I know it is not you even though you have withheld valuable information about the projects from us. This, too, is typical for someone trying to safeguard classified information."

"Then you are implying that the person is above me. No one below my level of access would know the information. Now, you're scaring me. What else did you discover?"

"We'll come back to this person later. Actually, I believe that there was a minimum of two people involved, one at a high level and one on site."

"That narrows it down to Dr. Smith or the two interns," Cyndi said.

Lander nodded. "You're right. It's not Dr. Smith. He's a true scientist and passionate about his work. He wouldn't engage in spying for another country. That leaves Kim and Shannon. Shannon was shot trying to escape, so I don't think it was Shannon."

"I can't believe Kim would do this," said Pasternak. "She seemed so thrilled to be working on her doctorate."

I spoke up. "Even good people can be turned for money. What was her financial status?"

Pasternak admitted, "She was having money issues; in fact, she couldn't have participated in the intern assignment if she hadn't received the fellowship money."

Lander said, "She deposited five thousand dollars in cash the day after the attack. Would her parents or a sponsor been able to do that?"

She replied, "I doubt it. I've never met them, but Kim has stated that her mom was single and had difficulty in meeting her own expenses; that was the reason Kim couldn't depend on help from her. I've actually bought her groceries a few times."

Lander said, "She is the main suspect in camp; however, there has to be someone above you who has been the real source of information. All Kim could do was to report current positions to someone."

Pasternak said, "That's probably true. What do you know about the actual project?"

"The background information on Dr. Yates was interesting. I know that she is a world-leading paleontologist. She probably knows more about ancient skeletons of dinosaurs than anyone else. That has been her passion for several years now."

Pasternak nodded, "Yes, all that is true, but . . ."

Lander continued, "But what does this have to do with the current situation? I also know that she is interested in what can be done with those skeletons."

"You mean in addition to studying and displaying them?" I asked.

"Yes." Lander looked at Pasternak. "I also know that she presented a paper at an international symposium last year on extinct animals."

Pasternak looked at him in utter surprise. "Do you know the focus of the paper?"

"Yes, I have read it. It is in this journal." He pulled the publication from an inside pocket and tossed it on the table. "Her focus was on the reviving of extinct animals."

I interrupted them. "Do you mean trying to reestablish those animals? I read something about that just recently. Someone was discussing trying to create a woolly mammoth from DNA or something. Is this what you are talking about? I think there was a scientific term for the process, but I don't remember it."

Lander lifted the journal and turned to a marked page. The title read, "De-extinction: The Moral and Scientific Implications."

"De-extinction. Dr. Pasternak, is this what Yates' excavation is about?"

Chapter 31

Each of the twelve monitors on the wall showed a different scene. "This is Pleistocene Park," said The Man. It will be the ultimate experiment of all history. What do you know of the work here?"

Ivanov shrugged. "Not much. Just rumors that a big project has been going on here for the last few years."

"Good! I hope you are being honest with me. Details of our work are not supposed to be public knowledge yet. Have a seat. This will take a while." He paused as Ivanov sat and then he continued. "You are one of the first to see the complete picture." He waved his hand and a tall Russian appeared with drinks. "Have a fresh drink," he said as he lifted one for himself and then sat down at the computer.

He clicked a key and the monitors all showed the same scene. It was a desolate, dreary-looking place covered with tall brush and trees. "This is the way the park looked back in 1988. Our great biologist Sergey Zimov received permission to develop the park to prove a theory he had about why the grasslands had disappeared ten thousand years ago."

Ivanov said, "This looks like the landscape outside the park now."

"Yes, it was all the same. In 1989, Zimov created Pleistocene Park; it was originally an area of one hundred sixty square kilometers surrounded by a six hundred square kilometer buffer zone in which there could be no developments. This is what it looks like now." The Man clicked a key and the monitors showed a picture of grasslands; the tall brush and trees were gone.

"How did he get grass to grow here?"

The Man leaned back in his desk chair and stared at the ceiling before answering. "This is close to what the whole area looked like at the end of the Pleistocene period. It was an area covered with grass and had an abundance of large animals, both herbivores and carnivores."

"Plant eaters and meat eaters?" asked Ivanov.

"Yes, I'm pleased to see that you know what I'm talking about. Anyway, at the end of the Pleistocene era, most of the large animals died out. The prevailing theory in the scientific community is that they died as a result of climatic change. After the long ice age where glaciers moved in and then retreated, the cold grasslands gave way to warmer and wetter tundra and forest.

Thus, they say, the large animals could not adapt to the different environment and became extinct."

"That sounds plausible to me." Ivanov was eager to agree with The Man.

"Yes, that makes sense, doesn't it? However, Zimov had a different theory. The reason he created the park was to test his hypothesis. He thought the others had it analyzed backwards. He did not accept the idea that the large animals died out as a result of climate change that others claim removed the grasslands. There was another important development about the same time that the ice age ended, not only here in Siberia but also in other parts of the world; North America was especially affected."

"What was this other development that our biologist believes led to the extinctions?"

"It was man. Zimov refers to it as a 'blitzkrieg hypothesis.' Humans migrated into the areas. They were smarter than the big, slow-moving animals and they had developed stone spear points to hunt with. Zimov claims that the hunters thinned out the herds so much that the grasslands disappeared."

"Why would smaller herds of large animals cause the grasslands to disappear? Am I missing something here?"

"According to Zimov, the great herds of large animals roamed all over the steppe. They kept the large brush and moss trampled down and the trees could not grow. They grazed and they fertilized the soil with their manure, enabling the lush grasslands to flourish. But when the herds were diminished by hunting, all that changed. No longer were there enough animals to keep the brush and trees stamped out, so the grasslands were slowly replaced with mossy forests and tundra. This, in turn, led to even fewer large animals that could thrive here. Only reindeer and moose survived."

"I like Zimov's idea. So why are we now seeing the grasslands rebound?"

"He felt that if the killing off of the large animals gave rise to the demise of the grasslands, then that process could be reversed. If we reintroduced large animals to the region, then the tall shrubs and mossy forests would be replaced with grasslands. It is a major initiative, one that could ultimately help to solve the global warming problem."

"How could it help to do that?"

"I will try to explain it to you as Zimov claims. It has to do with the permafrost."

"What is permafrost?"

"As the name suggests, it is ground that is frozen permanently. It is thought that beneath the permafrost are locked gigatons of organic carbon; it really is a large carbon reservoir. As long as the permafrost remains frozen, it cannot escape.

"An ambitious project, indeed! What animals do you now have in the park?"

The Man clicked another key and the monitors presented different views, many showing various animals roaming. "We started with the introduction of six horses and three moose. Obviously, that was not enough to impact the environment. We have many more now, including bison, musk oxen, moose, horses, and reindeer."

Ivanov watched in wonder as large herds of animals moved around the grasslands. "How does the package I delivered fit in with the project?"

The Man fixed his dark eyes on Ivanov. "That remains to be seen. Our project is just beginning." With that, he shut power to the monitors and stood up. "I hope that you have enjoyed your tour of our park. What you have seen and heard is not to be discussed with anyone. Do you understand this?"

Ivanov was well aware of the implied threat. "I will speak of it to no one," he said.

"Come; I will feed you before we look at the next phase."

Chapter 32

Yates followed Leonid down the hall; Leonid stopped at a locked door, placed his hand on the sensor, and watched the door open. They entered the room and the door closed behind them. The room was an elaborate lab. Leonid stood aside and let Yates walk around the lab inspecting the shiny, new equipment.

"Pretty impressive," Yates said.

"I know that you will be thrilled to work in such a lab," Leonid said. "I am sure you have nothing like this for your work."

"You're right. This is far beyond the facilities I am accustomed to working in. But what makes you think I am going to work with you?"

"I have several reasons to know that you will work with me. When we were at the conference last year, we talked at length about our work. You may be out digging up bones and you like doing that. But your passion is the study of ancient DNA and the possibilities that it offers. You want to do the same thing that I do: bring back some of the extinct animals that mankind eliminated. If you work through your system, it will be years before you are afforded that opportunity. Am I not right?"

Yates looked at him and then dropped her head. "Yes, I am afraid you are correct. We have so many roadblocks thrown up to stall real research. We have become so politically correct that almost everyone is afraid to step out and take any kind of risks now."

Leonid nodded his head. "I agree with you. If we cannot take chances—calculated, but risks, nonetheless—then we cannot progress. The U.S. has a good system. But one of your authors on leadership was correct: 'The enemy of great is good'."

I replied, "Jim Collins, one of my favorites. When things seem to be going well, most organizations or even individuals will not change, even when change is necessary to get to excellence. You said you had several reasons why I would help you."

"In addition to fulfilling your passion, what else is important?"

"My pledge to my country. I cannot do anything that will contradict the laws and procedures of the U.S. We have rigorous restrictions regarding working with foreign countries in the scientific areas, especially biological and chemical. There are harsh penalties for violating them."

"You remember that I told you that this joint venture has been signed off on. Suffice it to say that the person is high enough in your government to provide you not only permission to work with me but also grant you immunity for any problems that may arise."

"I don't believe you."

Leonid reached into his coat pocket and pulled an envelope out. He handed it to Yates, who looked at the return address printed on the top left. Surprised, she then moved her gaze to the addressee. It read simply, "Dr. Shirley Yates."

Yates removed the single sheet of paper and read it:

This document gives permission to Dr. Shirley Yates to enter into an agreement with Dr. Aleksey Leonid to work collaboratively on a project important to the U.S. and Russia. The project is concerned with the study of ancient DNA and the goal is to successfully create procedures to reintroduce to the world prehistoric animals that became extinct at the hands of mankind.

Due to the importance of this work, I assure Dr. Yates that she will be safe from any prosecution now or at any time in the future for collaborating with a foreign government. This project is protected at the highest levels of classification and security and is not to be discussed with anyone other than the principal investigators, namely Dr. Shirley Yates and Dr. Aleksey Leonid or me, or my designee."

It was signed by the President of the United States.

Yates looked in amazement at Leonid.

Leonid said, "This is such a secret that no one should know about the project except our respective presidents . . . and you and I, of course."

"If this is true, and I still don't believe it, why were the excavation sites attacked and people killed?"

"That should not have happened. I learned about those attacks by accident. There is a powerful man in my country that is running that part of the activity. He is in charge of Pleistocene Park and wants desperately to be the first to have extinct animals roaming the countryside."

"Who is this powerful man?"

"He was a high-ranking scientific official in the government and was assigned to be the administrator of Pleistocene Park. He received permission from our president for me to work with him. He was also at our conference last year and was in the audience for both our presentations; he observed us talking extensively during the free times. It was he who devised the plans to obtain the bones from the excavation sites and also to steal your notes to help me at the Park. He is known simply as The Man."

"If you were not a part of it, why didn't you warn me about the attacks?"

"I learned about them only after they occurred and his people had failed to get your information. The attackers were under strict orders not to hurt you; I think the shot was an intentional miss."

"It was close enough to shatter rocks and injure me."

"I can assure you that the man who fired the shot has met his punishment."

He continued, "I was going to approach you secretly to share the project details with you and to elicit your cooperation. Had I known about the assaults in advance, I would surely have notified you."

"How can you work with The Man at the same time that you are working with me?"

"My president, or our presidents, discussed this with me. My true work will be here in the U.S. with you in this lab. I will also work with The Man attempting to utilize the stolen bones. It will be a legitimate effort there; however, it will always be a step or two behind where we are here. I will occasionally travel to Siberia to coordinate their efforts."

"Won't that be extremely dangerous for you. What if he finds out that you are working here?"

"He knows that I will be working here. Even he thought it too dangerous to try to get you into

Russia. I convinced him that I would keep you secure here and spend a lot of time working with you, assuming that you would cooperate with us. He bought the idea of using your family as leverage to make you work with us. It will be a complex operation, but I think we can do it. I would count it an honor to work with you on this project."

"When the other man—my kidnapper—was here, you said that the project was to elevate Russia back into world dominance. That sounded political, not scientific."

"That was only propaganda for his ears, to convince him that I am committed to Russia's being first in this de-extinction project."

Yates considered this for a moment and then said, "I believe you. I remember how passionate you were in our discussions last year. I know you want to revive those extinct animals for the right reasons."

"You are right. When I look at the skeletons of great animals of the past, it's as if the bones are pleading with me. I can almost hear the echoes of those skeletons calling for help. That is what drives me."

"Echoes of those skeletons calling for help. That's an appropriate phrase. What are our plans if I agree to them?"

"My president is scheduled to visit the U.S. in two days. I suspect that we will have a meeting with them to finalize the plans."

"You said 'we'. Do you mean that both of us will meet with the presidents of the U.S. and Russia?"

"I am most positive of it. I have talked with both of them and they are in agreement that you are the one person in this country that could carry out such a project; they are very familiar with your work."

Chapter 33

My phone buzzed and I looked at the caller I.D. "It's McKenzie," I said, as I clicked the talk button. I listened a minute and then replied, "We'll be there."

"We need to be at the Ranger Station at two this afternoon. McKenzie and Spencer are going to interview Kim and they invited us to be there. I want to hear what she has to say. I assumed that you all would want to go, also."

Lander nodded in agreement. "I certainly want to be there. I think Kim knows more than she has volunteered."

I looked at Cyndi. "What about you? Are you going with us?"

"I don't think so. You two go. I want to do some more research while you're gone. But I do want you to do something first."

"I know; get you a Starbucks coffee. I can do that."

We parked in front of the Ranger Station at one fifty and made our way into the lobby. McKenzie's door was open and he shouted for us to come into his office. The day was clear and dry, with temperatures cool enough to be comfortable. McKenzie's window was open to the breeze and it felt good. No sooner had we sat down than the sheriff entered with Kim in tow. She looked surprised to see us there, but she recovered so quickly that I wouldn't even have noticed if I hadn't been looking for a reaction.

"What's going on? I thought you said the Ranger had a couple more questions for me." She addressed this to the sheriff.

"He does. I'm as surprised as you are to see these two."

McKenzie spoke up, "I asked them to come by to discuss developments with us. They've been involved since the beginning and really probably saved your life. If they hadn't shown up when they did, those attackers would likely have killed all of you. Do you have an objection to their being here?"

Kim hesitated, then she said, "No, not really. It's all right."

McKenzie said, "Good. Then let's get started. I've been over and over this case since it happened; something just doesn't fit."

Kim asked, "What do you mean?"

"Go back over the sequence of events, starting with the men entering the camp and ending with us finding you. Tell us exactly what happened."

Kim started her story. When she told the part about the men tying them up and leaving them,

McKenzie asked, "How did you get loose? Was it you or Shannon that escaped first?"

"I think it was Shannon who got loose first; yes, I know it was. She then untied me and we ran."

"Okay, go ahead with the rest of the story."

Kim picked up at the chase that ended with Shannon being shot and Kim hiding.

"Why do you think they shot Shannon and not you?" asked Spencer.

"I don't know; I was just lucky, I guess."

"May I ask a question?" I asked.

McKenzie replied, "Yes, of course; ask anything."

I looked at Kim and said, "When you came out of hiding, you were carrying a bright red hoodie. Why did you take time to grab it when you all escaped?"

She looked confused a minute and then said, "I don't know; it was lying beside me so I just grabbed it, I guess. Just force of habit."

"I have one more question. When you came out of the rocks, you said that it was a good thing that the man didn't know how to tie you up well, implying it was you who was able to get loose. A minute ago, you said it was Shannon that escaped first. Which was it?"

"I was scared and just talking when you found me. It was Shannon who got us loose."

Sheriff Spencer spoke up. "Then that's a problem. You see, Shannon has regained

- 187 -

consciousness and I talked with her. She was completely sure that it was you who got loose. In fact, she said that if you had been tied as securely as she was, there was no way either of you could have gotten free."

Lander had been listening to the conversation and now said, "When we were back at the excavation site and had just learned about the manhunt, you left for a minute. Where did you go?"

Looking scared now, Kim replied, "I don't remember. I guess I went to the bathroom."

Lander considered this a minute, then continued. "Kim, we have a major problem here. We know that someone, actually, probably two people, had to have been working with the attackers. Somebody in the camp was alerting them to some timelines. We think that person could have been you. Are we completely wrong here?"

Kim gasped and looked quickly at the door. "You are wrong. I don't know what you are talking about."

Spencer said, "Kim, we don't think you intended to assist in anyone getting hurt. We do know that you deposited five thousand dollars in your account. Do you want to tell us how you got that money? We know you have had a hard time financially working at the site and your family is in no position to help you."

Kim hung her head, her eyes filling with tears. "I didn't know anyone would get hurt. I needed the money and it seemed like it was safe. I thought all they would do would be to steal some of the bones. I took the money to tell them where the site was and who was in charge. I swear that was all."

"And you made a call to warn them about the manhunt?" Lander stared at her.

"Yes, but that is all. They said no one would get hurt."

Spencer asked, "Who gave you the money?"

Before she answered, a shot rang out. Kim's head exploded over her chair and into the wall and she slumped to the floor, silent forevermore.

Chapter 34

Romonov eased his car into the parking space directly in front of his motel room. It had been forty-five minutes since he had pulled the trigger, but his heart was still racing. Killing didn't bother him; in fact, he rather enjoyed it. He had pulled the trigger and watched through his scope as the head exploded. As soon as he confirmed the hit, he had pushed the stolen motorcycle to get away from the area and had switched to his car before coming to the motel. He knew they had not followed him because he had circled blocks and stopped briefly in various parking areas; no one could have tailed him without his knowing it. Although he had taken out the girl as The Man had instructed him to do, he still felt threatened by the new people. The sheriff and ranger he could handle, but there was something about that Lander man—and his cohorts. At some point, he knew he would have to eliminate them . . . and the sooner, the better.

He locked his car and paused at the motel door, checking the long hair he had taped across the entrance; it had not been disturbed, so he unlocked the door and entered the room. He sat on the bed and stretched his muscles, starting with his neck and working his back loose. He checked his phone for messages, looked at the time, and called The Man.

After two rings, the call was answered. "Da, go ahead."

"The girl has been taken care of."

The Man replied. "Good. I knew I could count on you. Wait for further instructions."

Romonov cleared his throat before speaking. "What about the other men—the ones that just happened on the scene?"

"They are just tourists, aren't they? In a few days, they will go back home and forget all about what happened. Leave them be for now."

Although Romonov knew it was dangerous to disagree with The Man, he said, "I'm not so sure about them. They seem to be everywhere we are."

"What do you mean?"

"They seem to have made themselves a part of the investigation. In fact, they were there today when I eliminated the girl."

"For now, do nothing. We don't need the investigation to expand any more than it already has." Romonov heard the phone go dead as The Man disconnected the call.

Romonov accessed his contacts and clicked on one. He spoke after the call was finally answered.

"Is this the Eastern Trading Company in Hong Kong?"

"Yes, it is. How may I help you?"

"I have a package that needs to be returned. It has been shipped out of Beaumont; standard procedures for getting it to you."

"Thank you. I will look for it. When it arrives safely, I will deposit the refund to your account. You did place the account information in the package, didn't you?"

"Yes, of course. I will look for the deposit and look forward to doing business with you again."

"I will contact you when it is time for the next transaction."

Romonov ended the call. He knew the package would be carried from Hong Kong to Shenzhen. In a few days, he would have more in his offshore account than he had ever dared dream. Although he could retire and live easily now, he was greedy and determined to stay on the payroll of both countries for at least another year. By then, he should be able to go and live anywhere he desired.

Chapter 35

As Kim fell to the floor, Lander yelled, "Get down!" As he shouted, he was already slipping through the office door and running for the front entrance. He ran to his left and paused at the edge of the building. He bent to his knees and eased his head past the corner so that he could see behind the station. He stood and his eyes followed the man on a motorcycle speed out of sight. As he watched him disappear, the others joined him.

"Did you get a look at him?" asked Spencer.

"No, he was almost gone before I picked him up. He must have fired from those trees back there. "Let's go check them out. Perhaps the shooter left a spent cartridge or some boot prints."

"It's still a little damp, so it's possible," said McKenzie. He looked at the distance to the trees and said, "Let's take the Jeep. It'll be quicker."

We found where the motorcycle had been parked; there were partial tire prints, but the area was mostly covered in leaves, so the prints were not good enough to get molds made from them.

Although we searched the area carefully, there were no other clues left behind. After thirty minutes of looking, we went back to the lobby, where Spencer called for an ambulance. We heard him tell the person who answered that there was no hurry—that they would be picking up a dead body.

"Maybe Shannon will have some idea of the person," I said. "She may have seen Kim talking with someone and not realized the implications."

"It's worth asking her about it," Spencer said. "I'll do that as soon as I get back to town."

No sooner had they sat back down than a car slid to a stop next to the front steps. Two men dressed in blue blazers and gray slacks stepped through the door. The lead man said, "Sheriff Spencer and Ranger McKenzie?"

Spencer and McKenzie walked toward them. "Yes," said Spencer.

"We'd like to talk with you a minute . . . outside, if you please." They turned and stepped onto the front porch.

McKenzie looked at Lander and me, shrugged, and followed Spencer.

Outside, Spencer said, "What is the meaning of this? But, first, who are you?"

The two men flashed I.D. badges. "Jeff Scout and Burt Green. We are here to ask you to abandon the investigation into the recent attacks on the excavation sites. All work from this point forward will be handled by the FBI"

McKenzie looked incredulously at the men. "Are you asking or are you ordering us to halt our investigation?"

Scout said, "Deal with semantics if you wish. We are asking that you stop; however, that request is an order."

"Order from whom?" asked Spencer. "You all don't have the clout to make that decision."

Green handed Spencer an envelope. Spencer opened it and read the one-page letter. He looked at McKenzie and said, "This is an order to cease all activity related to the case; it specifically names my sheriff's office and the ranger station . . . and it's signed by FBI Director Harvey Johnson."

Scout said, "I trust we can count on your cooperation." With that said, the two men turned, entered their car, and drove quickly away.

Spencer and McKenzie rejoined Lander and me. It was evident from the look on their faces that they had not received good news. Lander said, "Let me guess. That was an order from Washington that you stand down from the investigation."

Spencer looked at him in surprise. "You are right, but how did you know that was what they wanted?"

I half expected Lander to tell him, "If I told you, I would have to kill you." But he didn't say it. He replied, "It was pretty evident. A government-issued car, two men in typical agent clothes; when they asked to speak to you two, I was sure that was why they were here."

McKenzie said, "I'm sorry, but we have been ordered to close our investigation and not to talk with anyone at all about it. Nothing personal intended, but I'm afraid that includes you two."

Lander replied, "Nothing personal taken. It's a typical gag order issued when the feds get involved in a case. We'll leave now so we don't put you on the spot."

Lander nodded at me and we both shook McKenzie and Spencer's hands and then left.

As we drove away, I said, "Should we talk? Maybe they bugged our car." It was an attempt at a joke.

Lander answered and I noted that he was serious. "No, they didn't bug our car. I watched both of them from the time they arrived."

"What do you think?" I asked.

"You tell me," he replied.

"Teaching never stops, does it?" I thought and then answered. "This case is bigger than we thought. It's not just about a few bones being stolen and a couple of fatalities, is it? It's important enough to get the attention of the 'big dogs' in Washington."

He nodded. "Very good," he said. "Why would they order the locals to stop investigating?"

"The feds don't want the locals to realize the importance of the case. And I would guess that there might be classified information that may surface. They are stopping any potential leaks before they start."

"You are right. The current director believes in being proactive up front rather than reactive after the fact. It is easier to control information in that manner."

"So, we are through? And just when it was getting interesting!" I said.

Lander turned that look on me. "Who said we were through? We received no orders to stop doing anything." He smiled. "We are just getting started."

"What are our plans?" I asked, knowing that Lander was already two steps ahead of me.

"You tell me what our next step ought to be."

I considered what he said. "Well, I guess that we could begin to look for Dr. Yates. I hope that she is still alive."

"No," he said. "Dr. Yates is fine for the near future. Our next step is to grab some coffee and sit down with Cyndi at the motel and talk."

By the time we had gotten back to Durango, Lander had changed his mind. "Let's just eat and relax tonight. I need some time to think. We'll meet for breakfast and work out a plan."

Chapter 36

Cyndi and I were already at the table when Lander showed up. "Sorry, Guys. Another change in plans. I got a call late last night and have to leave for a meeting today."

"Where do you have to go?" I asked.

"I don't know. There will be a ride waiting to pick me up at the airport and take me somewhere. I should be back today. Do you want to take me to the airport or do you want me to drive?"

I looked at Cyndi and then said to Lander, "I guess you just drive. We'll slum around town here today. I'm sure that there are some shops we haven't hit yet." I knew better than to press Lander for details about his meeting.

He said, "Okay, I'm off. I'll fill you in when I get back."

Thirty-five minutes later, Lander pulled into the short-term parking lot. He grabbed his jacket, slipped it on, and headed for the front entrance to the airport. At the doorway, he noticed a man looking at him. He nodded twice and walked over to him.

"Mr. Lander. Please come with me."

Lander walked with the man through the lobby and out onto the tarmac where private planes were parked, some idling and some powered down. He was directed to a small jet. Entering the cabin area, he was met by another man who said, "Would you like something to drink?"

Lander said, "No, thank you."

"Okay. Please make yourself comfortable. We'll be departing shortly."

After several hours in the air, Lander recognized the airport as they descended. "Just what I thought. We're landing in Washington."

A man, waiting with a black SUV beside the plane as it stopped, met them. Although Lander was curious about the trip, he asked no questions; he understood that the people delivering him were just escorts and would have no knowledge of why he was here. They probably didn't even know who he was. The driver took the secret drive into the White House grounds and eased to a stop at the doors to a side entrance. Another man met the car and said to Lander, "Please follow me."

Lander went with him into the White House and paused. He went through the frisk and wand security procedures; he expected these and had gone through them many times before. Cleared, he walked with the man down a hallway. The man paused at a closed door, knocked, and then opened the door. He motioned for Lander to enter. At the conference table sat four people. Lander looked at each as he walked in, then suddenly stopped. "Dr. Yates! I am pleasantly surprised to see you here."

Yates was dumbfounded to hear Lander's voice. It was obvious that she had no idea that he would be joining them. "Mr. Lander? What are you doing here?"

"I'm glad to see you two recognize each other. Lander, you just can't keep out of trouble, can you?"

Lander glared at the source of the statement, then smiled. "Director Frazier! It appears that Kent has gotten me into another adventure. I'm glad to see you again." Lander went to him and shook his hand. "How are you, Sir?"

"Well. And you?"

"Doing better than I deserve."

"You mentioned the Kents. Are they a part of this, adventure, as you call it?"

"Yes Sir, Phil Kent was with me when we stumbled onto the attack at Yates' excavation site." As he spoke, the door opened and two men entered the room. There was complete silence as they took seats at the table.

Frazier said, "Mr. Lander, please have a seat and join us. I think you know most of the group." He pointed at Yates. "Dr. Shirley Yates. The man to her left is Dr. Aleksey Leonid. On her right is Harvey Johnson; he is Director of the FBI. Obviously, you know our President David

Branson. The gentleman that came in with him is . . ."

"Russian President Alex Kruschov," Lander said, as he nodded to him. "I'm pleased to meet all of you and am honored to be in such company."

"Mr. Lander, I want you to know that I objected to having you in the meeting," said Director Johnson. "But, as you can see, I was overruled." There was a noticeable air of tension around that statement.

"That's quite all right, Mr. Director. Depending on what's said, I may object to my being here, also."

Everyone smiled and relaxed a little. President Branson cleared his throat before speaking. "To set the record straight, Director Frazier and I asked that Mr. Lander join us." Yates looked at Lander with more respect. "I know that all of you are busy and I appreciate your meeting with us today. When I say us, I mean myself and President Kruschov." He dipped his head toward the Russian leader.

"Yes, I will concur with President Branson. I thank you for being here."

Branson continued, "We have a major problem. As all of you know, we have had several excavation sites targeted in the last month. Not only were irreplaceable bones stolen and shattered, but a number of our people were killed."

"Do you know who is behind the attacks?" asked Lander.

Branson looked at Kruschov, who replied. "I am afraid the source of the problem comes from my country. You may have heard about Pleistocene Park. It is a national project in Northeastern Siberia; we are attempting to re-create the grassland steppes that were destroyed during the Ice Age. Dr. Leonid is our foremost expert in paleontology and ancient DNA and he will speak more to that in a few minutes. The director of the project is a former high-ranking official named Peter Listovov; he goes by the self-imposed name of 'The Man'. I think it is he who is the man behind the plot. Dr. Leonid, will you tell us more about the project?"

"Yes, of course. The project was started in the late 1980s. The first goal was to re-create the grasslands that disappeared thousands of years ago. The Man was convinced that the grasslands had vanished not because of the climate, but because the herds of large animals that used to graze there had been depleted by hunters; he agreed with some scientists that the constant moving and grazing by the huge animals kept the trees and high brush from growing, thus leading to the plush covering of the grasslands. He introduced some animals to the Park to copy the ancient grazing patterns. In 1995, The Man—I have never heard his real name until today—approached me and appealed to me to come work at the Park. After touring the facilities and discussing the work with him, I agreed to do so. My chief goal was to reintroduce an ancient animal to the environment."

Lander said, "The woolly mammoth."

"Yes. It was a tremendous undertaking. But I was provided any equipment or supplies that I needed; all I had to do was request something and it was there in a matter of days. And the work, ah, the work, it was exactly what I wanted to do. How do you say, upfront? Upfront I emphasized to The Man that the project was a long-term goal and could not be accomplished in a short time."

Dr. Yates spoke up, "But he did accomplish it. Dr. Leonid discovered the skeleton of a woolly mammoth in the permafrost of Siberia. Because of the extreme cold, he was able to recover some cells containing some viable ancient DNA."

Lander said, "I thought that in order for ancient DNA to be viable, it had to have been flash frozen." Everyone present looked at Lander in amazement.

"You're right . . . or at least that is what most in the scientific community believe. It appears that the mammoth discovered by Dr. Leonid had gotten trapped in the frigid waters. The extreme cold of the water essentially quickly froze the animal. He was able to take some ancient DNA cells, introduce them to the sperm cells of an elephant, and then artificially inseminate a female elephant. At full term, a woolly mammoth was born. There are now five of them roaming the Park grasslands."

Johnson said, "It seems your project was successful. Then why the attacks?"

Kruschov started to speak, but Leonid spoke up. "After the success of the woolly mammoth, The Man got greedy. He wanted more and he pressed me to provide it."

Branson said, "What did he want you to do?"

"He wanted to de-extinct some of the most ferocious animals that ever lived. Understand this about The Man. He is not a typical thug; he is extremely intelligent. He became obsessed with the giants of ages past—both animals and man. He wanted, no, compelled, me to re-create those giants."

"Why did he come to the U.S. to obtain his bones?" asked Frazier.

Lander said, "Dr. Yates presented her work at the conference last year. And I suspect that The Man was there."

"Yes, you are right. He was in the audience for Dr. Yates' presentation and then saw us talking extensively about our work during free times. He has kept up with recent discoveries in your country."

"How has he kept up with our secret projects?" Frazier asked the question.

Leonid looked uncomfortable and looked to his President. Kruschov replied. "I have already discussed this with President Branson. The Man has a source here."

Lander said, "I thought so. That source has to be a high-ranking official, someone at a higher level than Dr. Yates." He paused and then added, "Is that why Dr. Pasternak is not here? I am convinced it is not she, by the way."

Frazier replied, "No, that is not the reason . . . at least, the only reason . . . she is not here. Go ahead with your story, Dr. Leonid. What is The Man's plan? I suspect that it is more than just exhibiting some de-extincted animals."

"You are correct, Sir. He has an ambitious plan and that is why Dr. Yates was kidnapped to help me."

"I thought you had recruited her," said Frazier.

Lander looked at him with surprise. He said, "I can't wait to hear the rest of this story."

Chapter 37

Ivanov followed The Man into a room that served as a conference room. On the table was set a meal for two. "Please, sit," said The Man. He pointed at one of the chairs. Ivanov sat, picked up the folded cloth napkin, and placed it in his lap.

A young lady entered the room. Ivanov thought she was as beautiful a woman as he had ever seen. She walked up to the table and asked, "What would you like to drink? We have iced tea, water, beer, or espresso. And, of course, vodka, if you prefer."

"I will have an espresso, double shot, if you will."

"But, of course. I will have it for you shortly."

The Man said, "Wait, Illya." He looked at Ivanov and said, "Have your espresso, but you have to also try the Khvanchkara; it is a semi-sweet wine from Georgia. It was Stalin's favorite drink. I will have one also." He nodded at Illya and she left. "Relax and enjoy your meal, Mr. Ivanov. I make it a rule not to discuss business while I eat."

Within five minutes, Illya was back with the drinks.

It had been hours since Ivanov had eaten, so he dug in. He recognized the dishes of borshch, shchi, tvorog, caviar, and pirogi; in addition, there were several others that he could not identify. He liked all but the tvorog; he had never cared for cottage cheese. He said, "This is excellent; the caviar is especially tasty."

"I'm glad you approve." As he spoke, Illya reappeared, carrying dishes of morozhenoe, or ice cream, tall drinks of vodka, and black bread.

The men ate the ice cream first. They finished the meal with the vodka, chasing it with the black bread.

Ivanov leaned back in his chair and sighed. "I could get used to eating like this."

The Man looked hard at him. "That is good. You could eat like this often. I want you to come work for me."

Ivanov replied, "I'm already working for you."

"Yes, you are. But you have been working only as I called you to do something. You have done well. I would like you to come here and work full-time. I have need for someone with your skills. You will be compensated well."

"What do you want me to do here?"

"You will do whatever I want you to do."

Ivanov knew it was a dangerous ploy, but he said, "May I think about it and tell you after we see the rest of the Park?"

"No, that is not possible. Your answer will determine how much of the rest of the project you will know. I must insist on an answer immediately."

Ivanov was not a wealthy man and was smart enough to know that opportunities such as this did not come every day. He also knew it would be dangerous to decline. It was a command disguised as an offer. He smiled and said, "Of course; I would be honored to work with you."

"Excellent! In that case, we will tour the rest of the facility. I assure you; you will not be disappointed. On the way, I will show you your cottage; I have taken the liberty to have it set up for you."

Ivanov smiled again, but thought, "I was right. If I had declined the offer, I would never have left the Park alive."

The Man led the way down the hall and paused at a recessed door, where he pushed a button. Ivanov heard a whirring and, in a few seconds, the door opened. "Another elevator. From outside, it looks like a one-story building."

"It is, if you are looking at it from the outside. After you."

The door closed behind them and Ivanov looked at the panel; he was surprised to see buttons for four floors. One button was lit, showing where the car now sat. The Man spoke in a low voice. "You are one of the very few to ever see this. You must hand me your phone. No one is allowed any type of camera in any area accessed by this elevator."

Ivanov surrendered his iPhone. The Man then pushed the button for the next floor down. The elevator shot smoothly down and eased to a stop. The door opened to reveal a gleaming white hallway. The Man stepped out and pointed to his left. "We'll start this way."

When he came to the first door, he pressed his thumb to a pad and then positioned his left eye up to a sensor. The door clicked and swung open. "This is one of our labs," he said.

"I thought we saw a lab on the ground floor."

"We did. That is the one that the public or press sees. It is a good lab, but nothing like the ones closed to outsiders. This one has the best equipment available in the world. It is the lab that has enabled our successful re-wilding of the Park. Walk around the room and see what we have here."

Ivanov left The Man standing there and moved through the room. He nodded to the five white-coated workers in the lab. Although he was no scientist, he recognized the quality of the equipment in the room. He saw not a spot of dust anywhere or a piece of paper lying around. It was as sterile a room as he could imagine. Off to one side, he saw another smaller room behind a locked glass door. Moving back to The Man, he asked him, "What is that room over there?"

"That is our clean room, absolutely sanitary; no one enters it without a chemical bath and putting on new sterile clothes. It is where we work with the ancient DNA. Let's look at the rest of this level."

Standing back in the hall, The Man pointed down the hall past the elevator. "The apartments there are where the workers on this level live. He turned and continued down the hallway. The next door opened to a wide-open area with tables and chairs. Spaced around the outside were large leather recliners. On the walls were large flat-screen televisions. Covering almost one wall were bookshelves. Ivanov walked over to them and looked at the reading material; most were non-fiction scientific books and there was also one shelf covered with the latest installments of the biotech journals. "This is the cafeteria and lounge area. The men take all their meals in here and can also come here for rest and relaxation. They are served almost anything that they could order. Although they have showers in their apartments, there are also restrooms and shower facilities in those two rooms at the back."

"Impressive," said Ivanov. "How many people work on this level?"

"There are twelve men and three women. They rotate shifts and work around the clock. There are always five scientists on duty."

"Who is their supervisor?"

"Dr. Leonid is the chief scientist, but he will no longer always be here. As you can see, there are cameras everywhere, here and in all rooms . . . except their apartments, of course. All activity is monitored and also recorded." Ivanov hoped that The Man didn't see him involuntarily flinch at this announcement. "Part of your job will be to supervise this area when Dr. Leonid is not here."

"Will I live down here, also?"

"You will have an apartment on this level, but you will have one on each of the other two levels as well. Your main quarters will be in another building. You will periodically stay in each of the apartments here—on a random schedule so that the workers can never know when you may be in residence. Let's move to another level."

After the quick drop in the elevator to the next level, The Man led the way through an identical setup. It could have been the same workers and the same facilities. The Man noticed the confusion on Ivanov's face and said, "It looks the same; however, even though the goals are the same, the two teams have different procedures to get there. This is new research, so there has not yet been a process that has proven to be the best procedure. We'll go to the next level now."

When the elevator door opened to the bottom level, a new sight met Ivanov. A brightly lit hallway led to the left; it was much wider than the ones on the other levels and ran in a straight line as far as Ivanov could see. Running directly down the middle was a rounded rail. But the item that got Ivanov's attention was the car. It straddled the rail and looked like no car he had ever seen. With smooth flowing lines and an aerodynamic shape, it looked built for speed. Looking at it, he couldn't tell which was the front of the car. "What kind of car is this?" asked Ivanov. "I've never seen anything like it."

The Man smiled. "It is a maglev car, the only one of its kind in the world. It was specially built for us."

"What's a maglev car?"

"Maglev is short for magnetic levitation. It travels along the guide rail you see in the middle of the road. It uses magnets to provide both the lift and the propulsion. By not touching the rail or roadway, there is no friction; this car can move at speeds over four hundred kilometers an hour." The Man placed his thumb on the car door's sensor plate and the whole side swung upward. "Get in," said The Man. As soon as Ivanov was seated, the door swung downward until it clicked shut. The Man repeated the process on the other side and entered the car.

Ivanov looked at the interior with awe. "Where is the steering wheel?" he asked.

"There is not a steering wheel. It drives itself."

He leaned forward and touched the built-in pad; at his touch, the pad sprang to life and a lifelike voice said, "Where do you want to go?"

The Man replied, "Take us to the remote science lab." He looked at Ivanov and said, "Hold on. You have never seen a car move like this one."

The car was suddenly moving, accelerating as if it were propelled by a jet engine, but with absolutely no noise. Within two minutes, the onboard voice said, "Speed, two hundred kilometers per hour. Destination: three minutes."

Ivanov marveled at the ride, but what he noticed mostly was the complete absence of sound; the two men could carry on a conversation in normal speaking voices. When the three minutes were up, the car eased to a stop. The Man touched a key on the pad and both doors swung open.

After both men were clear, the doors closed and the car moved ahead about ten feet and stopped. Ivanov followed his host through the only door visible and into a darkened room. As they moved from one area to another, in-floor illumination came on with diffused lights showing the way. Across the room was another closed door. The Man led the way to it, placed his thumb on the pad and the door opened into a large lobby. It looked like something from an elite Fortune 500 Company. On the far wall were painted murals showing a grassland scene with large elephants and a woolly mammoth grazing; horses stood a short distance away from them. The Man led the way and stopped in front of the mural. Suddenly, Ivanov's eyes opened wide and he gasped before he could catch himself! What he was looking at was no mural! It was a full-wall window looking out on a real scene!

Ivanov couldn't believe what he was seeing and asked, "You have created a woolly mammoth?"

"Yes, we have five now, thanks to Dr. Leonid."

"Then you have reached your goal. You have done it before anyone else. You will be the envy of the whole world. When will you announce it to the media?"

"We won't announce it yet. We have just begun our real project."

"What else do you want to do?"

"Let's sit here and I will tell you. Your life will depend on your keeping this a secret." The Man began his story. The further he got into his plan, the more astonished Ivanov became. When he finished, he asked Ivanov, "What do you think?"

Ivanov was almost speechless, but finally replied. "I think it is the most remarkable plan ever devised by mankind. I am honored to be working with you on this. It is a game-changer and will propel our Motherland back to its rightful place as the one true superpower in the world.

Chapter 38

Lander looked at Director Frazier and asked, "What do you mean you thought he had recruited her? She was kidnapped. I'm confused, Sir." He moved his eyes from Frazier to Yates. "Weren't you kidnapped?"

Yates smiled at him. "Yes, I was kidnapped . . . and I was recruited."

"We don't normally use those terms to describe the same event. Would someone please explain what is going on here?"

President Kruschov said, "Perhaps I can help. I'll start and if anyone wants to add something, please cut in."

For the next fifteen minutes, Lander listened to the story, breaking in occasionally to ask a question. Finally, President Branson said, "That's all we know at the present. And that's why we asked you to join us. We need your help."

Director Johnson spoke up. "I want to again express my displeasure for Mr. Lander getting involved in this case. He will get in the way of my agents. The FBI is certainly able to take care of a couple of murderers."

The President glared at Johnson. "This case has now moved to one of international importance. From this point, your men will no longer work on the case. It is being routed to Director Frazier and is now considered as a threat to our country from outside our borders. Mr. Lander, if he will do so, will work with and through Director Frazier. He—and the Kents—were instrumental in helping us thwart an international plot to kill millions last year." Branson turned to Lander. "Will you help us?"

"Of course, Sir. I will do what I can."

"Then that settles it. This meeting is over. I appreciate each of you coming. I don't need to tell you that this meeting is to be spoken of to no one outside this room." Johnson glared at Lander and then the President and started to say something. Finally, he muttered to himself, shook his head, and strode out of the room.

Director Frazier said to Lander. "You and I need to talk some more. Come to my office."

"Yes, Sir. I'll be right there." Lander went to the President and shook his hand.

Branson said, "Mr. Lander, I really appreciate your willingness to work with us on this case. We must stop this threat."

President Kruschov echoed his remarks. "On behalf of Russia, I want to also thank you. I remember what you did for us last year. It was not just your country that you saved from a catastrophe. Although Russia was not one of the targets, the weapons that would have been unleashed on the world came from us. It would have been a, how do you say, public relations nightmare for our government. If there is anything we can do to help you now, please let us know. President Branson and Director Frazier both have my direct contact information."

Lander looked around for Yates, who was still sitting talking with Leonid. He walked over to her and said, "I am really glad you are okay. We'll stop this man."

"I wanted to call you to tell you I was safe, but the President vetoed my talking to anyone. I was pleasantly surprised to see you walk into this meeting."

"No more shocked than I was at seeing you here. If you get any new information or think of anything that may help me, please give me a call. You have my number."

"Yes, I will . . . now that I know I can trust you."

Lander left the room and found Frazier's office. "Come in, Lander." He pointed. "You know where the coffee is."

Lander stepped to the side table and opened the drawer. He chose a half-caff and dropped the K-cup into the Keurig. Within a few seconds, he had his steaming hot coffee and moved to sit in his chair. Frazier walked to the door and told his secretary. "Hold all calls unless it is an emergency." He closed the door and sat in the chair opposite Lander. "Well, we are back in action. It's good to have you working with us again."

Both men had served together in the SEALs; they had been successful in many covert operations in some of the most dangerous countries in the world. Frazier had opted to remain in the service and quickly moved to the top position in the CIA. Lander had had enough and wanted to live a more normal life and left the service. Over the years, he had remained in close contact with Frazier and had even volunteered his services on occasion when Frazier needed someone with his skills to work a job outside the venue of the government.

"I'm happy to work with you again, Sir. This is an interesting project. What's the plan?"

"There is a lot at stake here; I'm not even sure we know the extent of it yet. I want you to lead the investigation. If you need any of my men to assist you, just let me know."

"I would rather work alone for now, or, if you don't mind, still let the Kents work with me. You know them from last year's adventure. They already know most of the story and will do what I ask without any problem."

"I hesitate to place civilians in danger."

"You forget; I am a civilian now. I will try to keep them away from potential fire. I will need to keep them in the intelligence loop if you consider this classified. We can work it the same way as last year."

"Yes, you're a civilian now, but a highly trained one! You would be sitting in my job if you hadn't left."

"I wouldn't want your job, Sir. Besides, your big butt fits these Washington desk chairs better than mine would. I would rather do what I'm doing and work with you on the side."

Frazier laughed. "My big butt, huh? You may have left the service, but you still have your charm. Use the Kents if they can help you. We'll follow the same communication pattern as last year; that worked out well, I think. Any communication to or from Washington will go through you only. You use your judgment as to how much to tell the Kents. For the time being, consider everything about this case to be classified."

"Yes, Sir. How did President Kruschov get involved and why is our President concerned with theft and murder? The President usually leaves those types of incidents to lower-ranking officials."

Frazier laughed. "You mean officials like me?"

Lander flushed at this remark. "I meant no disrespect, Sir."

"None taken. You may not know this, but Kruschov was a high-ranking scientist before he became President; he was in charge of their national science programs. He worked with Dr.

Leonid there. When he needed someone to head the research project for Pleistocene Park, he chose the best biotechnology person he could."

"And that person was Dr. Leonid," Lander said.

"Yes. Leonid was an expert in ancient DNA and was passionate about recreating the woolly mammoth. When Leonid learned of the ambitious plot of Listovov, he contacted Kruschov."

"Why didn't Kruschov just arrest Listovov?"

"He was going to, but Leonid convinced him otherwise. There were other people involved, but Leonid could not identify them. Kruschov agreed to hold off until they could get everyone in the plot. It seems that Leonid outlined the plan to get the rest of them."

"Did Kruschov contact our President?"

"Yes, he did. They have talked extensively about it. Kruschov was scheduled to visit the U.S. this week, so it gave them a chance to talk without raising the suspicions of The Man. They are convinced that both governments have high-ranking officials involved in the plot. That's why it's being played close to the vest here. They also are confident that the ultimate plot of Listovov is dangerous to both countries. President Branson is convinced that the illegal selling of classified scientific information to Russia is a direct threat to our national security."

"Is that why you sent for me? You don't know whom you can trust here, do you?"

"Yes, you are right. No one in Washington outside the ones in the room today knows anything about our actions."

"I don't think Johnson was happy about my being there."

Frazier laughed. "Johnson's not happy when anyone other than the FBI is even recognized. He's an ass; don't worry about him."

"Oh, I'm not worried about him. I think it's funny. He's a typical Washington bureaucrat."

"If there's anything you need, and I do mean anything, call me direct. I will be in contact with you as soon as I know anything new. Your ride is waiting for you in the hall. It's nice to see you, Lander. Be careful."

Lander stood and shook Frazier's hand. "Nice to see you, too. Kind of like old times."

Chapter 39

It was late afternoon when Lander returned to the motel in Durango. He had texted me that he would be there at five-thirty if Cyndi and I wanted to meet him for dinner. By the time Lander entered the restaurant, I had arranged for a table away from the dinner crowd so we could talk without fear of being overheard. We sat down and ordered drinks. When the server had gone, Lander asked, "Did you all have a good day? Get a lot of shopping done?" He smiled at me when he said this. He knew that we couldn't wait to hear about his trip and he was deliberately delaying that conversation.

I replied, "Yeah, we did. Cyndi wanted to get you a birthday present, but I talked her out of it."

Cyndi raised her eyebrows at this statement. "You know his birthday is not for another two months."

"Oh, I guess that's the reason we didn't get you a present. Okay, out with it. Where did you go today? Did it have anything to do with what's been happening here?"

"Yes, it did. But before I tell you about it, you have to assure me that what you hear remains with us."

I said, "Of course. What happens in Durango stays in Durango." Cyndi nodded her head to show that she was also in agreement. We both know that Lander sometimes shares classified, but necessary, information with us and we would never place his trust in jeopardy. "So, I am right. It does have to do with this case. You met with Director Frazier?"

As Lander started to reply, the server brought our drinks and asked, "Are you ready to order?"

Lander and I looked at Cyndi. She ordered the Tex-Mex Salad with grilled chicken; Lander ordered an elk steak, medium rare, and I ordered the steak fajitas. The server said, "I'll get those going right away," and walked toward the kitchen.

I asked again, "You met with Director Frazier, didn't you?"

"When I got to the airport, there was a private jet waiting for me. The pilot took me to Washington for the meeting. Yes, I met with Director Frazier. Dr. Yates was there. Also, . . ."

I interrupted him, "Dr. Yates. They rescued her?"

"Yes; no. I mean they didn't rescue her. It turns out that she didn't need rescuing."

Cyndi said, "You're talking in circles, Bill. Start at the beginning. This time, we won't interrupt you." She looked at me when she said that; I'm smart enough to know when she's telling me to shut up and listen.

Lander continued. "Dr. Yates was there. Also, there was a Russian scientist, Dr. Aleksey Leonid."

I said, "A Russian scientist! What was a Russian scientist doing there?" Cyndi glared at me. Maybe I wasn't as smart as I thought.

"Yes, a Russian scientist; he is their most respected paleontologist, specializing in ancient DNA."

"Other than Director Frazier and the two scientists, was anyone else there?" Ha! This time it was Cyndi who rudely interrupted him. I felt better.

Lander smiled, or maybe I just wanted him to smile. "There were others there. The Director of the FBI, Harvey Johnson, was there. He objected to my being there, by the way, but he was overruled, so I got to stay."

"Did Frazier overrule him? Is Frazier's ranking higher than that of the FBI director?" I had thought that those two positions were equal in the food chain.

"Yes. No, not really. The directors the FBI and the CIA are on equal footing as far as rank."

More circles! I'm going to get dizzy at this rate. I felt like I was on a merry-go-round. But I stayed quiet and let him think I understood exactly what he was saying. He continued with the explanation. "He was outranked by the President."

Cyndi exclaimed, "Our President was there?"

Lander smiled, and this time I knew he did so, and said, "Yes, President Branson was there along with Russian President Kruschov."

I considered this and then replied. "Is that all? Wasn't there anyone important there?"

Lander ignored my remark and Cyndi said, "Okay, tell us what happened."

He filled us in on the status of Yates. We already knew about Pleistocene Park, so that part of the story was not surprising to us. He did get our attention when he said, "But there is a deeper plot than that of re-wilding the grasslands in Siberia."

"So, The Man is up to more 'no good' than we thought," I said. That sounds a little awkward, but I knew Lander understood me when he replied.

"Yes, he is up to a lot more 'no good' than we thought. And Director Frazier and I are not sure we still know the extent of it."

"How did our President get involved? Did Director Frazier call him in?" Cyndi asked the question that I was going to pose.

"No, the Director did not. President Kruschov talked with him about the plot. As you already know, Leonid inadvertently learned about the extra plan—at least that there was more to the scheme—and revealed it to Kruschov. Leonid is the one who devised the strategy to let The Man continue with his plot so that they could learn the identities of the other players. Leonid is going to play both roles: he will continue to work for The

Man and head up the research at Pleistocene Park while he also will work with Dr. Yates. He will provide legitimate research information to The Man, but will always provide it a step behind where he and Dr. Yates are. He thinks that will keep The Man from being suspicious. Leonid will continue to let him think that Dr. Yates is only helping in order to keep her family safe."

I said, "You keep mentioning the extra plot. Just what does that plan entail?"

"Leonid and his President believe that it is to de-extinct the other animals whose bones they stole. The Park already has woolly mammoths grazing there; The Man would like to add other large extinct animals. It would be quite a draw for tourism for the Park."

I asked, "Is this what you believe?"

"No. Director Frazier and I think there is a darker side to their de-extinction project."

Cyndi asked, "What do you mean, a darker side?"

"We are not completely sure. That's the real goal for me, to find out what else is in the works. Director Frazier convinced the President that there might still be a real threat from the project. I am empowered to investigate in whatever direction it may take me. We'll look for the murderers and attackers for sure, but do it with the assumption that a much larger plan is unfolding."

Cyndi said, "You said 'we'll look'. Does that mean that we are still working with you?"

"Yes; they are fine with that. In fact, they appreciate your helping me again. You all made quite an impression with both of them last year. We'll set it up like last year. I'll be the only one to communicate with them but I can share information with you on a need-to-know basis."

"That sounds good. But what will the FBI think about our getting in their way?" I didn't look forward to working with them.

"We won't be in their way. The FBI has been removed from the case. It will be only us unless I request more help from Director Frazier."

Cyndi laughed. "So, the agents who so smugly told all of us to stand down have now been told that themselves. What goes around comes around. I love it! What about McKenzie and Spencer?"

"For now, they also are not in the loop. I'm sure that they will not like that. But this case is being looked at as a potential threat to our country, so, for locals, it's hands off. In fact, I cannot even tell them the developments so far."

"What about Yates' family? Will they be told that she is safe?" Cyndi wasn't afraid to ask Lander anything.

"They can be told very little right now. What they will be told is that we are pretty sure that the kidnappers will not harm her as long as she cooperates with them and that we'll continue looking for her."

I said, "If they know Yates, then they'll know that she wouldn't help her kidnappers under any circumstances."

"I hope they accept our explanation. If not, we'll tell them that even the strongest agents have cooperated with the enemy when their families are threatened. People are strong and will sacrifice themselves, but when it comes to their families, few are willing to allow that to happen."

"Okay, Boss. What's the plan?" I was ready to get started.

"I think you and I need to visit the other sites. We need to identify the attackers. If we can get them, maybe one of them will lead to the bigger fish."

"I thought that we knew the big fish. And you said you two were going to visit the other sites. What about me? What do you want me to do?" Was that a "left-out look" on Cyndi's face?

"I would like for you to do what you do best. Research and think! Find out everything you can about de-extinction and think about possible plot scenarios; what could bad guys do with large, ferocious animals if they are successful in de-extincting them?"

"Does that include the giant giant?" she asked. She was smiling at me. I swear that she can read my mind. I looked blankly at her and she just nodded.

I didn't even hear Lander reply to her question.

Chapter 40

Yates and Leonid were sitting in the conference room that doubled as their office space. Leonid said, "Let's set up our protocols for working in the labs."

"Yes, we need to do that to make sure we are working on the same page."

"What does 'working on the same page' mean?"

"It means that we agree on the same items; that we will follow the same protocols when we are in the lab. That's the only way we can be sure that we keep the lab from being contaminated. I have a list of typical standards for lab work in ancient DNA. Look it over and if there are any items you want to discuss, we'll do so." She handed a sheet of printed paper to Leonid.

He read the list:

- "The lab should be completely isolated from other labs, especially those for modern DNA.
- Ultra-violet light should be used to irradiate the lab.

- As much as possible, all equipment should be treated and cleaned with bleach.
- Any person entering the lab should have protective clothing on; this includes the wearing of face shields.
- If possible, all consumables should be irradiated with UV light overnight before use.
- All materials and transport equipment should be consumables."

She said, "Are you in agreement with those standards?"

"Yes, completely so. We must be very diligent to protect our work. Also, we do not have much material to work with and we may not be able to steal additional samples." He smiled as he said this.

Yates was beginning to like Leonid more and more. She thought to herself, "He does have a sense of humor, after all."

"We will have a total of three labs set up, each with its own equipment and consumables. All three labs will meet those same standards. And each will have its own samples to work with."

Yates looked surprised. "Where are the other labs?"

"This one, of course. Then I have the one in Russia; it is identical in every way to this one. We also have one in Virginia, just outside

Washington. We'll both work in this one; I'll be responsible for the one in Russia. You'll be responsible for the one in Virginia; it is also already set up for our work."

"You have been busy, haven't you?"

"Yes. Our superiors expect us to be working right away. We want to be the first ones to successfully de-extinct the other animals. We will have competition. There are several groups around the world striving to be the first; some are here in the U.S.; some are in the U.K., and there are others as well."

"I am aware that the Japanese and the Chinese are betting they will be the first. We'll have our work cut out for us if we are to lead the field. But we have an edge. You have already brought back the woolly mammoth."

"Yes, that is true. I need to show you the results of that project. The problem for us is that I was able to obtain viable ancient DNA from skeletons that had essentially been flash-frozen and then kept at a constant temperature for thousands of years; I was able to get samples of teeth, bones with blood that still looked like blood, and hair, all from an intact carcass. That's at least one good thing about the permafrost; it has kept the ground and everything in it frozen all this time. But these other samples did not come from a frozen environment."

Yates said, "You're right in all those items. But the study of ancient DNA has come a long way in the last few years. We now know that the preservation of ancient DNA depends on many things."

"Such as?"

"Well, for one, it depends on more than when the organism dies. Factors such as how quickly it's buried and the depth of the burial."

"I would agree; those are important elements."

"But latest research suggests that the most important element is the consistency of the temperature in the burial environment. So, although frigid temperatures may help preserve the bones, it does not seem like a requirement now."

"I agree with you. Although that is not common knowledge, the people who arranged to steal the samples here in the U.S. also know that."

"You're saying that The Man knows that. You didn't point that out to him?"

"No. It was not my plan to kidnap you. The Man is familiar with your work and he is aware that we spent some time at the conference last year discussing our work. I had told him that I needed to find someone to help me and he said he would take care of it. But, the thing is, if he knows it, then we must assume that others also know it."

"How do we travel from lab to lab? I am supposed to be kidnapped; I can't just go to the airport and travel back and forth to Virginia."

"I was told that we would be taken care of by Director Frazier, I think was his name. He was at our meeting. I'm not too good with remembering names. Anyway, someone will facilitate this."

"Okay. I'll just wait for someone to give me directions. Now, let's complete our discussion of our protocols. If we are going to work in multiple labs, it is more important than ever. Are we going to have any assistance?"

"Yes, we will need help; we'll discuss that later. I already have an assistant in Russia. But, let's get back to our discussion about protocols. These are the rules I used working with the woolly. Anyone entering the lab had to have PPE."

Yates knew that PPE meant Personal Protective Equipment, so she just nodded.

Leonid continued, "PPE has to be carried out by strict sequence and done before one goes into the lab. Shoes have to be removed and left out of the lab. Next, a pair of gloves must be put on. The coverall, including the hood, must be fully zipped to the top. Once it is on, then make a small cut in the wrist areas of the sleeves; this is to put the thumbs through to hold the sleeves in place. Follow this with either boots or disposable foot covers. After this, put on a facemask with an attached visor; it must be close-fitted. Then, clean the gloves with DNA remover. Finally, put on a second pair of gloves over the first."

Yates said, "That's good. Pretty standard protocol, and we need to follow it. To follow that, we should never remove any of the PPE while in the lab. Once we leave the lab, remove it and place it in the waste bin. Some labs reuse the coveralls, but I think dealing with the limited supply of ancient DNA samples, we should make coveralls disposable also."

"I agree. We aren't constrained by money, so we'll err on the side of safety. Anything we use that is not disposable must be cleaned with bleach immediately after use. By the way, you have a new laptop over there; I hope you like Macs."

Yates moved toward where he pointed and picked up the box. It contained a new MacBook Pro. "I know what I will be doing for the next hour or so," she said.

He replied, "It is already set up for you. Director Frazier took care of having that done. You can change your passwords, of course. Let's check it out."

She turned it on and almost immediately, it asked her for her password. She looked at Leonid, who said, "neverdead, all lower case." She typed the letters and the welcome screen appeared. Leonid continued, "Open Safari and go to this Website." He directed her and suddenly they were looking at a landscape copied from thousands of years ago.

She saw horses and elephants wander by, then sat up straight and exclaimed, "Woolly mammoths. These are the live ones you de-extincted in Siberia."

He smiled. "Yes, those are woolly mammoths. The first on the earth in thousands of years."

Yates slowly nodded. "Yes. That is a great accomplishment. But just wait! They haven't seen anything yet."

Chapter 41

Lander took a circuitous route to the lab; he had directions, but he wanted to be sure no one was following him. After circling several blocks and backtracking over some of the same roads, he pulled into a parking space in front of the lab. He sat in the driver's seat for a moment, looking all around. Seeing no one, he made his way through the front door and paused in the lobby. He heard the bell chime announcing his arrival and in a short time, a young lady came into the lobby.

"May I help you?" she asked.

Lander nodded, "Yes, I am looking for Dr. Lively," using the false name they had agreed on.

"Is she expecting you?"

"Yes, but she doesn't know the exact time I was to be here. "Tell her Mr. Lander is here to see her."

"Yes, Sir. I will be right back." She left the lobby and Lander heard the door lock click as she disappeared from sight.

In less than a minute, she reappeared and said, "Mr. Lander, please follow me."

She showed him to an office and asked him to be seated. As she left, the door opposite opened and Yates and Leonid came into the room. "Mr. Lander. I'm glad to see you. You remember Dr. Leonid, don't you?"

"Yes, I do. How are you, Dr. Leonid?"

"Fine, thank you. We are preparing to get started with our new project. What can we do for you?"

"I just wanted to come by and be sure that we were all on the same page."

"Ah, that page again." Leonid laughed and continued, "Dr. Yates has already outlined that page."

Lander reached into the bag that he was carrying and pulled two small boxes from it. "Here are phones; use them only to contact me."

Leonid shook his head. "I don't understand. We already have phones." He looked at Yates.

Lander said, "You may have phones, but these are new and clean. What you have may have been compromised?"

"What do you mean, 'compromised'?"

Yates said to Leonid. "What he is saying is somebody may have a way to check our phones for numbers and calls."

Lander continued. "She is correct. There are still people out there who might wish to do you harm. We don't want to let them know where you are via your phones. The phones have GPS tracking capabilities on them that may be used against you. I will call you only on the new phones. Don't use them to talk with anyone other than each other or me. Do you understand? Occasionally, when you are working in different labs, use your regular phones to talk with each other. But never divulge any classified information or breakthroughs on that phone. Leonid, periodically remind Yates that her family will remain safe only if she continues to work with you."

Leonid said, "Yes, I understand. These phones are private to only you and us." Yates nodded her agreement.

Lander directed his next question to Yates. "Do you still have your weapon?"

"No, it was left at the excavation site when I was taken."

Lander reached into the bag again. "Here; I think I remember that you use a Glock 21. I also have you an extra magazine and a box of cartridges."

"Thank you. I really appreciate this. I was feeling somewhat vulnerable without my handgun."

"Obviously, you can't take it with you when you fly. I have an identical one for you in the lab in Virginia. It's in a safe there and you'll have a lockbox here to secure this gun when you leave."

"Remember. When you travel, use your new identity. Your paperwork is good enough to pass any inspection; your new credit cards have no limit, but use them with discretion."

"Now, I have arranged armed security for both labs where you will be working. There will be three officers on duty at all times, one inside and two outside." He handed both scientists an electronic device attached to a necklace. "If you sense anything out of the ordinary, press this button. Wear it around your necks at all times—both of you." They looked at him and he said, "Yes, they will survive a bleach bath, so you can wear them in the lab."

"Does this button alert the security people?" asked Yates.

"Yes. The alert signals them and me."

Leonid said. "I am glad to have you help us. What is your role?"

"I'm working with Director Frazier. I intend to find the attackers first and foremost. I also want to determine the extent of the plot. Dr. Leonid, you can help me there. When you visit the lab in Siberia and meet with The Man, please make note of anything he says or who he talks to. I have a feeling that his ultimate goal is much more than the mere display of de-extincted animals."

Leonid said, "I will do so. I know that his intentions go beyond the re-wilding of the steppe grasslands, but I don't know exactly what yet. He may or may not confide his goal to me."

"If you hear anything at all, even if you don't believe it to be true, please contact me immediately. If I can't answer at the time, try again fifteen minutes later. I won't try to contact you when you travel to Russia; I don't want to let the Russians know I am communicating with you. Do either of you have any additional questions for me?"

Neither Leonid nor Yates had a question, so Lander continued. "Okay. Now, if you will, please give me a tour of the facility. I want to look at it from a safety standpoint. Your security agents will be on duty beginning tomorrow." He pulled some pictures from his pocket and handed a set to each of them. "These are photos of the agents. Study them carefully; you need to be able to recognize each one. If you ever see someone here—or at either of the other two labs—that you don't recognize or that gives you a funny or strange feeling, don't shrug it off; message my number immediately, and I do mean immediately, and put in the danger code of 911."

"Put those faces in your memories. Now show me around the building. I especially want to see any outside exits or windows to the exterior. I've walked around the grounds outside, but I want to get it from an inside perspective."

Leonid said, "All windows are reinforced and should be bullet proof. All doors, exterior and interior, have thumbprint sensors and iris readers. Both must be satisfied or the door will not open. Locks are deadbolts activated by the sensors, going in or out."

"What if the building loses power?"

"We both have keys that would enable us to override the sensors, but the keys should be used only as an exit precaution."

"I've seen a couple of cameras. What areas have them?"

"There are visible ones in the lobby, hallways, and labs. However, all the building has hidden cameras, so all points in the facility have camera coverage, both for visible light and infrared. Those recordings are stored in the cloud, so they cannot be tampered with here."

"Are they recording all the time?"

"No, only when sensors pick up either movement or heat. Then, each recording is date- and time-stamped. Also, each recording has the area or room recorded."

"Can they be remotely viewed?"

"Yes, I will give you the access information."

"This all sounds good. I'm also having external grounds covered by cameras. They should be effective beginning tomorrow afternoon. If they pick up anything, I will get an alert and can view what triggered them. Now, how about that tour?"

For the next hour, Lander was led around the building. He took pictures of each room, noted entrance and exit spots, and made notes on his iPad. He diagrammed all camera positions. When they returned to their starting point, Lander again warned them. "Stay vigilant at all times. Pros hit you when you least expect them. No one gets in unless I authorize it. When you need to leave one of the facilities, I want to know it beforehand. You will have security with you at all times. I know that this is an inconvenience, but it's a necessary evil. I don't need to remind you how important a project this is . . . to both our countries and to the world. These ancient giants will be re-born; we want to be sure that it is done under the right procedures and with the necessary restraints. If you need anything at all or you feel uneasy about anything or anybody, call me. I will be in and out, but will always be at your side as quickly as possible if the need arises."

"We appreciate that," said Yates.

Lander looked at Leonid. "You have a difficult task. You must keep The Man convinced that you are loyal to him and are being successful in keeping Yates in line to help you. Give him legitimate information, but keep it a step behind where you and Yates are. From what you say, he is smart enough to recognize faulty information if you feed it to him. If you need to get any information to your President, direct it through me. Both Director Frazier and I have direct access to him, twenty-four/seven."

Lander started toward the door, but paused and turned around. "Please be careful. And good luck with the project. If it is successful, your lives will change forever."

The two scientists looked at each other. Yates gave a slight shiver and said, "I'm afraid you may be right. But will that change be good?"

Chapter 42

The day following Lander's visit to the lab, all security was in place as Lander had promised. Yates and Leonid spent the day gathering and prepping all the materials that they would need to get started. Late that evening, Leonid's phone buzzed. He looked at the display and told Yates. "It's The Man. I have to take it; don't make a sound while I talk with him."

He clicked the talk button and said, "Zdravstvujtye." Yates knew a little Russian and recognized the term for "hello". She listened to the one-sided conversation for five minutes. Finally, Leonid said, "Do svidaniya!"

When he had ended the call, Yates asked, "Is everything all right?"

"Yes, it is good. He wanted to know if you were being a help or if we needed to make a visit to your family. I convinced him that you were fully cooperating. This was no lie, so it was easy for me to sound sincere." He smiled as he spoke. "He wants to know when I am coming to the lab there in Siberia."

"What did you tell him?"

"I told him I needed one more day here to be sure you were working as I requested and that I would travel there in a couple of days."

"Will that be safe for you?"

"Yes. He will not do anything to me. At the risk of sounding vain, I am too valuable to his plan. Without me, he cannot do what he wants to do."

"We need to let Mr. Lander know about the call and the trip." Yates was already dialing the number as she said this. Lander answered immediately and Yates told him about the call.

"I was expecting the call any time. Leonid will have to make several trips to Siberia as the project moves ahead. As long as he keeps his composure, he will be safe; he's too valuable to The Man's plans."

"You sound like Dr. Leonid. That's what he said."

"He's right. When he leaves for Russia, it might be a good time for you to go to the lab in Virginia. You could get it caught up while he is gone."

Yates replied, "That's probably a good idea. I'm eager to get started."

"Okay, I will visit you tomorrow with some travel supplies for you. Let me know if anything else develops."

"Okay, I will. Goodbye."

The next day, Lander and I went to the lab. I was driving and Lander had me to go through a series of moves designed to lose or flush out anyone tracking us. Again, we saw no one there. We parked and headed for the building; the new security people on duty stopped us before we reached the front door. Lander cleared us and we entered the lobby. Lander recognized the same girl who greeted him earlier and she went to get Yates . . . or Lively, as the girl knew her. Yates led us to the conference room. Shortly after we were seated, Dr. Leonid came in and Lander introduced me to him.

Lander asked, "When are you leaving for Russia?"

"I have a flight out tomorrow afternoon."

"How long will you be gone?"

"I'll be in Russia for about four days. I want to get them up to speed and ready to work with us. They'll follow the same protocols and they'll complete the same analysis that we do here, but I will keep them always a couple of steps behind. We have to ensure that they do not beat us to the, how do you say, finish line."

"Okay, that sounds good." Looking at Yates, he asked, "When will you be ready to go to Virginia?"

"I'm ready anytime. I would like to go either tomorrow or the next day."

"I'll arrange a flight for you tomorrow afternoon." He looked back at Leonid. "What time is your flight? I don't want both of you at the airport at the same time."

"My flight is at six-thirty tomorrow afternoon."

"That's good."

He said to Yates, "I can get you out at two thirty-five. That'll work out well and get you to your destination before dark." He opened an envelope and said. "Here are your identification papers. You have a driver's license, several credit cards, a voter registration card, and a passport—all made out in the name of Betty Lively. They are professionally done and should get you through any type of inquiry."

Yates looked through the papers and said, "These are remarkable. If I didn't know better, I would think that I am Betty Lively. What's this other document?"

"It is a short bio of Lively. Commit it to memory and then shred the paper."

"I think you have done this before, haven't you?" said Leonid.

"A few times. Here is the rest of your disguise." He handed her a dark red wig and some glasses with clear lens; then he gave her a small package. "I don't know if you can wear these or not, but it would be good if you could. Changing eye color is one of the best subtle changes you can do for a disguise."

"I wear contacts now, so that will be no problem." She looked at the package. "This green will look good with my new red hair. Seems stylist should be added to your long list of talents."

"I'll call you with the exact schedule. Kent and I will be here to take you to the airport, and I'll have some of my men to meet you on the other end to escort you to the lab."

We finished the arrangements and left. As we turned into the hotel parking lot, neither Lander nor I noticed the white van that had been following us.

Lander set Yates' flight up and called her to confirm the time. At eleven o'clock the next day, we stopped the Jeep at the lab and picked up Yates. Even though we knew how she would be disguised, we almost didn't recognize her. We drove to the airport and escorted her to her gate. As soon as she boarded the plane, we left the airport and headed back to Durango. The white van again fell in behind us unnoticed.

Chapter 43

Leonid was really tired; it had been a long trip and he was looking forward to catching up on some rest. He had never been able to sleep on a plane. Anatoly Ivanov met him at the airport and led him to the waiting Mercedes. As they turned south toward the Park, Leonid asked, "How are things going here? Is the lab set up?"

"Everything is ready to get started. We were just waiting for you to get here. We expected you a few days ago."

"I've been setting the labs up in the U.S. and convincing Dr. Yates that she needed to cooperate with us or her family would suddenly meet with some accidents. She is fully on board now."

"If she gives you any trouble, call me and I'll take care of the good doctor."

"I appreciate it, but I have it under control now. What time will I meet with The Man?"

"You can rest tonight; your meeting with him is at ten o'clock in the morning. After that, you will go to the lab and prep it for the project."

Following that brief exchange, there was no more talk for the remainder of the trip. For that, Leonid was thankful. He knew that when men get tired, they lose focus and get careless. Beyond that, he just didn't like Ivanov very much and felt sure that his feeling was reciprocated. As tired as Leonid was, sleep did not come easy; he was not looking forward to his morning meeting.

At ten o'clock the next morning, Leonid knocked on the door to The Man's office. "Come in," came the gruff reply.

Leonid entered and said, "How are you?"

"It's about time! I was beginning to think I would have to send Ivanov after you. Have you had trouble with Dr. Yates?"

"No, not now. She is fully on board. We have the two labs set up in the U.S. and are ready to start the project there."

"Tell me again why we need three labs doing the same thing."

"This is such an important project, one that, if successful, will be a breakthrough in ancient DNA revival. The experiments must be able to be replicated to be accepted in the scientific community. If something goes wrong at one of the labs—or even two of them—we will still have a valid project going and we won't have to start over." He looked at The Man and continued. "Also, if all labs are successful, then we will have three de-extinctions at a time. You wouldn't mind that, would you?"

"No, that would be remarkable. If you can do that, you will earn a substantial bonus. How can you run three labs at once?"

"I will oversee this one; Dr. Yates will oversee the one in Virginia; and both of us will work at the one in Colorado."

"Can we trust Yates by herself? You do have someone to keep her in line."

"She will be fine. There are security people with her all the time. She thinks they are there to protect her, but they really are there to ensure that she works." This was partially true, so Leonid felt sure that The Man would accept his explanation.

"I am holding you personally responsible to see that she does," The Man said. "Now, how often can I expect you to be at this site?"

"I will be here almost every week. I will typically spend two days at each site before moving on to the next."

"Can you get the project done by traveling that much?"

"Yes, I think so. You also said that money was no object in what we needed, so I thought I would hire three people at each site. It will cost to hire them and cost even more to buy their silence."

"How long will it take you to do that? We need to get started on the project."

"We have a list of possible names. With your blessing, we can have them in place within a week. But we won't waste that week; we'll get the project started in each site. It's important that all three sites are synchronized."

The Man said, "Yes, I agree, keep them on the same page. Now, go get this lab ready to go. If you need anything, let Ivanov know and he'll get it for you." He stood up, dismissing Leonid.

Relieved by the conversation, Leonid made his way to the lab. Larik, his full-time assistant, met him at the door. "Dr. Leonid, I am glad to see you. How have you been?"

"Great! How are things here? Are you ready to get back to work?"

"I am ready. Are we going to create another woolly?"

"No, not this time. We are going to work with other extinct animals. The short-faced bear is the first."

"That sounds exciting. I would like to see a live one. They were such ferocious animals. Do we have good ancient DNA for them?"

"We have a good sample of the femur bone from one; it looks as it has been well preserved. I'm sure that we will be able to get only fragments of viable DNA, so, of course, we will have to fill in the gaps. But with the more modern techniques of dealing with ancient DNA and using the latest equipment, I believe that we can re-create the big bear."

"The lab here is currently set up the same way that it was when we worked the woolly."

"There will be new microscopes and centrifugal machines here in a couple of days. They have already been ordered, along with new personal protection suits and all the consumables that we will need."

"It will be good to work with the latest equipment. When do we get started?"

"We will be working with two other labs so we can confirm all our steps and so we can triple our output."

"You mean we are going to create three bears on our first attempt?"

"Yes, if all labs are successful, we will have three big bears born at basically the same time."

"Where are these other labs? Are they all in Russia?"

"No, they are in the U.S."

"The U.S.? How did you manage that?"

"I have recruited a great U.S. paleontologist to work with us. I will be traveling to each of the labs to oversee the work and to be sure they are all on the timeline."

"The Americans would say 'all on the same page', wouldn't they?" said Larik.

"Yes, I guess they would. It is beginning to seem as if everyone would say that. When I am not here, I will expect you to carry on. Now, let's see what we have to work with."

For the next two hours, the men discussed their work strategy.

# # #

As soon as Leonid had left The Man, Ivanov entered the room. The Man asked, "Did you hear everything?"

"Yes."

"Is he telling the truth? Could you see his face?"

"I think most of what he said is the truth. I am not sure about the American scientist. He seemed a little too careful discussing her. I couldn't see his face, but I don't trust everything he said concerning Yates."

The Man started to reply, but the buzzing of his phone stopped him. He looked at the display and said, "I must take this call. Wait in the hall."

He watched Ivanov exit the room and close the door. Then he said, "Speak."

He listened for a moment and then replied, "I was afraid of that. They are going to be trouble unless we eliminate them. I will take care of it right away." He ended the connection and roared out, "Ivanov!"

Ivanov came back into the room. "Trouble?"

The Man replied, "No, not yet. But those civilians are still nosing around the lab."

"Was that Romonov?"

"No, the call was from my source in Washington."

"Do you want me to go to the States and take care of them? I might enjoy it."

"No, I will let Romonov prove himself. He should be able to handle three civilians."

"I thought there were only two of them."

"One has a wife with him. We might as well eliminate her also. She may know too much to allow her to live." He looked at his phone and tapped a contact. He heard the greeting and said, "Take care of the ones nosing around . . . yes, the three civilians. I want them to disappear before they cause trouble." He listened and then replied, "I don't care who does it. If you want your assistants to do it, that's fine. Just understand that I am holding you responsible. Let me know when you get it done. You have three days to finish." The Man stuck to his rule that no names were ever used on a phone call.

Romonov grimaced, but said. "You can count on me. Consider it done."

The Man disconnected the call. To Ivanov, he said, "Be ready to go if I need you."

"I am always ready to go . . . anywhere. I keep a suitcase packed. All I'll have to do is grab it and get into the car. Just give me the word."

Chapter 44

The next morning, Lander met Cyndi and me for breakfast. We ate and then walked back to the lobby. I directed Lander to one of the conference rooms and said, "Let's go in here; I have it reserved for the morning. We have a lot to discuss."

I followed Cyndi and Lander in and closed the door. Setting my backpack on the table, I pulled a stack of papers out, looked at them, and gave part to Cyndi. Lander gazed at them and said, "I don't think you all went shopping while I was gone the other day."

"You are so smart. Which clue gave it away?"

Lander looked at me and replied, "Because you didn't have a present for me?"

We all laughed at that. "Okay, let's get started. We spent the day on the Internet. It's a good thing we brought a printer with us. Cyndi, do you want to go first?"

"Sure. We thought that if we were going to do this investigation justice, we needed to get up to speed on the whole process. I thought de-extinction was a new and almost secret movement, but there is a lot of it going on all over the globe."

"What do you mean?" asked Lander.

"We really haven't heard much in the media about it, but it is a major undertaking in the scientific community."

"Of course, we had *Jurassic Park* a few years ago. It portrayed an environment full of dinosaurs. But this really is a much broader project than bringing back dinosaurs," I said. "Let's be sure we are defining de-extinction the same way."

Cyndi said, "It's the process of creating an animal or plant that is or greatly looks like an extinct species."

"Some people even use it to refer to the re-creation of an environment, such as the steppe grasslands of Siberia."

Lander asked, "How long has the process been going on?"

Cyndi answered him. "Really, in just the last few decades. Some have been concerned about the extinction of animals for many years, but science and technology are just now catching up so that de-extinction is becoming a real possibility."

I said, "Pleistocene Park is the project that may have garnered the most attention and it is the one that we are most concerned about."

Lander said, "According to Dr. Leonid, there are already woolly mammoths grazing there."

Cyndi looked at her notes and said, "And there are a lot of other animals there now; the environment is quickly evolving back into a steppe grassland. In addition to the woolly mammoth, there are woolly rhinos, steppe wisent, Lena horses, muskoxen, reindeer, and saiga antelopes. On the edges of the grasslands, there are moose, wapiti, Yukon wild asses, camels, and snow sheep. Those are all herbivores. The saiga antelope is especially critical to the area; it is prone to massive die-offs without any known precipitating causes. Whole herds numbering in the hundreds of thousands may suddenly die within a period of a few days. It is now on the endangered list."

"What about carnivores? Are they re-establishing them there?" Lander posed the question.

"Yes. Carnivores include Beringian cave lions, gray wolves, cave hyenas, brown bears, wolverines, and arctic foxes. At the edge of the grasslands, there are brown bears, wolverines, cave bears, lynxes, tigers, leopards, red foxes, Siberian tigers, and Amur leopards."

"The area is already evolving into grasslands," said Lander. "Leonid said that they used engineering tanks and eight-wheel drive Argo all-terrain vehicles to crush pathways through the willows and shrubs. How is this project supposed to help the atmosphere? How do grasslands help keep the permafrost in place?"

Cyndi answered, "Grasslands reflect more sunlight than tundra and helps keep the soil cold. In addition, herds of large animals trample the winter snows; this exposes the surface to cold air. Due to recent climate change, permafrost is beginning to thaw, releasing the stored carbon and forming what is called thermokarst lakes. When the thawed permafrost enters the thermokarst lakes, its carbon is converted to carbon dioxide and methane and is released into the atmosphere. As you know, methane is a potent greenhouse gas and has the potential to affect global climate change. This would lead to more permafrost thawing and just feed the cycle. If the large trees and shrubs can be replaced with grasslands, then the cycle can be broken. At least, that's the theory." Cyndi had done her homework.

"Does the permafrost have enough carbon stored in it to affect the global climate?"

"Yes. Permafrost has more than ten times the amount of carbon stored in it as is currently released into the atmosphere."

I said, "We also found out that there is a southern branch of Pleistocene Park; Wild Field is the public version and is south of Moscow. That's where visitors will be allowed."

"So, they can basically run any experiments that they want at the site in Siberia. That is where the rest of the plot will unfold," said Lander.

Cyndi said, "I sure hope that Dr. Leonid is really on our side. I would hate to have something bad happen to Dr. Yates."

Lander replied. "We have to trust him at this point. After all, he did go to President Kruschov, who then came to our President. You said that there were other projects going on other places. What are they?"

I looked at my notes. "One of the major projects is one in the U.S. itself. The passenger pigeon is on the verge of being de-extincted."

Lander said, "At one time, it was the most abundant of all the birds in the Americas, wasn't it?"

"Yes, it was. It is said that in the 1800s, flocks were a mile wide and as long as three hundred miles. It is claimed that it took a flock days to fly over a town; the flocks were so large that they blocked out the sun."

Cyndi asked, "Did climate change make them extinct?"

"No. Man made them extinct. The giant flocks were an easy target for hunters and furnished them abundant food. A couple of inventions helped in the harvesting of the pigeons. The telegraph gave a way for food companies to track the flocks; the companies hired trappers and hunters to head off the flocks. Also, about that time, the completion of the railroads provided the means to ship food out of the regions where it was harvested. Their feathers were used in bed mattresses and pillows; live birds were caught and shipped by the thousands to be used in trap-shooting tournaments. The last living passenger pigeon, a female named Martha, living in the Cincinnati Zoo, died on September 1, 1914. The bird was officially extinct. We basically hunted the passenger pigeon into extinction."

"How are they trying to de-extinct it?" asked Lander.

"There are several methods, depending on the status of the DNA. The passenger pigeon project is called The Great Comeback. Scientists will use the DNA from the passenger pigeon and compare it with the band-tailed pigeon, its closest relative. The first phase was to sequence the genome and analyze it; the goal was to identify the areas of the band-tailed pigeon that needed to be modified in order to produce a passenger pigeon. Phase two was to produce cells that could be used to engineer a living passenger pigeon genome. Phase three was to combine phase one genomes and phase two modifications to create the passenger pigeon genome. All that is done and the next phase undertakes to create a captive breeding flock kept in netted forest environments until they are able to thrive on their own. The last phase will be to reintroduce the pigeons into the wild. That's going to happen soon."

Lander said, "And a genome means what?"

I replied, "It's the complete set of genetic material of an organism; in the case of the passenger pigeon, all the genetics that make it a passenger pigeon."

Cyndi said, "That's similar to one of the projects I found. On Martha's Vineyard, there is a study underway to consider the possibilities and implications of trying to de-extinct the heath hen. The first step is twofold: one, to characterize the distinctiveness of the heath hen and two, to create the genomic resources needed for grouse conservation."

Lander asked, "Where are they in this project?"

The entire genome of the Greater Prairie-chicken, a close relative of the heath hen, has been sequenced; these can be compared to those of the heath hen to help determine what the modifications must be in order to most closely approximate the heath hen in the de-extinction process."

"Who is funding this process?"

"It actually is unique in that it is community driven and is funded by various contributors. Revive and Restore is backing the project."

Lander said, "Who or what is Revive and Restore?"

I replied. "Revive and Restore was originally created to de-extinct the passenger pigeon. It grew out of an idea that Stewart Brand had as he worked with the non-profit organization Long Now Foundation he had formed. He remembered the way his mother had talked about the passenger pigeon when he was a child and when he heard about the concept of de-extinction, he grew excited and decided to explore the idea. Revive and Restore's mission is to enhance biodiversity. They strive to do this through using genetics to save endangered species and to bring back extinct animals. The organization convenes meetings and serves as a resource to others. In addition, it works directly at times with projects and sometimes acts as a funder for ventures to de-extinct animals."

Cyndi said, "It sounds as if it could be really expensive to do all this DNA sequencing."

I replied, "Yes, very, although recent improvements in technology are bringing the cost down. That and more companies getting involved in working with DNA sequencing are creating competition, which also is bringing the cost down."

Lander asked, "Are there many companies doing DNA sequencing now?"

"Yes, more and more each year. The largest in the world is in China, a company called Beijing Genomics Institute, or BGI. A couple of years ago, it had one hundred and seventy-eight sequencing machines—at half a million dollars each, I might add—and accounts for at least twenty-five percent of the world's genomic data."

"It works with animals?" Cyndi asked.

"It sequences the DNA of many organisms: people, animals, plants, and microbes. One tech magazine had it on its fifty most disruptive companies for 2013. It does research on one hand and earns money on the other hand. It has over four thousand employees at its main facility in Shenzhen."

"That sounds like a powerful company. I'm glad they're not involved in this case," said Cyndi.

Chapter 45

As soon as the package was delivered to Chen Li in Hong Kong, he clicked a contact number in his phone.

"Wéi."

"Chen Li returned the hello. It is here. I will deliver it in an hour." He disconnected, grabbed his jacket, and spoke to his assistant. "I will be out the rest of the day. Reschedule any meetings I have." He carried the package and left the office building. In ten minutes, he was boarding the train that would take him the thirty kilometers to Shenzhen, just across the river from Hong Kong. Thirty minutes later, he left the train and walked the two blocks to an unmarked building. Looking around to be sure he was not followed, he walked into the alley on the left and knocked on a side door. It was quickly opened and Chen Li stepped into the darkened hallway and followed the man to a locked office door. The sudden light coming on almost blinded him.

"Let me see it." Ju-long could hardly contain his excitement as Chen Li handed him the package. He held it almost reverently as he looked it over. "Have you confirmed the contents?"

"No, I have not opened it. It is as it was delivered to me an hour ago."

Ju-long carried it to the conference table in the center of the room. "Come. Let's see what we have." He waited for Chen Li to join him and then, using his tactical knife, he sliced through the shipping tape. Next, he entered the code for the locked box and slid open the end. He looked at Chen Li, smiled, stuck his hand into the package, and pulled out the contents. He removed the bubble wrap and opened the final covering. Both men stared at the bone segments; each had a label taped to it. Ju-long picked up the one closest to him and read, "Sabre-toothed tiger." He turned it to every angle, looking for problems. Laying it aside, he hefted the second piece. "Short-faced bear." Checking it carefully, he placed it beside the first. The next one bore the label of "Epanterias."

Chen Li asked, "What is an Epanterias?"

"It is an extremely rare dinosaur." He laid it beside the others and picked up the last bone segment."

Chen Li said, "I thought we were getting only three segments."

Ju-long smiled and said, "Mr. Romonov is proving his worth. He has sent us a bonus—a piece of the femur of a giant. He may have just earned himself a nice bonus." He placed it with the others.

"Now what?" asked Chen Li.

"Do you know what this means? What we can do with this? If we can beat the Russians, we will be the envy of the world."

"Do you think Russia has anything like these bones?"

"I know they do. Romonov has sent them identical packages."

"Are you sure? How do you know this?"

"I have had him observed for the last month. He is working for a Russian called The Man."

"But Russia is behind China in DNA sequencing. Our largest company performs over twenty-five percent of the DNA sequencing models in the world. There's no way they can compete with us."

"The Man runs Pleistocene Park in Siberia. It is an area that they are modifying to match that of ten thousand years ago. He intends to re-create the large animals grazing on the steppe grasslands."

"You're talking about woolly mammoths? Does he think he can de-extinct one of them?"

"Yes, I am talking about woolly mammoths. And my sources tell me he has already completed the task. There are five woolly mammoths roaming the Park. He wants to add our specimens here to that."

"Why not eliminate Romonov for supplying the Russians?"

"No, not as long as he supplies us. Romonov is a capitalist; he is only making more money. I cannot fault him for that. But if he ever does double-cross us, he will quickly go away."

"Will you do the DNA work at the plant where you work? It is the best in the world."

"No, I have a special lab set up and I have the best ancient DNA scientist in the country to oversee the work. He is ready to go."

"Is he good enough to beat the Russians?"

"Yes, he is. But, as a precaution, I may have a way to slow the Russians down."

Chapter 46

After a break for lunch, we reconvened our meeting in the conference room. We had gone over a lot of information in the morning, but still had much to share with Lander. I kidded him and told him that he was the brawn but I was the brains of our group. He said, "I may very well be the brawn, but Cyndi is the brains of the team; you are just along for the fun of it—we have to carry you."

"I guess that I can't argue with that." Even Cyndi was shaking her head. "Okay, let's get with it. I don't want to be here all day."

Lander looked at me and said, "Okay, Einstein. What have you got? Educate me."

"Okay, pay attention. Where were we?"

"You and Cyndi were discussing some ongoing projects around the world. Do all the different projects use ancient DNA sequencing to reintroduce the animals? You said that there were different techniques."

"There are several techniques that have had some successes. The most familiar to the public is cloning. It has gotten a lot of media attention in the last decade or so. Everyone remembers the cloned sheep named Dolly."

"But that was cloning a living animal, wasn't it? How can you clone an animal that has been dead for years?"

"Many long-dead animals have had cell tissue cryopreserved."

"And cryopreserved means what in English?"

"It means the process of cooling and storing cells at a very low temperature in order to preserve the nature of the cells. Anyway, many animals over the last years have been cryopreserved. Scientists can use that super-cooled tissue to create viable eggs. The eggs are then implanted in closely-related animals; some of them then produce living offspring of the extinct species."

Cyndi spoke up. "There are several projects that are using cloning as a way to try to bring back animals. Have you ever heard of a bucardo?"

Both Lander and I shook our heads. "It looks like neither of us knows what a bucardo is," said Lander.

"Was," said Cyndi. "They are now extinct. But there have been efforts to try to clone one. The last one died in 2000. In 1999, she was captured and some tissue was extracted from her ear and was cryopreserved in liquid nitrogen. In 2003, a team attempted to clone the bucardo by transferring some of her tissue to eggs and implanting them in surrogate mother goats. One of them went full term and a baby bucardo was delivered by C-section."

"What happened to it?" I asked.

"It lived only ten minutes. It had a badly deformed lung, which is a common problem in cloning experiments. There are plans to try to clone the bucardo again." Cyndi looked at her notes. "Another cloning project is The Frozen Zoo; this one is a little more successful."

"Where or what is The Frozen Zoo?"

Cyndi looked at Lander and answered him. "The Frozen Zoo is a project of the San Diego Zoo. For the last thirty-five years or so, it has cryopreserved sample tissue from over ten thousand animals. Samples have been used in many studies. Two endangered species have been cloned from the collection. The Frozen Zoo has taken the lead in collaborating with scientists from all over the world in a project called 'Genome 10K'; the goal is to catalog full genome data for ten thousand vertebrate species."

Lander considered this and said, "So, if they have the full genome data of an animal and viable tissue cryopreserved, that animal could be cloned at any time in the future."

"Yes, you are right. Another one in Australia is called Project Lazarus, an attempt to re-create an exotic species of a gastric-brooding frog."

Lander said, "Gastric-brooding frog. What does that mean?"

Cyndi smiled, "Just what it implies. The frog swallowed its eggs and then gave birth to live frogs orally. The baby frogs were born through its mouth. By the way, the frog was declared extinct in 1983; scientists are using cell tissue stored in a conventional freezer for the last forty years to try to re-create it."

"Another technique is using selective back-breeding of existing animals in order to re-create a primordial ancestor. By intentionally focusing on certain traits, over a period of several generations, scientists can gradually return an animal to its previous state. One such attempt is being made on the aurochs, which at one time was plentiful in Europe and Asia. The aurochs was a huge ox, extinct since the early 1600s. The Taurus Foundation of the Netherlands is heading this project."

"That all sounds good, but what are we doing to keep other animals from becoming extinct?" Lander asked the question that many in the public have also asked.

"We are doing quite a lot, actually." I glanced at my notes. "Besides de-extinction, many people are working with nature preserves and re-wilding projects, here and abroad. European Wildlife is one organization dedicated to nature preservation and environmental protection. It wants to create a network of nature preserves to protect endangered species of plants and animals. It has at least two big projects: one is the European Center of

Biodiversity. It borders three countries in Central Europe and wants to create a type of 'Noah's Ark' for the majority of the European species. The second is a project trying to regenerate natural forests in the Mediterranean.

"Another major project is in the Netherlands. The Oostvaardersplassen is a twenty-three square mile nature preserve where an attempt to re-create a version of the ancient European landscape is ongoing. It is attracting large numbers of endangered species there. We see similar projects, perhaps not on as large a scale, here in the U.S. and in other countries."

I looked at my watch. "I think that's enough. Let's call it a day and go get a good dinner."

Lander said, "Good idea. We have a pretty good handle on what's driving the case now. The successful de-extinction team for the stolen bones will have a gold mine. People would flock to see those extinct animals. Can you imagine a real saber-toothed tiger, a breathing dinosaur, or even a short-faced bear?"

I nodded and said, "One that we haven't even mentioned. What are the plans for the giant? I don't think the public would stand for a person being displayed in a zoo, no matter how big he or she might be."

Cyndi and Lander considered my words and we all just shook our heads, wondering what we still had to discover about the case.

Chapter 47

The next day dawned bright and clear. Lander and I were on our way to one of the other dig sites that had been attacked. The saber-toothed tiger excavation project was northwest of Durango and would take us a couple of hours to get there. Lander asked me to drive. Before we left, he looked at me and asked, "Do you have your handgun?"

"Yes, of course. Do you think I may need it?"

"You always may need it. Be like the Boy Scouts! It's good always to be prepared. But, yes, to answer your question. You may need it."

"Why do you say that? Do you know something I don't?"

"I know a lot that you don't. There has been a white van following us the last few days. Two men in the vehicle."

"That's why you have been on high alert. Who do you think they are?"

"If I were guessing, I would say the two fake FBI agents."

"But you never guess. So, you're pretty sure that's who they are. How do you think they found us?"

"It wouldn't be hard to find us. It would be a little more difficult to follow us without our seeing them. That's why they put a tracking device on our car. I found it a couple of nights ago."

"Did you put it on an eighteen-wheeler going through town . . . or maybe on the train?"

His answer surprised me. "No, I didn't; I left it on the car."

"You want them to follow us today! Do you think they will try something?"

"I didn't want them hanging around town here with Cyndi by herself. Yes, I expect that they will make an attempt today. We'll be on isolated mountain roads most of the day. It'll be a good time for them to strike. And, it will be a good time for us to allow them to strike. Just keep alert. If I tell you to make a sudden move in the car, do it automatically and ask questions later."

"Yes, Sir!" I had enough confidence in Lander that if he told me to drive off the side of the road, I would do it. "Are you going to take them out? Or do you want to keep them alive to question them?"

"I would like to interrogate them, or at least, one of them. But, depending on the situation, we may not be able to do that."

"How will we know if they are following us? If they have a tracking device on the car, they can hang back out of sight . . . or even get in front of us and ambush us."

Lander smiled. "We'll know." He showed me his phone. A red dot was in line behind us and moving at the same speed we were.

"You put a tracker on their car!" I said. "When did you do that?"

"While you were asleep, I took a midnight cruise. Fortunately, they were sleeping, too."

"How did you know where to look for them?"

"I noticed where they picked us up on our earlier trips; there's not too many motels out that way. When we were on the way to the airport, I noticed a white van in the parking lot of one of the motels."

"How did you know that was the right van? There are many white vans; that's why so many bad guys use them."

"I had a talk with the night clerk. He confirmed it for me."

"I thought the clerks wouldn't identify guests. Did you have to force him to do so?"

"No, nothing that dramatic. It's amazing what a hundred-dollar bill will do for you. Anyway, he confirmed that the guests driving that particular van were registered as Daniels and Wilson."

"The FBI agents!" I said.

"The fake FBI agents," Lander said. "Watch everything, but we'll be safe for a while. They won't try anything until we get into the mountains."

Nevertheless, I reached under the seat and retrieved my Glock. I checked the magazine, pulled the slide to place a cartridge in the firing chamber, and carefully placed it on the front seat between my legs. "Boy Scout," I said.

"Just be careful it doesn't go off where it is." He laughed. "That would not be fun."

I moved the gun to the side pocket of the door as I said, "They still aren't sure what we are doing or who we are," I said. "Maybe they will follow us to see where we are going."

Lander's eyes lit up and he drawled in his best John Wayne voice, "Good thinking, Pilgrim." He smiled. "You may be right. They likely will follow us to the site, watch us there, and attack after we leave to come back."

"Does Dr. Lee know that we are coming there today? Is he back on site yet?"

"Yes, he is expecting us. Dr. Pasternak contacted him for me."

"Pasternak? Is she aware that we are investigating the incident?"

"She knows a little. I had Director Frazier to speak directly to her. She will cooperate any way she can. The site is not active again yet, but Lee will meet us there at ten-thirty."

"I'll have to hurry then, if I am going to get there by ten-thirty."

"Okay, but be careful. If you're going to hurry, I better take a nap. You drive better when I sleep."

He clicked something on his phone, reclined his seat, and pulled his cap down over his eyes.

"Hey, wait a minute. You need to watch for the van."

"You watch for it; you have to stay awake to drive—I hope."

He watched me squirm a minute, then said, "I have an alert set on my phone. If they get within a half mile of us, it will notify us."

"I hope it doesn't play *Taps* to alert us," I said. Lander only laughed and closed his eyes.

Nothing happened on the trip to the dig spot. Just before I slowed the Jeep to turn into the drive to the excavation site, Lander sat up. I swear I don't know how he does that, but that's typical of him. He glanced at his phone and said, "They are still with us, but about a mile away. They'll get closer while we are stopped, but position themselves to set up an ambush on the way out." I was glad to hear his words; we had a couple of hours of life left.

I parked the car at the end of the drive. Lee stepped out of the tent, looked closely to identify us, and then moved to meet us.

"Dr. Lee, thanks for meeting us here," said Lander. We all shook hands and then Lander continued, "Can you show us what happened?"

"Yes, as much as I can tell. I wasn't here, you know. But Dr. Pasternak called me and said to be completely honest with you. I'm not sure what your role is but she told me to ask no questions."

For the next two hours, Lee walked us over every inch of the site; occasionally, Lander glanced at his phone, but said nothing. The mess had been cleaned up after the attack, but, according to Lee, it had looked similar to the dinosaur location. He showed us the bag in which he had placed all the bone fragments. There was not a piece longer than one or two inches. "Those thugs don't realize how valuable these bones were," he moaned. "They were priceless."

Lander said, "Oh, they know all right. They just wanted to be sure no one else had a decent bone to work with. They have bigger goals than trying to sell a piece of bone. If that were what they wanted to do, they would have taken all the bones they could."

"What do you mean? What do you think they are going to do with the bone?"

Lander ignored the question and finally said, "I think we've seen what we came for. Dr. Lee, we appreciate your help. Please don't mention this meeting to anyone."

Lander looked at me and said, "We'd better get back on the road. No telling what we'll run into in these mountains."

I thought about dallying some more, but thought, "I've got the best sidekick a man could want." I said, "Let's go. I'm driving again."

He nodded and went to the passenger side. He looked once more at his phone and put on his game face. "Let's do it!"

Chapter 48

Ivanov knocked on the office door. It was opened almost immediately by one of the personal security men for The Man. After Ivanov was cleared, he entered the room and moved over in front of The Man, who sat in an overstuffed brown leather chair beside his desk. There was a similar chair about six feet to his left; a man Ivanov had never seen occupied it. The man was slightly built with a receding hairline. He looked as though he had never spent time in the sun although his face was covered with lines. His thick glasses made him appear bug-eyed.

The Man said, "Come in, Mr. Ivanov. I want you to meet the newest member of the project team. This is Dr. Mita Petrov." He pointed at Ivanov and said, "Dr. Petrov, this is the man I was telling you about: Anatoly Ivanov."

Ivanov walked to the man and shook his hand. "I am pleased you are joining our team. Welcome."

"I am honored to work on such a national project. Thank you for the opportunity."

The Man said to Ivanov, "Dr. Petrov is the man that I talked with you about when I outlined our plan. He is the final link to our success." He lifted the bottle of vodka and poured three drinks. He handed one each to Petrov and Ivanov. "Here's to success." After the toast, The Man said to Ivanov. "Take Dr. Petrov and show him around. Let him see the lab and then take him to his apartment."

"Yes, Sir. On which level is his apartment?"

"Put him next door to Dr. Leonid's apartment. They will be working together a lot, especially in the beginning stages of the mission."

The answer surprised Ivanov, but he suppressed any reflection of that in his facial reactions. He turned to the door and exited the room with Petrov right behind. For the next hour, he gave Petrov the same tour he had received. He ended it with the same ride in the maglev car and a view of the new steppe grasslands. The sight of the woolly mammoths grazing overwhelmed Petrov.

"There are rumors that Russia has succeeded in recreating the mammoth, but no one could verify it. This is amazing. How many are there?"

"We now have five, with three more in gestation. Our goal is to have a herd of twenty woolly mammoths in five years."

"I am thrilled to be working here."

"But the woolly is not the reason you are here, is it?" Ivanov knew what role Petrov was to play, but he wanted to check his discipline to not talk about the project."

"I cannot answer your question. I have explicit orders to say nothing to anyone, here on the facility or outside of it. That is a question you need to take up with The Man."

Ivanov smiled. "Right answer. All information about this project is to be considered highly classified and never to be spoken about. Let's go check out your apartment."

When they got to the correct door, Ivanov instructed Petrov how to unlock the door: first the thumbprint was verified; when that sensor turned green, he placed his eye up to the iris reader. There was a noticeable click and the door swung open. Ivanov followed Petrov into the room. Petrov looked around and then said, "Good. They have already delivered my luggage."

Ivanov handed him a phone and requested that he turn over his personal one. Petrov hesitated briefly and then handed the phone to Ivanov.

Ivanov said, "No one is allowed any personal electronics of any kind here. I'm sure that they told you not to bring your computer. Your new one is on the desk there."

"Yes, I was instructed to leave all electronics behind. I received permission to place all my pertinent files on a flash drive. I have it on me."

"Good. Did The Man explain the procedures to you?"

"Not entirely. He said that you would go over all the special rules with me."

Ivanov smiled at the realization that The Man was satisfied with his work and that he was empowering him to be the leader in charge of the project. "We have few rules, but it is essential that you adhere to all of them. There are to be no outside communications at all. You have a phone for one reason only: that is to communicate with Dr. Leonid. You answer to him and to me; I will be your liaison with The Man should you have a reason to contact him. You are to be only on this level; it is the one where you will live and the one where you will do all your work. You'll only leave this level with my permission and, even then, I will accompany you. You are never to access any social media sites; you have Internet access, but only for research purposes. Do you understand the ground rules?"

"Yes, they are exactly what I expected to encounter. May I use the phone to also get in touch with you if I need to?"

"Yes, I am the only person other than Dr. Leonid with whom you can communicate on the phone. Am I clear on that?"

"Yes." Petrov understood that his phone would be constantly monitored and he had no thoughts of abusing the rule. He harbored no death wish.

"By the way, Dr. Leonid will be here tomorrow. You will meet with him at eight-thirty in the morning. It is critical that the work gets underway immediately. Russia must be the country that leads the world in completing this project. I am sure you are cognizant of that."

"I am acutely aware of the importance of being first; that is why I am here." Petrov was sure that any type of failure would result in his never leaving Siberia. Although he convinced himself that the choice had been his, he knew that his involvement had been created with no alternatives at all.

He thought, *It will be tricky to fulfill my mission without Dr. Leonid knowing exactly how I would modify the work.*

Chapter 49

We turned from the driveway onto the state highway. I glanced at Lander's phone and saw that we were heading right for the red dot. As Lander had thought they would, they were stopped somewhere down the road and were setting up an ambush for us. Were we going to just ride right into it? Knowing Lander as I did, I was sure he had a plan; nevertheless, I was getting pretty anxious the closer to the dot we came. I put my hand on my Glock. Lander saw me do that and said, "We'll stop just up the road here. There is an old logging trail off to the right; turn onto it. It should be a hundred yards around the curve coming up."

I thought, "So Lander does have a plan." I gave a sigh of relief and instantly felt the tension start to ease. I drove around the curve and just where Lander said it would be, there was an overgrown logging trail to the right. I slowed and steered the Grand Cherokee off the road.

"Stop here," said Lander.

I stopped the car and Lander quickly jumped out. He moved to the front of the car and dipped out of sight. After a few seconds, he stood up again and motioned to me to join him. "Here is their tracking device," he said. He showed it to me and then said, "Get my backpack out of the car."

I retrieved the backpack and followed him over to a tree. He glanced at his phone and then reached for the backpack. He pulled out a small tin and opened it. He used a small stick to pull a glob out of the container and spread it on the back of the tracking device. He then placed the tracker on the back side of the tree and said, "We'll let them track this tree while we set up our own trap. They'll know we stopped and after a while they will come to check it out. We'll be ready for them." We started to leave and Lander said, "Wait. Change of plans." He went to the tree, removed the tracking device, and wiped it clean of the adhesive on the back of it. "We'll leave it on the ground in the middle of the trail. They'll think it came loose from the car from the bouncing on the trail." He dropped it in one of the ruts and said, "Let's get on up the trail here."

The trail was rough and after a short distance, I engaged the four-wheel drive. After that, the trail posed no difficulties for us to travel and we followed it up a steep incline. "Stop up here on the top. We'll leave the car here and walk back to the spot." We left the car and started down the slope. "Wait a minute. I need my backpack." I watched

Lander hurry back to the car to get the bag. He glanced at his phone and said, "We need to hurry. They are on the move."

When we got back to the trail intersection, Lander looked down the road and said, "It's clear. Hurry to the other side of the road." We ran across the road and stopped in a copse of trees. "We'll wait for them here," Lander said as he looked at his phone again. "They should be here in a couple of minutes."

The white van slowed and then stopped just past the trail cutoff. We watched as the driver reversed his direction and stopped at the intersection. The van eased onto the trail where the driver cut the engine and the two occupants exited the vehicle. We couldn't see them clearly until they walked to the rear of the van. "They are Daniels and Wilson, the fake FBI agents," I said. Lander merely nodded and placed his finger to his lips, signaling me to be quiet.

Daniels bent into the back of the van and pulled out a rifle. We saw both of them check their handguns. There was no doubt what their plans were. They slowly moved forward, hoping to surprise us where our car was supposedly stopped. Suddenly, Wilson stooped down and picked something up. "They've found the tracker. Let's hope they think it vibrated off the car," whispered Lander. The two men looked around and then whispered to each other. We watched them separate and begin walking down the trail, one on each side and each leading with his handgun.

"What now?" I asked as the two men disappeared around a bend.

"We wait for a few minutes. They'll follow our car tracks down the road, maybe all the way to where we left it."

After five more minutes, Lander motioned for me to follow and stepped out on the road. "We'll wait for them at their van. When they come back, remember what you have been taught about using your handgun. Aim for body mass and, if you have to shoot, shoot to kill. We're not in a video game here. Those men intend to kill us and we're not going to let them do that. If they wind up dead, it'll save us having to tie them up and get them to a holding area."

"I thought you wanted to interrogate one of them."

"If one lives long enough, I'll do that. Right now, our primary goal is to be the ones driving down the mountain."

Lander opened the rear door of the van. "Well, look here. They have enough fire power to arm a small unit." He put on gloves and lifted out an AK-47 and checked it out. "Good weapon," he said. "Here's a Glock, a Smith and Wesson revolver, a Colt Special Combat Pistol. There're three more rifles and a double-barrel shotgun. These guys mean business."

"What if they call in reinforcements?"

"They won't do that. Those two think they're far superior to just a couple of vacationers who happened to be in the right place at the wrong time. They greatly underestimate us."

"Underestimate you, maybe."

"You know a lot more than you think you do. When they come back, if one is leading, I'll take him; you take the other. If they are side by side, I'll take the one on our right; you take the other. I'll call out 'Drop your weapons'. If they don't do it immediately or they make a move to raise their weapons, shoot. Just like on the range, body mass; but don't miss. Do you want this shotgun?"

"No, I'll stay with my Glock. That's why I got it." I checked the slide to be sure that a cartridge was in the chamber. "I'm ready."

In about four minutes, Lander held up his finger and pointed. "They're coming. Fire on my signal."

We watched the men appear on the trail, still one on each side. They were moving quicker now. When they got within twenty feet of the van, Lander called out: "Stop where you are and drop your weapons! Now!"

They quickly stopped and looked toward the van. Suddenly they made a move to raise their weapons. Lander reacted immediately and said, "Fire!" Our handguns went off almost simultaneously and I saw both men fall to the ground. Lander was already moving and ran to his target first, the one with the handgun and rifle. He kicked both weapons away and then sprinted to the other man, who lay moaning and holding his chest. Lander grabbed the handgun from the ground where it had landed and removed the magazine.

"Good shot, Kent. You can come out now."

I moved to the spot where Lander was checking my target. "He's still alive, but it'll be touch and go. Here, tie him up. Don't worry about trying to be easy on him." He moved to the other assailant while I slipped the paracord bracelet off my wrist. I freed the six feet of cord and secured the man while Lander did the same to the other shooter. He then placed compress bandages over the wounds and tightly secured them with tape.

"Do we need to call the sheriff or ranger?" I asked.

"No. I'll call Director Frazier. He'll arrange a pickup of the men here and transport them out of here. We'll stay with them until then." He checked the pocket of the man and found a set of keys. "Here. Get the van over here. But put these gloves on first. Try not to touch anything with your bare hands. They'll check the van for prints or other DNA evidence."

I drove the van off the road and stopped it near the men. Lander said, "Help me put them in the van." We loaded the men into the back of the van. Lander got into the driver's seat and motioned for me to sit in the passenger side.

He slowly drove the van up the trail. When he got close to our Jeep, he steered the van off the trail into a small clearing. He checked the GPS coordinates and called Frazier back. "You'll find the van with the two injured men in it; I don't think that they'll be going anywhere." He listened a minute and then responded. "Okay, we'll clear out before the helicopter arrives. As soon as I hear it, we're gone." He gave him the coordinates for the van and then disconnected the call.

"Let's check the men out," Lander said as he opened his door. We opened the rear door and looked at the men. Neither one was conscious and I wasn't sure whether either would survive.

Lander closed the door and I followed him to our Jeep. We retrieved it and drove it back to the spot where the van was. "As soon as we hear the helicopter, we will leave. When they get through with the site, there will be no indication that we were ever here."

"Where will they take the men?"

"They will probably take them to the hospital at Fort Carson Army Base near Colorado Springs. They can treat them there and then, if one or both survive, Director Frazier can have them interrogated and held there."

Twenty minutes later, we heard the thump, thump of the helicopter. Lander looked at me and said, "Are you all right?"

"Yes, I'm fine." I'm not a big proponent of violence, but some people just need to get what's coming to them. These men had murdered before and had intentions of killing us, so no, I don't feel any remorse about our actions."

"Good. You're still driving. I need a nap. Just be careful; you've got valuable cargo here." He smiled and reclined his seat.

"What will we tell Cyndi about today?"

My question went unanswered and I had valuable time to consider our next steps.

Chapter 50

After a long and tiring flight, Ju-Long walked the covered exit from the plane to the lobby of Denver International Airport. His large glasses and floppy hat would conceal his identity from all but his closest associates. He had traveled as a Chinese businessman he knew back in Shenzhen. Although Romonov had hesitated when he had contacted him, he knew that he would meet him here. He had traveled light with only a carry-on bag and would be returning to his country on the first flight out the next day.

Ju-Long walked through the airport to the front drive and looked for the shuttle to the Hyatt House. After a short trip from the airport, he walked up to the check-in counter and spoke to the clerk, a young attractive girl. "Reservation for Chen Wie."

After looking at the computer, the clerk said, "Yes, Sir. I have you booked for one night. Is that correct?"

"Yes, I will be leaving early tomorrow."

"The room has been prepaid. Breakfast begins at six o'clock off the lobby." She handed him a key and pointed to the elevators. "Your room is 800, a corner room as requested."

"Thank you. I will be retiring shortly. Please hold all calls to my room."

"Yes, Sir. Have a good night and thank you for staying at the Hyatt."

Ju-Long walked to the elevators and pushed the up button. He exited on the ninth floor, checked to be sure he was not followed, and took the stairs back to the eighth floor. He quickly entered the room directly across the hall and used the chain to double-lock the door behind him. He tossed his bag on the bed and took care of business in the bathroom. Feeling better, he approached the door connecting him to the room next door and knocked on it. It immediately opened and Ju-Long was looking at the man in the adjoining room. Although he had never personally seen Romonov, he had no doubt that it was he standing there. Ju-Long pushed past Romonov and quickly scanned the room and bathroom. Seeing no one, he came back to Romonov.

"Mr. Romonov. It is a pleasure to finally meet you after doing business with you for the last two years." Instead of the traditional custom of bowing, he extended his hand to shake that of Romonov.

"The pleasure is mine, Ju-Long. What is the purpose of this visit? I trust that you received the package and that it was acceptable."

"Yes, it was exceptional. And I appreciate the extra item you sent. You will be well compensated for that. It may prove more valuable than all the others."

"I thought you would welcome it and appreciate its value! After all, some historians believe that the ancestors of the North American giants originated in China. We have evidence of multiple skeletons of giants discovered here."

"Yes, I believe that to be true. As for this meeting, I have a proposal for you, one that I could not discuss over the phone, even on a secure connection. Come to my room and let's sit while we talk." Ju-long walked to the room phone. "But we need something to drink first." He connected to room service and said, "Please send a carafe of hot tea to my room. I need it as quickly as possible. Thank you."

Romonov knew that the culture of the Chinese during formal meetings called for small talk before the actual topic was addressed, so it didn't surprise him that Ju-Long began by asking about Romonov's family. Within five minutes, there was a knock at the door and they heard, "Room Service."

Ju-Long looked through the peephole and opened the door. "Please set it on the table." He took the bill and signed for it. As soon as the server had left, he again secured the door and walked back to the table. He lifted the carafe and poured each of them a cup of tea. The conversation stayed casual until they had finished their tea.

Romonov recognized the signal to begin the discussion of the topic for the meeting and said, "You said you had a proposal for me."

"Yes, I do. One which I hope you will seriously consider."

Romonov considered Ju-Long's words. He thought to himself, "Was there an implied threat there? If so, it was so subtle that most would not distinguish it." But Romonov was not like most; he had not survived in dealing on the global black market by being reckless and had developed a keen sense of undertones. He reminded himself to be on high alert and was thankful he had a handgun in his concealed shoulder holster. He responded, "I am honored you wish to include me."

Ju-Long continued, "I know that you have also sold the same specimens to the Russians." At that statement, Romonov looked intently at Ju-Long, but knew that one did not interrupt a Chinese talking. Ju-Long noted the look and said, "I don't have a problem with that. You are an entrepreneur and want to make money. I would do the same thing."

Romonov noticeably relaxed and nodded to Ju-Long.

"As I was saying, I know money is your motivation. I am going to offer you an opportunity to triple what you have already made. That is, if you are interested." He paused while Romonov considered his words and finally nodded. "I thought so; you are an ambitious man. Cautious, but ambitious. Am I right?"

Knowing that Ju-Long was waiting for an answer, Romonov said, "Yes, you are right. Will your proposal cause me a problem with the Russian?"

"You expect an honest answer? Only if The Man finds out about your involvement."

"How do you know about The Man?"

"How I know is irrelevant. That I know is important. I know about him; I know about his plans; I know about the labs here and in Russia. I know about Drs. Leonid and Yates. I even know about the official in the U.S. government who is helping The Man."

Romonov was scared now. "But how could you know all this?"

"I told you that is irrelevant. I will remind you that the Chinese have the most advanced methods in the world to mine information. Do you want to know what you are to do?"

Romonov noticed that Ju-Long no longer phrased it as a request. "Yes, tell me what you want."

"First, you are to continue your work and contact with The Man. It is essential that you project no difference in your attitude toward him. If he discovers that you are double-crossing him, he will have no qualms about eliminating you."

Romonov didn't doubt that at all. "What if I decide I can't help you?"

Ju-Long smiled. "Then The Man will have no qualms about eliminating you for selling me the items you have already delivered. I won't have to do anything."

Romonov recognized the threat for what it was . . . and he completely agreed with Ju-Long's assessment. If The Man knew he had delivered the packages to Ju-Long, he would have assassins in place within hours. Romonov had no choice and Ju-Long knew it. Ju-Long spent the next thirty minutes proving to Romonov that he knew everything he claimed. He neared the end of the speech and said, "Of course, Dr. Leonid and Dr. Yates must be terminated. If we play it right, we can make it seem like an accident while someone is trying to rescue the lady; after all, it seems as if she were kidnapped."

Romonov was astounded. Ju-Long knew everything. "Lander and Kent won't be an option. They are being eliminated today."

"That attempt will fail. Your two clowns are no matches for them. Lander and Kent will remain obstacles." He handed Romonov another phone. Use this only for communication with me. I will make the first contact. Wait for my instructions before you do anything." He stood to his feet and said, "It will be nice doing business with you. Do it well and you will have enough to retire anywhere in the world that you wish. You may even decide to come to China. Close and lock the door between our rooms."

Chapter 51

I had been driving about an hour when Lander's SAT phone buzzed. He immediately opened his eyes and looked at the caller display. "Frazier," he said.

"Yes, sir," he answered. "I am still in the car with Kent. Is it okay if I put it on speakerphone so he can hear? He listened to the reply and clicked the icon for the Bluetooth; the call was now coming through the speakers in the car.

"Where are you? You were able to vacate the scene without any trouble, weren't you?"

"We are about an hour out from our hotel. No problems. Thank you for cleaning the site. I would not have liked trying to explain what happened to local authorities."

"Yes, this will keep it much cleaner. By the way, neither man made it. Be at the airport at five-thirty in the morning; I will have a ride for you; the Kents, too, if they can make it."

Lander looked at me and I nodded. "Yes, Sir. I will be there. I'm not sure about Cyndi; she's doing much better after her last back surgery, but mornings are still tough on her."

"That will be fine. She's welcome to come if she feels like it; if not, then I'll see you two tomorrow. By the way, Lander, be sure no one follows you this time." Before we could reply, he had ended the connection.

When we got into Durango, I pulled through the Starbucks and got Cyndi a decaf; I didn't want her to drink alone, so I got one, too. Lander just looked at me with that stupid smile, but he did get one himself. *He needed the caffeine; all he did was sleep when he was with me. At least, when he wasn't killing people,* I thought.

Cyndi looked up and said, "Yea, Starbucks." She stared at me—trying to read my mind— and then said, "Okay, what did you two get into today?"

Lander looked at me and I said, "Well, we drove to the site, met with Dr. Lee, and drove back. Oh, and we killed a couple of men and the CIA retrieved them and cleaned the site. Other than that, not much happened. Well, except that our friend here slept through most of the trip and we have a meeting tomorrow, probably in Washington. Just another day at the office!"

I didn't know whose eyes were bigger, Cyndi's or Lander's. Finally, Cyndi said, "I can't let you two go anywhere by yourselves, can I?" I really expected her to ask if we were okay, but she didn't. I guess she could tell that we had survived since we were talking with her. She's smart that way.

Lander had to get his two cents in. "Phil keeps getting me into trouble. Here I was, trying to take a nap so I wouldn't have to watch his driving in the mountains and the next thing I know, two men are trying to kill us. I don't know how he does it."

We all laughed at that and the tension eased. Cyndi said, "It's obvious that you two are all right." I told you she was smart. She continued, "Let's sit down and you can tell me about your adventure." I was glad I had brought her the coffee.

I started telling her about the two men waiting for us. "Wait a minute, how did they know where you were going?"

"They probably didn't know where we were going; they were following us again."

"What do you mean 'again'?"

I nodded at Lander. "You explain this."

He said, "They have been following us for the last three days. Today, we went to an area where they thought they could ambush us without there being witnesses."

"Are you telling me that you couldn't lose two men that you knew were following you? Are you slipping? You couldn't get lost in the mountains?" She was still looking at Lander but I wondered if that was a reflection on my driving she was mocking.

I said, "Lander didn't want to lose them; besides, we couldn't see them. They had a tracking device on our car."

"What do you mean, 'Lander didn't want to lose them'?"

I sighed and said, "After three days, he wanted them to make a move . . . and they did."

"That still doesn't make sense. How did you know they were following you if you couldn't see them?" Cyndi reads a lot of spy books.

"Lander put a tracking device on their van. We could tell they were following us."

Cyndi laughed. "You all were tracking each other? That's a first, even for you two. When did you put the tracker on their car?" She addressed that question to Lander.

I answered first. "It seems that he knew that they were following us the last couple of days because he spotted the same van we had seen before. He sneaked out late at night and found it at a local motel. That's where he put the tracker on their van."

"How did you know it was the same van following us? It was probably a white van, the most common on the road?"

Lander was still slow, so I answered her again. "He used his manly skills—and a hundred-dollar bill—and got the motel clerk to identify the men. You'll recognize the names: Daniels and Wilson."

"The FBI agents?"

"The fake FBI agents." Lander was quicker this time.

Cyndi looked at Lander. "Why didn't you tell us about the van?"

"I didn't want to worry you until I was sure they were up to no-good. I should have told you what I knew."

Cyndi replied. "Don't worry about worrying us."

Lander blushed slightly. "Yes, Ma'am. No more secrets."

I picked up the story again. "Anyway, Lander found the tracking device on our car and decided to leave it so that they would follow us today and not hang around town with your being here alone. He convinced me that they wouldn't try anything until the trip back and he was right. We tracked them tracking us." I went on to explain how we had tricked them into finding the tracker that "fell off our car." I ended the story with an account of the gunfight.

"Did you have to kill them?"

"We gave them a chance to give themselves up, but they decided to go for their weapons instead. We were faster."

"Then I don't have a problem with that," Cyndi said. "Just don't get used to it. Did you leave the bodies in the mountains? Oh, wait. You said the CIA cleaned up the scene, didn't you? Is that what you meant? Did they retrieve the bodies?"

"Yes, they picked up the bodies and the abandoned van. It will never make the local news. Not even McKenzie or Spencer will hear about this incident."

"So, it's relegated to 'incident status'? Do you think this will end the trouble?"

Lander replied, "No, I don't. These two were just the foot soldiers. Someone else is pulling the strings. The disappearance of these two will in all probability escalate the attacks. We also will no longer be able to fly under the radar; this will warn them that we're not just average sightseers. We'll need to be extra vigilant from now on. I don't want to alarm you, but don't assume anyone or anything is safe."

Cyndi smiled and said, "Forewarned is forearmed."

Chapter 52

At five o'clock the next morning, Lander and I were parking at the airport. Cyndi had elected not to go with us; she said she would stay around the hotel and read or something. I interpreted the "something" as she was going to do some more research. She was good at it and enjoyed it. Or maybe she just enjoyed being able to tell Lander and me information that we didn't know. When we entered the airport, Lander saw the same man who had met him on his previous trip. We made our way over to him. He shook our hands and said, "Please, follow me."

We followed him to the waiting private jet and within five minutes, we were speeding down the runway. Other than the pilot and our escort, we were the only ones on the plane. That felt pretty good: having a private jet to ourselves. We helped ourselves to the fruit and drinks set out for us and then reclined. I asked Lander, "What do you think Director Frazier will have to say?"

Hearing no answer, I looked at Lander and shook my head. I was starting to worry about him.

Four-and-a-half hours later, we began our descent and were on the ground within minutes. The jet taxied over to a private hanger and after walking down the steps, we followed our escort to a waiting black Explorer. A short time later, we entered Director Frazier's office.

"Lander; Dr. Kent. Please come in."

"Just Kent or Phil," I said.

"Kent it is. Please have a seat." After we sat down, Frazier instructed his secretary to hold all calls and closed the door. He addressed us again. "Coffee, tea, water?"

I started to decline, but Lander quickly said, "We'll have coffee."

Frazier pointed at the Keurig and said, "Cups and pods are in the drawer there. Help yourself." We made our coffees and then sat in the chairs facing Frazier.

"I appreciate your both coming today. Bring me up to date on what's going on. Start at the beginning with your adventure the other day."

I nodded at Lander and he began. "The two men that attacked us were introduced to us as Brett Daniels and Jeff Wilson, almost certainly fake names. They claimed to be FBI agents and had warned all of us off the case. Have you been able to get anything on them after your men cleaned up the site?"

"You're right—they are fake names. Their real identities are George Fannin and Doyle Ayers. A couple of hit men who've worked for a number of unsavory characters over the years. They have been suspects in several crimes, but have never been convicted. They were arrested last year for a murder in D.C. but were released on a technicality. I'm not sure with whom they are—or were— working. The van provided no clues to anyone else."

Lander continued. "I suspected as much. They had been following us for at least three days and had managed to place a tracking device on our car."

Frazier raised his eyebrows at this statement. "You let them put a tracking device on your car? Is this the Lander I used to work with?"

Lander just laughed and replied. "The operative word is 'let'. I wanted to keep them close to us."

"Did you consider that might be a dangerous situation: their being able to track you? You're good at eluding followers, but if they have a tracker, then they don't have to stay close enough to allow even you to make them. And you've got to remember; staying close to you is staying close to the Kents, also. Are you slipping?"

"I thought the same thing, Mr. Director. However, I found out that Lander had placed a tracker on *their* van. We were able to track them following us. That's how we were able to flip the ambush they had planned for us in the mountains."

Frazier horse-laughed at that. "Maybe you're not slipping, after all." He wiped his brow in an exaggerated motion and said, "Whew! That's a relief! Now, go ahead with your story. What else have you been able to uncover?"

"Not much at this point; mostly just supposition. We know that the two deceased perps were working for someone else, someone with contacts and resources. I'm certain that someone high in Washington is providing information. That person has to be a top official in the National Science Foundation or in one of the agencies that can get highly secretive information from the NSF. At one time, I thought it might be Pasternak or Lee, but I'm now sure that they are not involved. Whoever the spy is, it's unlikely that he or she is the one that is at the helm of the project to steal the ancient bones. That person is probably the man in Russia who is heading up the re-wilding project for them. What was his name?"

"Peter Listovov, although he has adopted the name of The Man."

"That's right; he's The Man. I'm still not convinced that he has devised this elaborate plot in order just to get samples of bones to repopulate his park there. There's got to be another level."

I thought about saying something about peeling away the layers of an onion, but decided it wouldn't add to the conversation, so I kept my mouth shut.

Frazier said, "You're right. There are more layers to this. My intelligence has uncovered a rumor that the Chinese may also be up to something."

"Related to the ancient bone thefts?" I shook my head. "First the Russians; now the Chinese."

"Yes, we picked up a conversation between a person here in the U.S. and someone in China."

"If it was on a phone, can you ID the owner?"

"No, it was a throwaway phone and hasn't been used since. The call originated in the New York area."

Lander asked, "Do we know how the stolen bones were delivered to The Man in Siberia?"

Frazier shook his head. "Nothing definitive at this point. We don't think they were shipped commercially there."

Lander considered that. "Would someone have been able to just carry them on an airplane without the possibility that they would be discovered?"

Frazier said, "Perhaps, but it wouldn't be a hundred percent that it could be done."

"What if it were someone with private transportation or someone who doesn't have to clear customs?" I asked.

Both men looked at me and then Frazier spoke. "Good idea, Kent. We have a group in New York that do not have to clear customs . . . coming into New York or when they travel to their countries."

Lander said, "Diplomats! One of them could carry a package out of the country knowing that it would not be inspected."

Frazier said, "We'll seriously consider that. I'll get intelligence on it immediately. That would be the simplest way to carry a valuable package from the U.S."

Lander said, "And you are following up on the possibility of the Chinese involvement also, aren't you?"

"Yes, of course. Are you learning anything from Yates and Leonid? Do you think he's on the level working with us?"

"We've met with them, and, yes, I think he is committed to helping bring The Man down. Don't you agree, Kent?"

"Yes, I think so. He is above all else a scientist. He is passionate about his work and wants to keep the politics out of it."

Frazier asked, "Did you discover anything new at the site you visited before the ambush?"

"Not really; we are planning to visit the other sites within the next few days."

"With Daniels and Wilson out of the picture, I wish I could tell you that it will be safer from now on. However, I think that they were just dispensable hit men and they are probably already replaced. Be on high alert. If anything feels suspicious or uncomfortable, act on that feeling;

don't take any chances. I'll let you know any new information I get. You have my number; check in with me anytime." He stood up and I realized the meeting was over.

Chapter 53

Leonid said, "Is the lab in Virginia ready to go?"

"Yes, all the equipment is there. I have my assistants in place and have met with them. They are waiting for directions to proceed. What about Russia?" Yates paused for an answer.

"It is ready to go. The Man has hired someone to oversee the lab work; I think he is there to monitor and assure that we are all working. He looks like Russian Mafia to me. They are expecting quick results from us. We may be the best in the world at ancient DNA but we're not miracle workers."

"We have to convince them that we are working at maximum speed and that the Russian lab is in sync with what we are doing here. Where do we start?"

"Let's start with the bear. It may be the simplest to re-create. Where did this bone come from?"

"Southeastern Colorado. It was found buried deep in the side of a cliff, in an isolated room that in the past had been part of an underground series of connected caves. A recent earthquake caused part of the mountain to collapse. A local archeologist discovered a bone and there was a newspaper report about it. It was in an area where there were rumors of an extinct type of bear that once lived there. The archeologist contacted the NSF, who forwarded the report to Dr. Pasternak. Southeastern Colorado was one of the places on her radar, so she organized an advance team to check it out. The team became excited about the spot, so it became a legitimate excavation site of the NSF. They had been there about three weeks when it was determined that newly discovered bones were indeed those of a short-faced bear."

"What type environment had the bones been preserved in?"

"This area was once an active volcano site with all kinds of fault lines running through it. The mountains are part of the Sangre de Cristo Range and have the highest sand dunes in North America connecting to them. It appeared that the bear had been in the cavern when the mountain partially caved in during an eruption. The bear was covered with several feet of sand and rock and the opening to the cave was sealed, placing it in an airtight tomb. It remained there for several hundred years until the recent earthquake provided access to the area."

"So, the bear was buried alive and the burial chamber should have had pretty constant temperatures over the years."

"Yes; that is why Dr. Pasternak was so excited about the find. She thought it possible that the site would yield enough viable DNA to re-create the bear."

"Well, let's find out, shall we?"

They retrieved the bear bone from the storage facility. It took them fifteen minutes to don their personal protection suits. They pulled their masks over their faces and put on the second pair of sterile gloves, which they cleaned with DNA remover. Only then did they enter the lab. Everything in the room had been scrubbed down with bleach and treated overnight with UV light.

Yates laid the bone on the worktable. Even though the skeleton had remained in a constant-temperature state for its buried life, it still did not contain enough viable DNA to allow a simple cloning of the bear. She stared at the bone fragment. This finally was what she really wanted to do as a paleontologist; she almost entered a dream-like state as she considered the passage the skeleton had gone through over the years: As with almost all bone fossils, the most difficult obstacle to overcome was that the natural processes of dying and the effects of the environment damages the DNA. When an animal dies, cellular enzymes called nucleases start to break down the DNA. This process takes energy and as soon as the oxygen is depleted in the body, then it stops. The result is that the DNA strands are broken down into smaller and smaller segments. After this, then bacteria, fungi, and insects work on the skeleton, destroying much of the DNA but not all of it. Finally, the environment of the skeleton continues to chemically affect the DNA. If there is water present, then the bones are subject to hydrolysis and oxidation. Hydrolysis breaks apart the DNA while oxidation destroys it.

She came back to the present when she realized that Leonid was addressing her. "Dr. Yates. Dr. Yates. Are you okay?"

She shook her head to clear the cobwebs. "Yes, I was just overcome with the reality of the moment; it is the answer to my dream—what I have studied for all these years. And we are really going to do this." She couldn't hold back her laughter. Finally, she said, "Are we certain the cameras are on? We have to be sure to document everything we do."

"Yes, they are recording, both audio and video. Here, you do the honors." He handed her a small power saw. "We'll only have small DNA fragments. For my woolly de-extinction, I used bones recovered from the permafrost; almost fifty percent of the DNA recovered was that of a true mammoth. I expect only about three to ten percent of the DNA we find here to be endogenous. The rest will be from outside organisms."

She took it and shaved off a small bit of the bone. "But we can take those small fragments and, with the new technology and advances in sequencing, we can fill in the gaps and re-create the bear chromosomes. Once we have that, we can eventually create a sperm and artificially inseminate a close surviving relative of the short-faced bear."

"Yes, that is the plan. What we will get will not be a one hundred percent short-faced bear, but it will be close, so close that we can label it as such."

Yates placed the shaving in a mortar. Leonid stood by with two tubes. He said, "We'll make up two primer sets."

Yates replied, "Three would be better. That will allow us to do two and use one as a control set."

"You are right. Three would be better. I'll let you have the privilege. While you do that, I'll prepare the master mix."

Yates used a pestle to grind and crush the bone. She then divided the crushed bone into three equal sets and labeled each container. She waited until Leonid came back with the master mix and watched him place the appropriate amount in each tube. "There. That should do it," he said.

Yates then carefully placed into each tube the DNA extract. "Okay, they're ready for the thermocycler." They took the samples to the thermocycler outside the room.

"I am eager to see how this new machine works. I understand that it is a major upgrade from those I used just two years ago," said Leonid.

"I've just read about them; many of my colleagues refer to them as DNA amplifiers. Give me a quick tutorial," said Yates.

"This particular machine has room for six sample tubes; we'll only use three at a time. You know that the thermocycler raises and lowers the temperature. At the high point—about ninety to ninety-five degrees centigrade—the DNA strands will break and fall apart. As they cool, they will use the master mix we put into the tubes and re-create two new DNA ladders. By cycling through the temperature range from twenty to thirty times, we will make millions of copies of the original DNA."

"So, in a day's time, we can create enough DNA to move to the next step."

"Yes; that's right. When we are finished with the thermocycler, it will be critical to store the samples at four degrees centigrade; that's why we have a new refrigerator/freezer in here."

"When will we insert the sequence into the sperm of a living bear? Which bear did you decide to use to carry the egg?"

"There's only one surviving species from the lineage, the spectacled bear, Tremarctos; it is found in the Andes Mountains of South America. We have one in the attached holding room in each lab. We'll sequence the DNA and introduce it into the sperm. Then we'll artificially inseminate the egg."

"How close to the actual short-faced bear will our cub be?"

"It depends on our success in sequencing the DNA. If we do a good job, it will be pretty close."

"What about the size of the bear? What can we expect?"

"The ancient short-faced bear was estimated to weigh over a thousand kilograms."

"Wow. That's over twenty-two hundred pounds, almost five hundred pounds heavier than an average male polar bear."

"As soon as we are finished here, we'll go to Virginia and get that one started. I want to have the two bears in the U.S. a couple of weeks ahead before I inseminate the one in Russia."

While the DNA amplifier cycled the samples through the temperature range, Yates and Leonid finished the preparations for the next steps. As soon as the thermocycler finished, it provided an alarm to notify them that it was through. They removed the tubes and placed them in the freezer.

"Let's get some rest; we have a full day tomorrow," said Leonid.

"I'm so excited that I may not be able to sleep."

Chapter 54

We sat down with Cyndi and discussed our trip to Washington. "We really didn't find out anything new," I said. "Frazier mainly wanted a face-to-face meeting with us concerning our recent attempted ambush. What's the term? I forgot it."

Lander added, "Debriefing."

"Yeah, that's the word," I said.

Lander continued, "Director Frazier also mentioned that some recent Intel that he had indicates that the Chinese are also probably involved."

Cyndi said, "Great! We're going up against the Russians and the Chinese. And that's in addition to the American thugs out to get us."

I looked at Lander and said, "Just another day at the office . . . for you."

Lander replied, "Not so much anymore. Remember that we can call in additional troops from Frazier anytime we want to. If you all want to bow out of the picture, I completely understand. It is dangerous for you to be involved."

Cyndi looked at me and said, "It seems that we are already involved and our adversaries know who we are. It would be safer to work with you and assist all we can."

I nodded agreement. "In for a penny, in for a pound."

We discussed going to the other sites to see if we could uncover any additional clues. Lander and I decided to go to Alamosa, the closest town with motels to the site of the short-faced bear excavation site. Even though we would be gone a couple of days, Cyndi decided to stay in Durango and do further research. It was a good three-and-a-half-hour drive and we wanted to spend the afternoon at the dig site.

Leaving Cyndi at the hotel, we walked to our car. "Do you want me to drive so you can sleep?" I asked.

Lander just looked at me like I had insulted him and then said, "You're driving." What a surprise!

Don't tell Cyndi, but we stopped at Starbucks on the way out; I thought that drinking hot coffee would keep Lander awake, at least for a short time. I didn't want him to drink alone, so I got some, also. I turned east on Highway 160 and before we passed through Bayfield, Lander had finished his coffee, reclined his seat, and was out cold. He managed to stay asleep through Pagosa Springs and even until South Fork, where he awoke long enough to say, "You're doing a good job, Kent." Two minutes later, he was snoring again. Finally, when we saw the signs for Alamosa, he awoke and adjusted his chair.

"How do you do that, wake up at exactly the time we get to where we're going?"

"If I told you, I would . . ."

I interrupted him. "I know. So, you're well-rested now and ready for an exciting afternoon," I said.

It really wasn't a question, but he answered anyway. "Yep, I'm ready to go now. It's amazing what a little nap can do for me. It allows all the disconnected pieces of our puzzle to begin to align a little."

"What did you solve? And don't tell me you heard the bear growling—that was you snoring."

He answered me as he usually does, by misdirecting our conversation. "There should be some motels here in Alamosa. San Luis is closer to the dig site, but I'm not sure it has accommodations there."

After a few more minutes, we saw a sign for Comfort Inn & Suites. "What about this one?" I asked. "It looks pretty nice and most of the ones I have stayed in are clean and comfortable."

"It'll do. As long as it's comfortable enough that I can sleep, I'm fine."

I looked at him and laughed. "As though you need somewhere plush to be able to do that!"

He returned my grin and said, "Okay, as long as it is clean, I can sleep there."

"It's only one o'clock. Do you think they will let us check in now before we go on to the dig site?"

He said, "Probably. Looking around, I don't see many cars lined up to stay here tonight."

I pulled in front of the office and stopped. We went into the lobby and approached the front desk. "Can I help you?" said the young female clerk. She looked Mexican, but spoke flawless English.

Lander said, "We'd like a room for tonight, one with two queens or doubles, non-smoking."

She replied, "I have one with two queens on the ground floor if that is okay. And all our rooms are non-smoking," she added.

"Can we go ahead and check in? We want to go see the Sangre de Cristo Mountains and may not get back until late."

"Sure. No problem. Just fill out the paperwork here." She passed the paper to Lander and he handed it to me.

"What? Am I your secretary now?"

"Yeah. Just fill it out while I think," he said.

We put our overnight bags in the room and changed from our shorts and tee shirts into something more suitable for a hike in rugged mountain terrain. We pulled on jeans and long-sleeve shirts; hiking boots were next. Snakes were a real threat this time of year, so we carried snake-proof chaps and gloves with us. We checked our handguns and left the motel. Lander had directions to the excavation and had arranged for the local sheriff to meet us there.

Forty-five minutes later, we pulled into the site. A tall, dark man in a uniform watched as we got out of the Jeep and walked up to him. "Sheriff Anderson?" Lander asked.

"Yes; you must be the person I talked with on the phone. Lander. That right?"

"Yes. Bill Lander and this is Phil Kent. We appreciate your meeting us here."

"No problem. After your call, I got a call from Washington requesting that I help you any way I can. What do you need?"

"If you would, show us around the site and walk us through the attack."

The camp was set up somewhat like the others that we had already seen. There were two tents and signs that some excavation had taken place. However, this location was covered and surrounded by rocks and debris from the mountain. We had to pick our way over and around large rocks in order to get to the dig site.

"This is where the bones were discovered. You can see how the entire place was vandalized. Nothing was left intact . . . including the bones that had already been recovered. I would have thought it was just a group of kids drinking and out for a good time except for the murders. Even drunk kids usually don't go as far as killing someone."

Lander replied, "You're probably right. This is only one of four such attacks in the last few weeks. It seems as if someone is after ancient bones."

The sheriff asked, "Do you know what type bones were here? No one has ever said. I know Colorado has given up some dinosaur bones, but I'm not sure these were dinosaurs; they are usually found more west of here, I think."

Lander said, "We were told that all the sites were different types of bones, but we'll have to verify that statement before we release any information." That seemed to satisfy him for now, so we let it go at that.

I asked, "What about the victims? Who were they and how many were there?"

The sheriff answered, "The director of the site was killed, executed with a shot to the forehead. Two other workers were also murdered. One died from a wound to the back of the head and the other was shot in the back as he tried to run to safety."

"Did the shooters leave any clues?" Lander beat me to the question.

"We found a couple of boot prints, but they weren't distinct enough to get good imprints made. Other than those, we found nothing. Just a lot of bones and equipment destroyed."

"Did you find a computer or any notes from the workers here?"

"We did recover a computer, but it had been thrown against a rock."

"Where is it now?" I asked.

"It is at our office. We tried to turn it on, but it wouldn't even power up. We didn't think it would relate to the attackers at all, so we didn't pursue it."

Lander said, "We'll come by and pick it up later; you're probably right, but we'll have some technicians to take a look at it anyway. Where is your office?"

"It's on Main Street in San Luis. You can't miss it; there's not too much downtown." We continued to search the site, but found nothing new. After a few more minutes, the sheriff said, "Well, you've seen pretty much everything; not much left of it. Is there anything else I can help you with?"

Lander answered him. "No, you've been a great help. We'll just wander around and look a little more; then we'll drop by to pick up the computer."

We watched him drive away and then Lander led me back to the car, where we put on our chaps and grabbed our gloves. I was glad because if we were going to explore the area surrounding the site, I wanted protection from the snakes.

Lander led me back to the center of the site and gazed around. After a minute or so, he pointed up the slope and said, "Let's check it out."

We made our way up the side of the mountain. It was rough going and, in some areas, we had to pull ourselves up over rocks and downed trees. I was glad we had dressed for the terrain. "What are we looking for?" I asked.

"Anything that seems out of place. I suspect that the killers set up an observation point so they could attack the site when everyone was present. If you were watching them, where would you be?"

I paused and gazed around the slope. "I would hide behind those rocks over there," I said, pointing to my left.

Lander nodded and said, "Why would that be a good place?"

"It's out of their normal movement area. It has a good visual to the camp and is plenty big and thick enough that they could not be seen from the site."

I led the way over to the spot. There was nothing evident, but that didn't mean the killers had not been there. We searched the spot carefully. Finally, Lander dropped to his knees and ran his hand in the crack between two rocks. "Well, look here. We may have just gotten a break."

Chapter 55

The Chairman wants to know how you are progressing. Are you still sure you can beat the Russians and Americans?"

Ju-long glared at his visitor. "We have the best DNA facilities in the world. Our scientists are excellent. We will succeed!"

"But your scientists have never de-extincted any animal. The Russian has five woolly mammoths to his credit. Do you really think you can catch him? Maybe it is time to take additional safeguards."

"Do you mean eliminate the Russian?"

"Yes, and the American also. She is working with Leonid and we can now assume that she knows all that he knows about de-extincting the ancient giants."

"Does the Chairman agree with the killing?"

"Yes. In fact, it is his idea to accelerate the action. He does not want to take the chance that they succeed in beating us."

"Do we have a plan to dispatch them?"

"Yes. We will use the fact that the Russians kidnapped the American and are forcing her to help them."

"Can we get some of our people into America to take them out?"

"We don't have to; we have two agents already there. They are good and they have carried out similar missions for us in the past."

"How do we communicate with them?"

"You leave that to me. I need you to concentrate on reviving the animals. Which are you working on first?"

"The easiest and quickest one should be the bear. It has a surviving relative in the Andes Mountains of South America. I have arranged for one of them to be sent here by the end of the week."

"Why do you need a bear from South America to de-extinct an ancient bear?"

Ju-long sighed and looked at his visitor. "The sequencing of the ancient DNA is only the first step. I must have a host for the gestation period. The best chance for success is to place the embryo in an animal as nearly identical to the ancient one as we can find. And, for the short-faced bear, that is the spectacled bear, Tremarctos."

"How long will it take?"

"Only a week or so to prepare the DNA; then the implanted egg must go through the gestation period. For large bears, it could be eight months or longer. There is usually a correlation between the time of birth and the size of the species."

"Now you're confusing me. I don't know what correlation means."

"It means a relationship."

"A relationship? I don't understand."

"Just leave it at that. You worry about ending life and I will worry about beginning life."

"I will be glad to do that. I think I have the easier task. I will tell the Chairman that you are advancing but we need to put our contingency plan in place."

"Keep me informed on your progress."

Chapter 56

Yates and Leonid were eating their breakfast the next morning. "Why did you create five woollies?" asked Yates. "Wouldn't one have given you the display specimen you needed?"

Leonid replied, "Ancient woolly mammoths were social animals. It would have been cruel to have just one roaming the grasslands—it would never survive alone. With five, they can adjust to the grasslands within their group."

"Do you have both male and female or will you have to clone the living ones in order to expand the population?"

"We have two males and three females. It is our hope that they will repopulate the herd on their own."

"That's exciting—seeing an animal that hasn't lived on earth for the last ten thousand years."

"That's not technically correct. The last herds of woolly mammoth to roam Siberia vanished with the death of the grasslands ten thousand years ago; however, the last woolly died about four thousand years ago."

"Where was this? I didn't know about mammoths' being alive that recently."

"They survived on Wrangel Island off Siberia's northern coast and were genetically much less diverse than their earlier ancestors. This was undoubtedly the result of inbreeding and probably was the final cause of their extinction."

The sound of an alarm cut off their conversation.

Outside, the two men had moved through the forest, staying out of the sightline of the windows. "How many security men do you think are here?" asked Lu Sung. At only five feet seven inches tall, his broad body nonetheless gave the appearance of superior strength.

His accomplice, a wiry man almost six feet tall, answered. "I know that there are two outside; I would guess that there will also be at least one on the inside." As he spoke, he pointed at the large tree just outside the fence. "This is where we wait. One of the guards will walk this perimeter shortly."

The two men in camouflage settled down behind the tree to wait. After a few minutes, Qiang whispered, "Get ready. Here he comes."

Lu Sung shifted his body so he could access the pockets in his backpack. He chose two tranquilizer darts and retrieved his lightweight gas-based projector. He was an expert in the use of the quiet darts to either immobilize or kill his targets. He loaded one of the darts and checked the power setting. It would be a close-range shot as the guard would walk the fence line and be within ten feet of Lu Sung when he fired the dart. The men watched as the guard walked by. Just as he passed him, Lu Sung fired the dart. The guard slapped the back of his neck, thinking a bee had just stung him. As his fingers closed around the dart, he fell to the ground. His last conscious thought was to sound the alarm to stop the two men rushing toward him. He never was able to push the button on his radio.

Qiang grabbed the guard's radio and said, "Quick! Let's get him out of sight. We have ten minutes before the other guard comes this way."

Lu Sung held the fence open while Qiang pulled the guard through the hole they had created. They left him lying behind the big tree and settled down to wait for the other guard to make his pass. After eight minutes and another well-placed dart, they pulled the remaining guard outside the fence and left him with the other one. Qiang said, "Let's go. That should be all the security outside. There will be one more inside."

"Piece of cake," said Lu Sung. "Let's go finish this job."

Qiang paused and looked at the two fallen guards. "No, wait. Let's put on their uniforms. They look like they should fit us pretty close. Hurry and get changed."

In three minutes, they slipped through the fence. Qiang said, "Remember, meet me at the front door in five minutes." They separated and went opposite directions along the fencerow.

They paused at the front door. Qiang pulled his handgun and opened the door. He looked left and said, "Clear."

Lu Sung followed, checking the right. "Clear," he said. Both men moved forward toward the inner office.

The receptionist saw them approaching and spotted the guns they were holding. She reached under her desk and pushed the button. The alarm was sent simultaneously to the lab and to Lander.

Yates heard the alarm and said, "Something's wrong."

Leonid said, "What do you think it is? We have security men on duty."

Yates moved to the door and assured herself that it was locked. "I have no idea what the problem is. We'll just wait here until we get clearance." She was glad that she had elected to keep her handgun with her. She pulled it from the holster at her back and chambered a round. Leonid watched her with fear evident in his eyes.

The receptionist started to leave out the back door. Qiang said, "On, no, you don't. You're not going anywhere!" He brandished the gun and said, "Where is the inside security man?"

"Right here! Put your weapon down!" He stepped toward Qiang, not noticing Lu Sung. The shot echoed in the room as the guard's head exploded in a mist of red and gray.

The receptionist screamed and then fainted. Qiang told Lu Sung, "Here. Pull her out of sight behind her desk and tie her up. Gag her, too. You brought the zip ties, didn't you?"

"Yes, of course."

While Lu Sung secured her, Qiang went to her desk and looked for keys. He found them in the second drawer. Next, he looked for a diagram of the building. Finally, he lifted the desk calendar and he saw it taped to the desk. The lab was outlined in yellow and was marked with a number four. He looked at the set of keys and found the key labeled with the number. "Let's go, Lu Sung. I have it."

The two men paused at the door. "Remember, both must die. You shoot the woman and I'll take care of the man." Bypassing the biometric safeguards, Qiang slipped the key into the lock and turned it slowly and quietly. He nodded once to Lu Sung and pushed the door open. Both men sprang through the opening, raised their guns, and two shots rang out.

Chapter 57

The next day, Lander met us for breakfast. He had left in a hurry yesterday afternoon and returned late last night. I tried then to get him to tell me what had happened, but he told me it would wait for this morning. We sat at a booth in the back corner, away from everyone else. After we had ordered and received our coffee, I looked at him and said, "Okay. Out with it. What happened yesterday?"

He looked at Cyndi and then me. "The lab was attacked. My security men were killed and the attackers were able to get into the lab."

Cyndi gasped. "What about Dr. Yates and Leonid? Did they kill them?"

I added, "Were you able to get there in time?"

"When I got there, I went directly to the lab. There were two bodies on the floor, both dead."

Cyndi said, "Oh, my God! Both scientists dead?"

Lander dropped his head; then I saw just a trace of a smile. "No, the scientists were fine. Both attackers were dead. In fact, Dr. Yates almost shot me, too, when I rushed into the room. She was still holding her weapon ready. Remind me never to take on a female scientist that's packing."

I asked, "What happened? How did they get past the guards?"

"We found the outside security men; they were both dead. It seems as if the attackers waited outside the fence. When the guards made their way around the fencerow, they were shot with poisoned darts and dragged behind a large tree. The attackers changed clothes with them and walked right into the building. The receptionist saw them on the monitors approaching the building but, because they were dressed in the security uniforms, she didn't recognize the situation. When they started toward her office, she noticed that the uniforms didn't fit the way they should have and she saw them carrying weapons. That's when she pushed the alarm button. That probably saved the lives of Yates and Leonid. Yates said that when she heard the alarm, she immediately checked her handgun and had it ready for use. I got the same alarm and immediately hurried to the lab; however, I was too far away to be of any help to them in this situation."

Cyndi said, "What a tragedy! How are the scientists holding up?"

Lander laughed. "Dr. Leonid was shaken up pretty badly; however, he will be ready to go again in a couple of days. Dr. Yates took it in stride—she said she's ready to continue now. She's one tough lady."

"Were the men Russians?" I asked.

"No, they appeared to be Chinese."

"Chinese! So, they *are* in the picture. Director Frazier said he had intelligence that they were also suspected of trying to get involved."

"Yes. With both groups attempting to kill our scientists, I underestimated them. I will have a much more robust security team set up tomorrow." It was evident that Lander was holding himself responsible for the near-tragedy. "They'll not get close to them again."

I could tell he was committed to that. "We had planned to visit the last site tomorrow. Do we need to postpone that trip?"

"No, not unless something else happens. I'll get the security set up today and be ready to go tomorrow. We need to get a handle on the big picture here. I'm hoping something new pops up at the giant site." He looked at Cyndi and said, "We've not had a chance to talk much the last couple of days. Have you discovered any new information? What can you tell us about giants? I know you were researching them while we visited the bear site the other day. By the way, I'm sure Phil told you: we found nothing there to help us."

She replied, "Let's go up to our room and continue this. I'll go on up while you all make a run for coffee."

I said, "You just had coffee with breakfast."

"You're right, but it's not the same."

As Lander and I went to get the drinks, I said, "I should buy stock in Starbucks."

When we got back to the room, Cyndi had a stack of papers divided into three sections. "You asked about giants. No pun intended, but that was a big assignment. It seems as if world history is replete with stories of giants. Evidently, they were much more prevalent than we have been led to believe."

"So, you believe some of the legends; they're not all just old folk tales like Paul Bunyan?" Lander smiled as he said this.

"There are too many accounts with too much similarity for them to be all made up."

I jumped into the conversation. "Is there any substantial evidence to prove the existence of them?" I then quickly added, "I mean, other than the bones that were stolen in our case?"

Cyndi answered, "William Turner, naturalist and Dean of Wells, is reputed to have seen a tribe of very gigantic naked savages on the coast of Brazil; one was estimated to be twelve feet tall."

"Did he get pictures or any concrete evidence?" I asked.

"No, he didn't. This sighting was alleged to have occurred in the mid 1500s. He had no camera or smart phone with him."

"What else do you have?" Lander asked.

"Captain George Shelvock is supposed to have seen Indians who were nine to ten feet tall on the

Island of Chiloe off the coast of Chile. There were reports of other giant sightings over the years. Even Magellan's crew is said to have seen a giant, supposedly so tall that the tallest of the crew came only midway between his waist and shoulders."

"What about North America? Do we have a history of giants more recent than those of South America?"

Cyndi looked at me and replied. "I'm glad you asked. There have been many reports of giants in North America."

Moving to the obvious question, I asked, "Then why haven't we heard more about them? It seems as if giants would be front-page news."

"There are many who believe that the reports and even recovered bones have been intentionally covered up."

"What do you mean? Why would they be suppressed?" I shook my head.

Lander had remained mostly quiet during the discussion of the giants, but spoke up. "Actually, for a number of reasons. Conclusive proof of giants would be unsettling to many people. For many others, it may trigger diggings all over an area where giants were reported."

I added, "Do you have any idea of the modifications that would have to be made about our history, not only in North America, but in all the world, if we had proof of civilizations of giants?"

Lander nodded and continued, "In addition, many religious beliefs would be questioned."

Cyndi shook her head. "No, I disagree with you. The Bible itself speaks of giants."

I said, "Yeah, Goliath was a giant. But that was just an exaggeration, wasn't it? He looked big compared to the boy David."

"No, I don't believe so. David wasn't a little boy and Goliath was reportedly over nine feet tall. Goliath was from a Philistine camp in Gath; his brother and son were also men of great stature. There are many other accounts of giants in the Bible, especially before the great flood which killed all living mankind except Noah and his family. And then there were the Nephilim."

Lander was engaged now and asked, "Who were the Nephilim? Were they described in the Bible?"

Cyndi nodded. "Yes, they were. Some think that they were the fallen angels."

I asked, "Why were they called the fallen angels?"

"It seems as if they disobeyed God when He told them to watch over the people of the earth but not to interfere in their affairs. They visited the earth and saw beautiful women and fathered children with them. Because these angels were more than normal size, their children became some of the giants of the earth, only to be destroyed in The Flood."

"Okay, I believe you about the giants in the Bible. You were going to tell us about some examples in North America."

Cyndi handed me a stack of papers and passed one to Lander. "Here. Look over these. I don't want to do all the talking." We looked over the printouts while we sipped our coffees. After several minutes, Cyndi said, "I'll start."

"Much of the oral history of Native Americans includes stories of giants. Some of the North American Indians believed that the first race of humans were giants. It is said that the autobiography of William 'Buffalo Bill' Cody includes a description of a giant thigh bone of a human being that was found. When he asked an Indian where such a bone might have come from, he was told that long ago a race of giants had lived in the area. Those early giants were reportedly three times larger than normal men, could outrun a buffalo, and even carry one in one hand. According to the legend, this race of giant men denied the existence of a Great Spirit and subsequently was destroyed in a great flood."

"Interesting," I said. "But you said that there were some reports that had been suppressed. If there have been a lot of reports, shouldn't there be evidence available from some of them?"

"According to reports, as Americans migrated westward, there were many instances of large skeletons found. Supposedly, many of them were reported in local newspapers."

"Are we able to access any of those articles?" Lander asked the question before I could.

"Unfortunately, most of them were in smaller towns and do not have all their archives available electronically."

"It would be interesting to see those original stories. But go on."

"According to at least one report, the Smithsonian sent a team of archaeologists to West Virginia to analyze a South Charleston Mound; giant skeletons were found with one of them seven feet, six inches tall. In Wheeling, a report says that a group of giant skeletons were found, ranging in height from six feet, seven inches to seven feet, six inches. On Cheat River in 1774, a group of settlers found numerous skeletons, one of which was an eight-foot male."

I looked at my papers. "Here is an example from New York. In 1871, a newspaper reported that in Cayuga, some two hundred skeletons were found. Only a few were less than seven feet; some were up to nine feet tall. In Ohio, there were skeletons found from eight to ten feet. In Newark, there is a claim that an eight-foot queen was found." I looked at my next sheet. "In Indiana, skeletons from six feet, nine inches to nine feet were found; some of them had double rows of teeth. Skeletons up to seven and three quarters feet were discovered in Popular Bluff, Iowa." I looked at Lander. "What do you have?"

"In our home state of Tennessee, a deceased eight-foot giant was found a few miles from Sparta. Louisiana had its share, also. Near Winnsboro, supposedly a race of giants was found, some up to seven and a half feet. Texas reportedly gave up a skull twice the size of a normal skull." He shuffled his papers. "Here's some interesting information. Around the California and Nevada border, there's an area called Death Valley Temple of Giants. It's a complex of thirty-two caves and it is said that eight- to nine-foot skeletons were found there. Then, on Catalina Island, a crew was supposed to have exhumed over thirty-seven hundred skeletons of blond-haired giants; the average height was seven feet tall with some up to over nine feet tall."

Cyndi said, "Lovelock Cave is in Nevada. In that area of the state, stories have been handed down by Native Americans that tell of red-haired giants, some as tall as twelve feet." She looked at her last sheet. "Wisconsin is also represented. Near Lake Delavan, skeletons may have been found, ranging from seven and a half feet to ten feet; some have double rows of teeth . . . a new wrinkle here: these skeletons were supposed to have six fingers and toes. Near Madison, a grave yielded a skeleton over nine feet. Giants were also found near Potosi and West Bend."

I held up my hand. "Okay, I believe you. Surely, all these are not hyperbole—especially if there are actual newspaper accounts of many of them."

I looked at Lander and smiled. He said, "I know, I need to find some of those articles. It would liven my classes."

Cyndi laughed and I just nodded.

Lander said, "Enough conversation. I have to go get my security set up for the lab. I'll see you two later."

Chapter 58

It was a five-and-a-half-hour drive to the Grand Canyon from Durango, so Lander and I decided to fly. We made the early morning flight and had just settled in. "Did you get the new security people in place?" I asked.

"Yes, I met with the new guards late yesterday. They should be able to protect the doctors from any attack."

"Are Yates and Leonid both ready to resume their work?"

"Yes, Dr. Yates is a calming influence on Leonid. They actually have finished the bear DNA sequencing and only need now to implant the DNA into a viable sperm cell and inseminate an egg cell in a live bear. Then we wait for the pregnancy to come to term."

"Wow. That was fast. For some reason, I expected an extended period of time to do this."

"With the modern technology, if there is some viable DNA, the sequencing can be done in a day or two. As soon as they artificially inseminate the bear, they will begin on the next project."

"Which will they do next? Have they told you?"

"No, I don't know. If I were to guess, it would be the dinosaur. That is really Dr. Yates's primary passion."

"It's exciting to be involved in such a scientific endeavor, isn't it? Not many people in the country—or even the world—can say they are associated with trying to revive extinct animals."

"I agree. But we've got to remember that our objective is to protect the scientists. We can't get too engaged with the allure of the development."

"Who do you think is the greatest threat, the Russians or the Chinese?"

"They both are extremely dangerous. Both are utterly ruthless and have no regard for human life. Don't misunderstand me. There are good Russians and good Chinese, but the subgroups we are dealing with are the lowest of the low."

"What do you think will be their next move?"

"The Russians will in all likelihood let the project play out. They think that Yates is helping them and, as long as they think that, they will be hands-off. The Chinese, on the other hand, already tried to eliminate them once. They will come back with a stronger force because they know that they have no scientists that can beat Yates and Leonid. They will try again as soon as they can assemble their assets."

"So, our main concern is with the Chinese."

"Well . . . not exactly. As far as the threat to Yates and Leonid, that's right."

"But you're saying the Russians will come after us."

"Yes; as far as they are concerned, we are a threat to them. They believe that we are still looking to rescue Yates. They may not even realize the Chinese are in the picture yet."

We landed in Flagstaff and rented a car for the drive to the Grand Canyon. We drove north on Highway 180 for about two hours; I drove while Lander . . . well, you know. As we pulled into the Visitor Center, Lander awoke and said, "We are meeting the local ranger here; he will take us to the site." He looked at his watch and said, "He should be here in about ten minutes. Good job, Kent."

We exited the car and walked around, stretching stiff muscles. Shortly, a ranger's green car pulled into the space beside our car. The man got out of his car and looked at us. Lander nodded to him and we walked to meet him. After introductions—his name was Bob Driver—he pointed at his car and said, "Hop in. I'll drive."

As Driver maneuvered his Ford Explorer out of the lot and turned north, Lander asked, "What can you tell us about the recent attack?"

Driver stared at Lander for a few seconds before responding. "You must have some pull; my boss said to tell you everything and give you anything you need. I'm not sure what is going on here."

Lander said, "I appreciate any help you can give us. As you may or may not know, we have had a series of attacks on excavation sites, all with basically the same M.O. Artifacts and skeletons were destroyed and workers were executed. The only thing taken from each site was part of a femur bone."

"That is essentially what happened here, also. However, the attack occurred while everyone was gone, so we had no fatalities. But we had several priceless artifacts destroyed."

"Where is the site?" I asked.

"It is a good hike down the North Kiabab Rim. There is an old path that the Hopi Indians used at one time. The find was deep in a cave that was just rediscovered a few months ago. It may even connect to the underground complex that has already been excavated. I'm sure you've heard about that one."

Lander looked at me and answered him. "We know about the one that was supposedly found in the late 1800s, the petrified body of an almost twenty-foot giant."

"That's not it," Driver said. "The one I'm talking about had all kinds of ancient Egyptian artifacts and hieroglyphics there."

I thought, *Is this one that slipped by Cyndi?* I said, "You said ancient Egyptian. How old is ancient?"

"It was estimated to be at least three thousand years ago. And this last discovery had similar items and even some of the hieroglyphics."

Driver parked his car and said, "I'm glad you have on your hiking boots. It's not an easy trek down there. Keep a watch for loose rock and also be on the lookout for snakes." He handed us each a spotlight and said, "Clip these to your belts; you'll need them."

We picked our way down the ancient path that snaked down the steep slope of the canyon; I felt like I was on Lombard Street. Well, not really; San Francisco may be more dangerous.

After a descent of thirty minutes, Driver paused and pushed aside some limbs, revealing the entrance to a cave. We followed him into the opening and turned on our flashlights. We were standing in a room about five feet wide. "It's a way back to the site, so pay attention; there are some side passages, but if you follow the chalked line, you won't get lost. We had some people working in here that were not used to working in caves, so we put down a line for them."

We followed Driver for about ten minutes. The path gradually sloped downward and narrowed to about two feet before opening into a large round chamber. "This is the spot," he said, shining his light around the walls of the room; it was, I guessed, about thirty feet in diameter, with walls that climbed about twelve feet to the roof. I could see fragments of artifacts that had been smashed into tiny pieces.

Lander asked, "Did you find any clues to the perpetrators?"

"No, nothing was found."

"Still, I want to look around if that's okay with you," Lander said.

"Help yourself. I hope you can find something. I want these men caught."

I started to ask Lander what we were looking for, but I knew what he would say, "Anything that's not natural, that looks out of place, anything suspicious."

We spent forty-five minutes searching the cave for clues, but found nothing, not even a boot print. Finally, Lander said, "We're wasting our time here; there's nothing. Let's go back to the entrance."

When we exited the cave, Lander paused. He looked all around the path and locked his eyes on a spot just below the entrance to the cave. He said, "If you look carefully right there, what do you see?" I knew he was asking me the question. Training quiz number thirty or something.

I stared at the spot. " The rocks there are a little different, almost as if someone slipped on them."

"Not 'almost as if someone slipped on them'; someone did slip on them." He pulled a length of para cord from his pocket and handed one end to me. "Here, hold on to this." He wrapped the other end around his waist and began the descent.

When he reached the spot, he pushed aside some brush. "Aha! We may have a break here." He disappeared behind the brush for a moment before reappearing. He held up a phone and said, "If we're lucky, this may give us some information." He removed a zip lock bag from his pocket and placed the phone in it.

It took us almost an hour to get back to the car. Driver asked Lander, "Do you need anything else?"

"No, just take us back to our car. I'll have the phone checked for prints and for a call log."

"Will you let me know what you find out?" asked Driver. "Here's my card with my contact information on it."

Lander took the card and handed him one of his. "Of course; I'll let you know what I can. If you discover anything else or think of something, give me a call."

We retrieved our car and made our way back to the airport. By early evening, we were back at the hotel having dinner with Cyndi. "Any luck today?" she asked.

Lander and I took turns telling her about our day. Although we told her about the ancient Egyptian discoveries, I didn't rib her about missing it in her research. I thought about it, but decided it wasn't the right thing to do, so I bit my lip. She was excited about the phone find and asked Lander, "What are you going to do with the phone?"

"I'm overnighting it to Director Frazier. He will have his men go over it with a fine-tooth comb. If there is anything there, he will find it."

I said, "That sounds like a plan to me. What's our next step?"

Lander looked at Cyndi and said, "I don't want you to go anywhere without Kent or me with you?"

She smiled. "What about the bathroom? Can I go there by myself?"

"Yes, as long as it's the one in your room."

"So, you think we're still in danger?"

Lander explained the conversation we had about the threats.

Cyndi replied, "Bring them on. I have my men here to protect me."

Chapter 59

The next four days went by with no further problems. Yates and Leonid had gotten back to work and had successfully implanted the DNA into a bear sperm cell and used it to artificially inseminate an egg in a bear.

Leonid said, "We will now wait to see if the procedure was successful. Let's move on to the tiger. I would like to have both embryos in place before I go back to Russia. If we do that, I will complete the bear sequencing there and then come back. They will be convinced that we are on equal tracks in all the labs."

In two days, they had completed the procedures with the saber-toothed tiger. Leonid said, "It is time to move on to the other labs and get them started."

Yates asked, "When will you go to Russia?"

"I have a flight booked for tomorrow morning."

"Then I will get a flight to Virginia tomorrow. How long will you be gone?"

"Probably three days. I want to get the bear project completed. If I don't, then The Man will become suspicious of my intentions."

"I'll do the same with the lab in Virginia. That will give us three embryos for the bear. I'll wait for you to return to begin the tiger in Virginia. This is exciting. I need to call Lander to provide him our plans."

Yates used the secure phone and dialed Lander. He answered after two rings. "We have completed the first procedure here and need to go to the other labs to get them going."

"When do you want to go?"

"Dr. Leonid already has a flight tomorrow morning for him. He will be on the eight-fifteen flight."

"Okay, I will arrange a flight to Virginia for you and get back with you. We'll need to provide escorts for both of you to the airport." He paused and then added, "In fact, we may go to Virginia with you."

"You think someone may be waiting for me there?"

"Probably not. But we could leave you working in the lab there and go meet with Director Frazier. I could call him, but I prefer to meet face to face when possible. I want you to still wear your disguise when traveling."

"Okay; I'll get things ready to go here and be ready to go whenever you say."

Lander ended the call and turned to us. "Are you all up for a trip?"

"Of course." I looked at Cyndi to be sure I had answered correctly. She nodded, as I was sure she would. "When are we going?"

"I'll have to make reservations for us. We'll check out in the morning and make hotel reservations back here in a couple of days. We'll just keep the car rental and park it at the airport." Lander dialed the airport and booked flights for them.

He then called Director Frazier and placed him on speakerphone. "Mr. Director, Lander here. I am with the Kents and have you on speakerphone. How are you?"

Frazier replied, "I'm good. How are you all doing? Has anything else happened?"

"No, nothing yet. We are accompanying Dr. Yates to her lab in Virginia tomorrow. I was wondering if we might come in to meet with you a few minutes."

"I have a meeting tomorrow afternoon; how about the next morning?"

"That will work; we'll be on the plane most of the day tomorrow, anyway. What time?"

"Let's meet at eleven o'clock. Let me know where you all are staying and I'll send someone to pick you up."

"Will do. We're flying into Richmond; it's the closest airport to the lab. We'll see you in a couple of days."

"Sounds like a plan. Good timing. We have some information that may help you." He ended the conversation.

Cyndi said, "Where do you want to stay? I have some possibilities here." She had been busy on her iPad while we talked with Frazier and she pointed at it.

Lander looked at the list and said, "What about this Holiday Inn Express? It's close to the interstate and will be easy getting in and out of."

"I'll go ahead and make us reservations, then. How many nights? And do I need to make reservations for Dr. Yates?"

"Make them for three nights. Dr. Yates is planning to work there for a couple of days. It'll be too late tomorrow when we get there for her to get started. Make her a reservation for the first night; after that, she will stay at the lab until we leave."

We watched as Cyndi clicked a couple of keys and then she said, "Done!"

The next morning, we picked Dr. Yates up at six o'clock. She had done a good job on her disguise and it would be hard for anyone to recognize her. We arrived at the airport for our eight-fifteen flight. I let them all out at the door and went to park the car. In fifteen minutes, I rejoined them at the gate for our carrier. The flight was about nine and a half hours with layovers in Denver and Newark. We landed and, because we only had carry-on bags, went directly to the car rental booths and arranged for a car. We stopped at a Red Lobster and ate dinner. By seven-thirty, we had checked into our motel. Lander called Director Frazier and told him where we were. Frazier told us he would have someone to pick us up at eight o'clock the next morning. We were all tired, so we said our "Good nights" and went to our rooms, promising to meet in the on-site restaurant for a six-thirty breakfast.

Lander already had us a table when we entered the restaurant the next morning. We had just sat down when Yates joined us. We ordered and as the waitress moved away, Lander said to Yates, "I have a couple of my security people coming to take you to the lab. They'll be here at seven-fifty, so I will be able to be sure that they are legit before we leave."

By seven-thirty, we had eaten and left the restaurant. We told Lander that we would meet him in the lobby and went back to our room. A few minutes before eight, we stood in the lobby looking for him. After a couple of minutes, he walked through the front door and made his way over to us. "Dr. Yates got off safely. Our ride should be here in a couple of minutes. Let's wait for it outside."

The black limousine slowed and pulled to the side of the drive directly in front of us. The passenger door opened, a man stepped out, and said, "Mr. Lander?"

Lander replied, "Yes."

The man opened the rear door and nodded to us. "Please get in." Lander moved to the car and looked in.

He raised his eyebrows in surprise. "Mr. Director. I didn't expect to see you here." He listened to the reply and then motioned to us. "Let's all get in."

Cyndi and I slid into the back seat and Lander sat beside the Director. The car moved away from the curb and Director Frazier pushed the button that closed the privacy window to the front seat. He pushed another button and a top slid open to his side. He reached into the opening and lifted out a cup. He handed it to Cyndi and said, "I think you like the hazelnut."

Cyndi took the cup of Starbucks and said "Thank you. How did you know I liked this one?" We all just looked at her until she realized that she was talking to the director of the CIA.

He retrieved another and handed me the half-caff vanilla. He then gave Lander a cup of strong coffee and took one for himself. He then said, "Now that we have the important things taken care of, bring me up to date on your investigation. We've not talked since you sent me the phone."

Lander outlined the events of the last few days, focusing much of the conversation on the Chinese who had attacked the lab. Frazier was especially intrigued by the report that it had been Yates who had single-handedly stopped the assailants.

"You have upgraded your security, I expect?" Frazier stated it as a question.

"Of course. It would take an elite team to get to the scientists now."

Frazier placed his index finger on his lips, considering his response. "Don't rule that possibility out," he finally said. "I'll arrange for extra agents to secure the outer perimeters of the labs. Let your teams focus on the interior and the grounds inside the fences. They will be in place this afternoon."

Lander said, "Thank you, sir. All help appreciated. We don't need any more close calls. Now, do you have any new information for us?"

"Yes. Some good news here! The phone you found may be what we need to stop this operation. It belonged to a man known to operate outside the legal boundaries. We have an extensive search for him now."

Lander replied, "I suspect that if you find him, he'll be unable to talk."

I said, "You mean he was a loose end that has been taken care of, don't you?"

"Yes. Once he delivered the goods, he was expendable." He looked at the Director. "Were there any contacts on the phone or were you able to trace any recent calls?"

Frazier smiled. "Yes. There was only one number that had contact with the phone. It was to an unregistered phone—a throwaway."

"Then how will that help us?" asked Lander.

"We identified the location of the calls. They just happened to be in an area that had some security cameras located. I had my men to analyze those recordings and based on the timestamp of the calls, we have identified the man."

"Do you have him in custody then?" I asked.

"No, we don't. We have him under surveillance and have tapped the electronics he has on him. We want him to lead us to his boss."

Lander said. "That's great. Who is he? Does he have contacts in the NSF or the United Nations?"

"The man goes by the name of Romonov. He is on our watch list, suspected of supplying corporate secrets to rogue countries."

"Do we know with whom he is working?" Cyndi entered the conversation.

"We are gathering Intel on his contacts now. As far as we can determine, he has had no communication with anyone at the NSF."

"But he has had contact with someone from the U.N.?" Lander had picked up the clue in the unspoken statement also.

Frazier considered his response. "Yes, we have a possible link there. We are verifying it now." As he spoke those words, the limousine pulled to the curb in front of our hotel.

I asked, "Would Romonov work with both the Russians and the Chinese?"

"Yes, he would . . . and he has. He will work with anyone who can meet his financial demands."

"Thank you, Mr. Director," said Lander as the door was opened for us to get out. "If anything happens, I'll let you know. One more question. Where is Romonov now?"

"He followed you yesterday. He is in Richmond now. He is extremely dangerous, so keep your guard up."

Chapter 60

After what seemed like a week of traveling by plane, Leonid walked out of the airport. His ride to Pleistocene Park was waiting for him at the front entrance. "This way, Dr. Leonid," said Ivanov.

As they wound their way to the Park, Ivanov spoke for the first time since they had entered the car. "I trust you are ready to proceed with the project this time."

"Is everything ready to go?"

"Yes; all supplies and equipment have been delivered and set up to your specifications."

"Then we will begin the procedure first thing in the morning."

"Good. That is the correct answer, Doctor."

Leonid swallowed nervously and thought, *What have I gotten into?*

After a night of fitful sleep, Leonid entered the lab to find his assistants already there. "Good morning," he said. "Are you ready to get started?" He looked at each of them and paused when he got to Petrov. "Who are you?"

"I am Dr. Mita Petrov. I am to work closely with you throughout the project." He bowed slightly and continued, "I am happy to work with such a distinguished scientist."

"Who brought you into the project?"

His answer did not surprise Leonid. "The Man convinced me to join your team. I look forward to the work."

"What is your background?"

"I work at the cellular level. I have experience in modifying cells to produce planned mutated generations of animals."

Leonid said, "Good. That is exactly what we are doing here. Welcome to the team." He repeated his earlier question to the group. "Are you ready to get started?"

"Yes, Dr. Leonid. We are anxious to begin."

Leonid walked around the lab, assuring himself that all was ready. Coming back to his assistants, he said, "It is all ready and in good shape."

He spent the next fifteen minutes outlining the procedures to his assistants. "Does anyone have any questions?"

"Do we have to be that careful with all the protective clothing? You're making it sound like we are working in a nuclear facility."

"Yes; you must treat the project as if you were working in such a facility. It is not for your protection; it is for the protection of the bones and the DNA. I will tolerate nothing less than complete adherence to sterile conditions. Do you understand?"

They each looked at each other before his primary assistant spoke. "Yes, Dr. Leonid. We understand and will be diligent in following your directions."

"Good. You know where the bones are stored. Someone, retrieve the one marked as 'bear'."

One of the younger assistants stood and said, "I will get it."

Leonid said, "Thank you. Please keep it secured in its container until you bring it to me." He handed the helper a key. "And be sure to lock the freezer back up when you get the container."

When the box was delivered to him, Leonid said, "Okay. Now all of you should put on your protective gear. Be sure to follow the checklist absolutely. Mark off each step as you complete it." After everyone was dressed and ready, Leonid opened the lab door and they all entered. He sat the container on a workbench, unlocked it, and removed the bone. "First, we'll . . ."

In another room, The Man sat watching and listening to the scientist. Ivanov pointed to the monitor and said, "This is a good idea. We are able not only to watch them and listen to their conversation, but we can also record the proceedings. If he tries to deny anything, we will have it on the disc." He looked again at the computer, assuring himself that it was indeed recording. He smiled when he saw the red light indicating a recording was in process.

The Man darted a look at Ivanov. "You seem not to trust Dr. Leonid."

Ivanov replied, "I don't trust him. He's a scientist; he doesn't want to be involved in the politics of our country." He watched the video for a moment and then said, "What is he doing with that saw? Is he going to destroy the bone?" Ivanov stood in preparation for storming the lab to stop the scientist.

The Man laughed. "No; he is not going to destroy it. He must take a small piece of it to extract the DNA from it."

They watched as the doctor directed his team to take the sample and crush it.

Petrov was still a mystery to Ivanov; he wondered why The Man had brought him into the project. After they observed the scientists working for a while, Ivanov decided to risk it. "What is the role of Petrov?"

The Man chuckled. "What do you think he is doing here?"

"I think that he is more than an assistant—and that you have another motive for his being here." Ivanov quickly followed that with the thought, *Did I go too far with that statement? Have I crossed the line with The Man?* He held his breath while he waited for The Man's response.

"You are right. His job is to make one more modification to the embryo than what Dr. Leonid directs."

"How will he be able to do that if Leonid is with him all the time? I am assuming that it must be done without the knowledge of Leonid."

"You know that Leonid will be here only for a couple of days at a time. Petrov assures me that he can accomplish his objective after Leonid goes back to the U.S. You must allow him access to whatever he needs after Leonid leaves."

Ivanov watched The Man's face morph into an evil mask. "And don't question Petrov or me again about his role. Your position is one that does not afford you that information." He laughed heartily. "You might just live longer if you don't know everything."

Ivanov just nodded, indicating that he had understood the implied threat.

Chapter 61

Ju-long stood in front of his assistants. He had been thinking about which animal would be the first to have its DNA sequenced in preparation for the de-extinction project. Over the last few days, he had gradually modified his original plan. Yesterday he had met with the Chairman and presented his new strategy. The Chairman had listened politely, giving no indication of whether or not he agreed with the change in plans. When Ju-long finished his presentation, the Chairman dropped his head, considering the implications. Finally, he looked up and smiled.

"Proceed."

It was only a one-word response, but the one that Ju-long hoped for.

The original plan was to work with the saber-toothed tiger first and then move quickly to the dinosaur. The de-extinction of those two great animals would have brought much needed respect to China's scientific community. The country's technology program was second to none, but the biological and other real natural sciences were lagging far behind the world leaders. Short term, the revelation of success would have been good for the country.

However, Ju-long was looking long-term and the modified plan he had presented to the Chairman would be in the best interests of China's continued assent. He felt it only fitting that the revival of a long-absent species would resurface in China.

After all, many knowledgeable people in the world think that the early giants originated in China. And, unlike the animals, with the plan he had devised, giants would be able to actively participate in the scheme to elevate China to that of a true world power. Also, he couldn't ignore the fact that along with the success of the plan, his own status would skyrocket.

All eyes in the room were on him, waiting patiently. Finally, Ju-long spoke. "We are going to revive our great ancestors. The fact that there were giants that once roamed the earth is well documented. It is also known that the original great men came from China. We will bring them back to their rightful place in our country. Let us begin."

All stood and reverently bowed, expressing their respect for Ju-long and his plan.

Ju-long lowered his head, basking in the glory of their admiration. He thought to himself, "If they only knew the complete plan! It was true that he wanted to re-introduce a race of giants to China, but he intended to create a superior fighting force, an elite group of true warrior giants—and he would be in charge of their activities."

Chapter 62

Ambassador Serhat ducked into the open doorway of the bookstore. He picked up a book and seemed to be looking through it although his eyes were staring out the window at the sidewalk. He ceased his search when he found the tall man in the tan fedora. Although he now wore a hat, the Ambassador was almost sure he had spied him earlier. His first thought was, "Was the tall man following him?"

He jumped when he heard the deep voice. "May I help you find something, sir?"

Serhat relaxed when he realized the question came from the clerk. "No, not yet. I'm just browsing right now. I'm not sure what I want."

"Take your time. If I can help you find something, let me know."

Serhat looked back out the window. The man was gone. "Now what do I do?" he wondered. "Should I wait here or should I go back out and confirm that he is following me?" His thoughts were screaming through his mind. Finally, he swallowed roughly and decided. "After all, this is

New York City. He will do nothing in broad daylight." His mind made up, he eased out the open doorway and quickly turned left, still moving in the direction he had been going before he entered the bookstore. He crossed the street, slipping rapidly between moving cars. He stopped in front of a window and used it as a mirror to check behind him. He did not see the man so he took a chance and turned his head to look more closely. "Not there," he thought. He breathed a sigh of relief.

Serhat walked to the next corner and turned down Broadway. Once he turned the corner, he speeded up and forced his way through the crowds, putting distance between him and his imagined follower.

Across the street, an average-size man in tan shorts and an "I luv NY" tee shirt moved in the same direction; he would have passed for one of the many tourists in the city. He raised his wrist to his mouth and spoke into the tiny microphone. "I have him now. Back off for a while. He may have made you back there."

"I hope so. We wanted him to think he was being followed."

Serhat continued moving down the block. In his casual dress, no one not intimately familiar with him would identify him as an Ambassador. He had no fear of being recognized; he was in one of the most diverse cities in the world and, although he looked nothing like an American, he was just one of thousands on the sidewalks of New York who fit that bill. He kept glancing around, looking for the tall man in the fedora, but, if he were following him, he seemed to have lost him.

At the next corner, Serhat crossed the street to the left, passing directly in front of the tourist, who also turned the same direction. Halfway down the block, the Ambassador paused, then pushed open a door to a small deli, and then entered. He moved immediately to the small, round table in the back corner and sat down across from a person wearing dark sunglasses.

The person smiled and then said, "What's wrong with you? You look like you've seen a ghost."

"Nothing, I guess. I thought I was being followed, but maybe I was wrong."

"Followed? Who would be following you? Are you a spy or something?"

Serhat jerked his head at this question. "I don't want anyone to know that I am meeting you. Americans are still somewhat leery of these relationships."

The tourist just walked right by the deli, not even looking in the window. He looked intently at his phone, snapping a picture through the window of the two. He keyed his mic and said, "Suspect just entered the Uptown Deli. He is meeting with a woman. I am sending the image to the Director. Go in and put some pressure on him; let's see how he reacts."

Within a minute, the tall man in the fedora walked into the deli. He paused as soon as he was in the restaurant and looked all around. He made eye contact with Serhat and immediately stepped toward him. Stopping in front of the Ambassador, the man gazed intently at Serhat, who looked as if he wanted to bolt from the deli. Finally, the man removed his hat and spoke, "I'm sorry to have bothered you; for a minute, I thought you were the Ambassador from Turkey, but, on a closer look, I see that you are not. Have a good day." He put his hat back on and walked quickly out of the restaurant.

As soon as he was outside, he keyed his mic and said, "Mission accomplished. He looked like he wanted to sink into the floor. He'll make his call soon."

Back in the deli, Serhat was having trouble breathing. His companion said, "What is wrong with you? Why did he think you were an ambassador? You're just an accountant in a big office building."

Serhat felt as if his whole world were suddenly crumbling around him. He had to get out of here. "I'm not feeling well. I'm sorry, but I need to go."

"Are we still going to stay at the hotel tonight? You'll feel better when we get to the room and can relax. Her foot brushed Serhat's leg under the table."

"No; I can't tonight. We'll make it next week at the same time. I've got to go." With that said, he stood and hurried from the deli.

He looked both ways, but was so rattled, he failed to spot the two men standing behind the sign. He pulled his phone from his pocket and hit the speed dial.

The tall man in the fedora spoke into his mic. "He's making a call now."

Director Frazier replied, "We're on it. Let's see if it is to who we think his contact is. I got your image; I'm having it run through our files now."

Romonov looked at his display. His anger almost kept him from responding. Finally, he answered. "What do you want? It better be important to call me on this phone." He listened to Serhat for a minute and then asked, "He said he thought you were the Ambassador from Turkey? You're sure he said exactly that?" Romonov obviously did not like the answer. "Then you are made. Get off the streets now and back to your safety zone."

Frazier raised his fist and yelled, "Yes. We have him. The Ambassador from Turkey is our courier." He pushed his mic and said, "Pick him up and bring him to Langley. Don't let him call or talk to anyone."

The Director smiled. "Finally, a break!" He pushed the call button and waited for an answer. "Lander, we have him. Our man is the Ambassador from Turkey. We are picking him up as I speak and will take him to Langley. Romonov knows the Ambassador has been identified, so he may feel pressured to make a move, so watch your six. You're still in Virginia, aren't you?" He waited for Lander's reply and then said, "If you want to be in the conversation with the Ambassador, meet me at The Farm at ten o'clock tomorrow morning." He paused before adding, " In fact, I do want you there; I'll have you picked up. Be ready at eight sharp."

Chapter 63

Lander brought us up to date on what Director Frazier had told him. I felt pretty good because it was I who had first broached the idea that the rogue agent might be an Ambassador. I said, "You're going to meet the Director tomorrow for the interrogation of Serhat . . . aren't you?"

"Yes. He has strongly suggested that I be there; he is sending someone to pick me up at eight. Do you think you all will be okay here for awhile while I go?"

"Of course. I think you need to go. You might be able to get information that the others can't acquire. We'll be okay. We have the car and may spend the day sightseeing."

"I don't know. Director Frazier said that Romonov followed us here. You may need to stay in while I'm gone."

"If Romonov is here, he will follow you. Maybe we need to go to protect you."

Lander didn't respond, but he thought, "I hope he does follow me; in fact, I am counting on it."

The next morning dawned gray and cloudy; heavy rain was forecast for the evening. Typical weather for the area in summertime: hot and humid with a chance of late afternoon thundershowers.

Lander got into the black SUV and it immediately pulled away. I continued to watch, looking for another vehicle leaving to follow him. When it was almost out of sight, I saw a small black Nissan turn from a cross road and move in the same direction. I called Lander. "You have a tail, in a black Nissan Juke."

I went back into the restaurant and sat down. Cyndi asked, "Did you see anyone following him?"

"Yes, maybe. Someone in a black Juke went the same way shortly after Lander left."

"You think it was Romonov?"

"I don't know; I couldn't get a good look at him. You've looked at the picture of him that Lander gave us, haven't you?"

"Yes, unless he drastically changes his appearance, I will recognize him. Where is Lander meeting the Director?"

"Lander didn't say, but I suspect that it may be at The Farm."

"What and where is The Farm?"

"It is thought to be a covert CIA training facility near Williamsburg, at a military reservation called Camp Peary. Supposedly, agents are trained in all types of spycraft and techniques of espionage. It is a highly secure location and has a room designed for tough interrogation situations. If anyone can break the Ambassador, it will be done there."

"Did you let Lander know someone was following him?"

"Yes, I did. He sounded like he expected that."

"Well, if Romonov is following Lander, we should be safe enough to act like tourists today. What do you say?"

"I say let's go. We may even run over to Williamsburg; we've talked about going there for several years. I don't expect Lander back before tonight."

"Sounds like a plan. But take your Glock just in case."

"Always!"

# # #

The driver looked at Lander and said, "I think we've got a tail."

"You're right. Black Nissan Juke. Should be one man in it."

"Do you want me to lose him?"

"Not yet. I want him to follow me for a while. Keep your eyes on him. If he starts to close the gap, let me know. We'll take him when we get to an isolated area. That's where he will try to make a move."

"Yes, sir. I'm on it."

"He'll be armed, probably with an assault rifle."

The driver smiled. "Good. That will make it more interesting!"

Lander said, "I'm beginning to like you more and more."

After twenty minutes, the driver slowed the SUV, turned into an overgrown trail, and began the gradual slope to the top of the hill. Lander asked, "Did our man follow us off the highway?"

The driver checked his mirror. "Yes; he is still with us, about thirty seconds behind. Can his little car navigate this rough road?"

"Yes, it is probably a four-wheel drive and it sits up pretty good. There's a sharp turn just ahead. After you make it, I will slip out and wait for our friend."

"Do you need a weapon?"

"No, I've got one." Lander pulled his handgun and checked the magazine. He pulled the slide, chambering a cartridge. "I'm good to go. When I bail, you keep going until you see the next turn. Stop the car there. He'll have to stop also. Hopefully, we'll have an addition to our little chat with Serhat."

The driver glanced at Lander's handgun. "H & K? That's a good one." After the sharp right turn, he slowed for a couple of seconds, allowing Lander the chance to exit the car. As soon as Lander eased the door shut, he accelerated back to his normal speed.

Lander ducked and slipped behind a large tree. He watched the SUV get to the next turn just as Romonov came around the curve. As soon as the SUV stopped, the Juke slid to a stop also. Romonov leaped from the car, and carrying what looked like an AK47, moved quickly behind his car. He was so intent on watching the SUV that he never saw or heard Lander approach from his rear.

"Drop your weapon. Right now!"

Romonov spun to his rear, raising his rifle. The shot rang out before he had a chance to pull the trigger. He dropped the weapon and grabbed his right arm. Almost immediately, his hand was covered in blood. Lander walked up to him and kicked the rifle away, keeping Romonov in his sights the whole time. "Don't move. The next one will be a kill shot. Put your hands on the car and spread your legs." Lander quickly ran his hands over Romonov, looking for additional weapons. Finding none, he said, "Now, get on your face on the ground and put your hands behind your back."

"But I'm bleeding. I can't do that; I'll die."

"You'll die if you don't. You can take your time or you can hurry; I don't care. If you hurry, I'll get a bandage on that wound."

Romonov stared at his arm dripping blood and then he slowly lay down on the ground and placed his hands behind his back.

Lander pulled his zip ties and secured Romonov's hands; then he also zip tied his ankles together. When he had finished, he stood in the middle of the road and signaled the driver of the SUV, who backed the car the short distance to Lander. "Bring me the first aid kit you have in the back. I know you have one."

The driver opened the rear cargo lift and grabbed a soft-shelled bag. He walked to Lander and handed the kit to him. Lander looked inside and selected a roll of gauze and some tape. He took his knife and cut the sleeve away from Romonov's wound. He placed a compress bandage on the injury and wrapped it tightly with the tape. He helped Romonov stand and said, "Let's go. In the back seat! I'm glad you were able to make this date."

Chapter 64

As soon as they had Romonov secured in the SUV, Lander moved the Juke off the trail and the driver turned the SUV around. In a short time, they were back on the main highway, heading for the facility known as the Farm. Lander contacted Frazier and alerted him to the fact that they were delivering Romonov. When they arrived at the facility, they were stopped and IDs were checked. The Director had communicated with the guards and a security officer in a military Jeep met them at the gate. They were escorted to the isolated facility where interrogations were carried out. As Lander exited the car, two more agents approached and took control of Romonov.

Director Frazier said, "Come in; help yourself." Lander looked to where the Director was pointing and moved to the Keurig, where he started a coffee. "So, you had some excitement on the way here; things are getting interesting, aren't they?"

"Yes, we had an incident. Romonov is now in our control. Here is his phone; you can have it checked."

"You allowed him to live? That somewhat surprises me; are you getting soft in your old age?"

Lander chuckled. "As far as my age, just remember that you are right there with me. You wanted him alive, didn't you?"

"When did what I want stand in your way?"

"You're top brass now. You could make me disappear at any time."

Frazier laughed. "You overestimate my power, I'm afraid. Enough chitchat. I'm glad you're okay. We'll interrogate Serhat first. Do you want to handle it or do you want to observe?"

"I'll observe if you don't mind. I may have a question or two as the session develops."

Frazier keyed a mic and said, "Take Serhat in." Lander followed Frazier to a back door and went into a small room. The walls were of unfinished cinder blocks and the floor was unpolished concrete. There were no windows in the room and the one light dangling from the ceiling provided a dull light to the room. In the center of the room, one rectangular table set, surrounded on each side with one metal chair. On closer inspection, Lander could see that all the furniture was bolted to the floor. Another door opened and Serhat was led to the table. His shackles dragged behind him and were loud in the silent room. He seemed almost on the verge of panic, which is the mindset

Frazier and Lander wanted to see. The guard pushed Serhat roughly down into one of the chairs. He unlocked the handcuffs and pulled Serhat's hands behind the chair, where he cuffed him to a chain that was itself bolted to the floor. Frazier nodded to the guard who went out the same door he had entered.

Frazier and Lander sat down at the table and said nothing for a good two minutes. This was by design, as they wanted Serhat to anticipate the worst possible scenario. Suddenly, Frazier slammed his fist down on the table, stood, and moved his face close to Serhat. Serhat jumped at the sudden noise and tried to scoot his chair backward, but to no avail. His squeezed his eyes completely shut, trying to make the scene disappear.

Frazier said in a low voice. "We have you, Serhat. You might as well talk to us."

"I'm a diplomat. I demand to be released."

"If we have knowledge that you are actively working to damage our country, we can keep you locked up—and you'd better believe we'll do that. Now, you might be able to help yourself. With whom are you working?"

"I don't know what you are talking about. I have done nothing to what you call 'damage' your country."

Lander held up his hand. "If I may, Mr. Director, could I speak to our guest?"

"By all means."

Lander looked at Serhat. "We know you have corresponded with a man named Romonov. And we know that you have met with him and helped him."

Serhat said, "I don't know a Romonov."

Lander smiled and said. "We have Romonov in another room. We have not talked with him yet. But I can tell you, the first one that comes clean will come out ahead." He looked to Frazier for confirmation. Frazier nodded his assent.

Lander looked at his watch and said, "Mr. Serhat. You don't have to talk to us. We are going to drink a cup of coffee while you think about it. We'll be back in exactly one-and-a-half minutes. At that time, you just tell us you don't want to talk to us and we'll let you go back to the room where you were. We'll bring in Romonov and give him the same chance. Do you think he will go down protecting you?"

Lander and Frazier walked to the door, paused, looked one more time at Serhat, and then left, closing the door with a dull thud.

"You still know how to raise the anxiety level, don't you?" said Frazier.

"Some people will react to that; others won't. I really don't think Serhat is a bad person; I believe he only acted as the courier in order to make some cash. I doubt if he even knew what he was carrying." They stood sipping their coffees for a bit. Then Lander said, "Well, let's go see if our absence had any effect."

When precisely ninety seconds had passed, Lander and Frazier reentered the room. Lander walked over to the chair where Serhat sat. He glared at him before saying, "Okay, Mr. Serhat. I will ask this only one time. You will answer in no more than fifteen seconds. If you don't, you will immediately be escorted from the room. Who knows, if the good Director here wants to, he may ship you to Gitmo on suspicion of being a terrorist. Do you understand what I am saying?"

Serhat shook his head violently. "Yes, I understand."

"Do you know a man named Romonov?" Lander looked at his watch. "Time starts now."

"Yes, yes. I know him."

"Okay; that's better. What did you do for him?"

"I delivered a package for him. That's all; I swear."

"What was in the package?"

"I don't know. He didn't say and I was afraid to look."

"Where did you take the package and who did you give it to?"

"I took it to a man in Turkey, to a city called Samsun. The man took a boat across the Black Sea to Sochi."

"What was his name?"

"He goes by Anatoly Ivanov."

"For whom does Ivanov work?"

"I don't know. He's the one I always meet. I don't know what he does with the packages after I deliver them to him?"

"So, you have done this before?" asked Frazier.

"Yes, about two times a year. It was easy for me as a diplomat. But I didn't think it was anything that could be dangerous to the U.S. I was just making some extra money; diplomats don't get rich, you know."

Lander stared at him. "You mean they don't get rich if they only do their job."

Serhat said, "That's all I know. I swear to you."

Frazier spoke into his radio. "Come remove this prisoner."

The same guard entered, released the cuffs from the chain, and led Serhat from the room.

"What do you think?" asked Frazier. "Is he telling the truth?"

"Yes, I think so. He's so scared I don't think he would hold anything back. Let's see what Romonov has to say."

"I doubt if he'll talk so readily. I don't think he'll scare so easily."

Romonov was brought into the room and secured to the same chair.

Frazier began the conversation. "Mr. Romonov, I am happy you joined us. Have my men been taking care of you? I see they have stopped your bleeding."

Romonov just glared at him.

Frazier continued. "I think you know Mr. Lander here. I would have thought you were smart enough not to try any of your little games with him. You're not in his league!" The Director nodded to Lander.

Lander said, "Mr. Romonov. I hope you will share some of your knowledge with us."

"Then you will be disappointed."

"Mr. Romonov. I'm sorry you are taking that tone with us. You see, you're facing life in prison at the least. But, probably, you're facing death for capital murder and working with foreign governments to cause harm to the U.S. That may even be considered terrorist activity."

Frazier spoke up. "Had you rather be put to death for murder or executed as a terrorist?"

"You can't prove anything!"

"Well, let's see. We have you for killing scientists at the excavation sites. You do know what excavation sites I am talking about, don't you?" Frazier paused to see if Romonov would answer him.

"What's an excavation site? I don't know what you are talking about."

"Oh, I think you do. We also have proof that you have been supplying foreign countries with classified scientific materials."

"And how was I supposed to have done that? I haven't left the country in the last year."

Frazier said, "We know you hired the Ambassador from Turkey to carry some bones to a contact from Russia. And we have traced you to Beaumont, Texas, where you shipped similar items to Hong Kong to be delivered to China."

Lander looked at Frazier in surprise. "Once we identified him, we had the most likely ports checked. We picked up your shipper yesterday, and, guess what . . . he admitted mailing a package for you not too long ago."

Lander looked again at Romonov. "So, I guess you get to pick your poison. I know that you were the one that also kidnapped Dr. Yates. She has picked you out in a photograph. In fact, she has a picture of you on her phone."

"Why would I kidnap a scientist? If I had the bones, I wouldn't need her, would I?"

"Yes, you would. The Man hired you to kidnap her and coerce her into helping Dr. Leonid de-extinct the animals. You threatened her family if she refused to help the Russians."

When Romonov realized that they knew about the kidnapping and knew about The Man, his whole demeanor changed. "What do you want to know? What's in it for me?"

"Still trying to sell secrets, aren't you?" Lander looked at Frazier and said, "What about it? Does he know anything worth bargaining for?"

Frazier shook his head. "I don't think so. I believe we know everything he has done; what we don't know, we can probably get from his phone records. He's in no position to bargain."

"No, wait. I do have more information; I used throwaway phones for most of my contacts. You proved you know who the Russian is, but do you know who is leading the Chinese project to use your bones? If you don't stop them, they will beat Yates and Leonid. The Chinese are leading the world in using DNA."

Lander said, "Maybe in using contemporary DNA, but I don't believe they are better at ancient DNA sequencing than Leonid or even Yates. You know Leonid has already de-extincted the woolly mammoth. The Chinese can't compete with them." He looked at Frazier and said, "You're right; he has nothing to bargain with. I think we're through here." He got to his feet and signaled Frazier, who also stood.

"No! Wait! I can tell you who your high government official is. He's been helping the Russians for the last five years."

Lander and Frazier both sat back down. "Maybe you do have a bargaining chip after all. Go on. Tell us who he is."

They listened to his answer. Frazier said, "Well, I'll be a son-of-a-gun! I would never have thought that." He immediately pulled his phone from his pocket and quickly left the room, leaving Lander sitting in shock.

Chapter 65

We were just sitting down to dinner when Lander walked into the restaurant, spotted us, and then made his way over to us. He sat down and asked, "Did you order for me? I'm starving."

"No, we didn't. You didn't bother to let us know you would be here." I stared at Cyndi. She usually left those types of remarks to me.

Lander looked suitably chastised. "I'm sorry. I should have called you. A lot has happened today and my mind is still whirling with it."

"Okay, you're forgiven," I said. "Out with it! What happened?"

The server interrupted us and we ordered. As soon as he left us, I said again, "Tell us what happened today."

He considered my words and looked around us; the dining room was full. "Not in here. It'll have to wait until we've eaten and gone to your room." He read the disappointment on our faces and said, "I'm sorry. It's too explosive to take a chance on someone overhearing us."

"Now how do you think we're going to enjoy our meal after your saying that?"

"While we're waiting for our food, tell me what you all did today."

"We drove over to Williamsburg and toured it. It's pretty interesting."

Cyndi added, "It was really enjoyable. We had been talking about visiting Williamsburg for the last few years, but had never made the decision to do so. Something always seemed to pop up to keep us away."

"I'm glad you all had fun while I worked." Lander sounded serious, but he put that warp-sided smile on his face.

Before I could reply, the server began to bring our meals to the table. I don't have to tell you that we ate the quickest meal we had ever had. Well, at least, since we had been in college.

We entered our room and Lander hooked the security chain on the door. Cyndi dropped her shoes at the door and padded barefoot to the bed. Lander and I followed, with him sitting in the side chair and me balancing on the edge of the bed beside Cyndi.

I said, "Now, Mr. Lander. No more delay. What happened today? From the start! I know that you set it up so that Romonov would follow you. Did you see him?"

"Yes, he followed me, as you well know. In fact, you called me to warn me. You don't remember that?"

"Of course, I do. But I wasn't completely sure that it was Romonov in the Juke."

"Well, it was. We let him follow us to an isolated area. When we were out of sight around a sharp curve, I bailed out and waited for him. He thought he had us cornered and was just setting up a shot at our car when I came up behind him."

"He just gave himself up?" Cyndi asked.

"No, he didn't. But I got a shot off before he could target either of us."

"Did you kill him?"

The answer surprised me. "No, I only wounded him. We were able to take him to The Farm to join Frazier and the Ambassador. We had good interviews with both of them."

Cyndi could barely contain her excitement. "What did you learn?"

"The Ambassador was really scared. He told us everything he knew, which wasn't much. He was the one that slipped the bones out of the country to the Russians, but he had no idea what was in the package he delivered. He was only the courier and making some side money—quite a bit, I might add. He did give us Romonov as his contact here. He passed the package to a man in a city on the Turkish coast to take across the Black Sea to Sochi. From there, Serhat had no idea where the package would terminate."

Cyndi tilted her head, thinking. "Sochi. That's where the Russian Winter Olympics were, wasn't it?"

I shook my head in the affirmative and then asked Lander, "What about Romonov? I bet he wasn't as eager to talk, was he?"

"You're right. Romonov is a hardened criminal. He may have not pulled the trigger, but he was certainly a party to the murders. He also kidnapped Dr. Yates. And that's not all. He has conspired to sell classified scientific information—and priceless ancient bones—to foreign governments. He's looking at a lifetime behind bars. He may have bargained for his life."

"What did he reveal that would be a valuable trade-off?" I couldn't think of anything that important.

"He gave us two valuable items. One was the identity of the Chinese group and where they are located."

"Can we do anything about them? The bones are already there, aren't they?"

"I don't know. I'll leave that to Director Frazier to sort out.

I said, "You said Romonov gave up two important information tidbits. What is the other?"

"Are you sitting down?"

We listened to his revelation. "Are you sure?" Cyndi looked wide-eyed as I asked the question.

"Yes. It seems accurate. Director Frazier is following up now. This will shake the country if it gets out. This is one of those items which you have to consider classified. Don't even hint it to anyone else."

Chapter 66

The three men huddled together in a hotel room in Hong Kong. T.J. stabbed at the map on his iPad. "This is the lab. It's a one-story block building on the corner."

Lance pointed to the rear of the building. "Is this an alley behind it?"

"Yes. It is a service and delivery route for the businesses in that block." He paused and then said, "And, yes, there is a rear door to the lab."

"What about security?" This came from Allan, the tech expert in the group.

"As far as we can determine, only the usual for China. Double locks; no cameras; no live guards. Should be easy to get into."

The next ten minutes were spent on the planning for their operation.

"When do we go?" Lance was the tough guy and stayed ready for live action. He hated this part of the mission.

"As soon as we get the signal. As we planned, it will be a night operation. We need to get in without being seen, set the fire, and get away. We want it to look like an accident, not an attack."

Lance said, "Wait. If it's a block building, it won't burn."

T.J. replied. "It is block outside, but the entire interior is paneling and wallboard. The clean room is newly redone, all with wood. It will burn enough." T.J.'s eyes focused intently on his two comrades. "We do not want to engage anyone; under no circumstances do we want to leave bodies behind."

Lance laughed and replied, "Not unless they're Chinese bodies."

"Do we have infiltration help?" Allan asked.

"Yes; that has all been arranged. At our call, he will meet us on the waterfront and drop us near the Chinese mainland."

"Near? Does that mean we swim into shore?"

"Yes; he will have diving gear for us so we can remain submerged until we hit shore. After he drops us, we will have two hours to get back."

"What happens if we're delayed?"

"Then we're on our own. Now I suggest you get some sleep; if we get the green light, it will be a long night." Within five minutes, all were sound asleep.

The trio was an elite group of covert operatives and all had experience in slipping into foreign countries; most missions were rescues but there were also occasional targets to dispose of. T.J. had handpicked his two companions and had no qualms about being successful. During their experience, they had trained their bodies to relax on a moment's notice. "Sleep when you can and eat when it's available" was the mantra. Three hours later, T.J. awoke at 2230, feeling refreshed and ready to go; he looked at the window and confirmed that it was a dark night, overcast with no moon, perfect for a covert incursion. He glanced at his phone and saw the message: "Green for tonight!"

He spoke. "Okay, guys. We have a go! Get ready. We leave in two hours." T.J. pushed a button on his phone, waited for an answer, and then said, "It's on—meet us at 0100. " He immediately ended the call.

The men took showers and ate the snack that T.J. provided. They checked their equipment and reviewed the plan one last time. Thirty minutes before time to leave, they began to dress for the mission. Their uniforms for this operation consisted of black cargo pants with a black, long-sleeved tee shirt. Black boots and black toboggans finished the clothes. Allan was the first dressed and removed a round tin of black waterproof face paint. He needed no mirror to expertly cover his face with the gel. When all were finished, they inspected each other to be sure no bright spots were left that would reflect a light. They put on their mics and did a quick communications check.

T.J. checked his watch and picked up his weapon and backpack. "Let's go, men," he said.

Moving to the window, he separated the curtains enough to peek through. "Looks clear. Check the door, Allan."

Allan cracked the door and peered out. "All clear." He led the way out and the men moved quickly to the path that led down to the waterfront. Staying in the bushes that paralleled the path, they crept toward the landing area. Off to the southeast, they could see the lights of the planes as they landed and took off at Hong Kong International Airport. Suddenly, the South China Sea lay before them. They waited out of sight until they saw the running lights of a speedboat approach. The captain of the boat flashed a light twice, paused for a count, and then flashed it three more times.

T.J. whispered into his throat mic, "That's it. Let's go." He led the way to the boat that had bumped up close to the deserted dock. One after the other, they jumped into the boat. As soon as the last one landed, Allan pushed the boat away from the dock and the captain eased it away from land. T.J. handed the man a thick envelope. "It's all there."

The captain weighed it in his hand, smiled, and then said, "Same plan?"

T.J. answered the captain. "Yes, get us as close to Shenzhen as you can. Did you bring the dive equipment?"

"Yes, it is under the tarp. I didn't want anyone to spot it." He pushed the throttle forward and the boat quickly accelerated to fifty knots. The captain guided the boat between the mainland on his right and the small island on his left. The island was the home of Sha Chau and Lung Kwu Chau Marine Park and, although the captain was pretty confident that no one there would notice the boat this late, he stayed a good distance away from it. A few minutes after he was past the island, he angled the boat into Deep Bay. He said to T.J., "You all need to put on your dive gear. When I say 'Go', hit the water; I will not come to a complete stop. I will return for you in two hours. If you are not here, I will wait only fifteen minutes. I can simulate fishing for a short time. If I leave, you are on your own."

A short time later, the lights of Shenzhen began to appear. The captain steered the boat northeast and pointed. "The golf club is directly ahead. You have a road that comes down almost to water's edge west of the course. There will be a small car parked off the road. Here are the keys. You know the way to your destination?" The captain had no idea why the Americans were here and didn't want to know. All he cared about was the thick wad of U.S. dollars that was in his pocket.

T.J. secured the keys in a pocket and zipped it shut. He did not want to lose the keys when they were in the water. He stood and motioned to his men. He said to the captain, "Stay two hundred yards from shore. Turn the boat slowly. Halfway through your turn, we will jump." He clicked the button for his chronograph and the two hours began ticking away.

On T.J.'s signal, the men eased into the water, floated while they adjusted their buoyancy, and then sank out of sight. A few minutes later, they stood in the shallows of the bay. With all the vegetation, it was still dark here. They found a spot to leave their dive gear and covered it with limbs. Unless someone stepped on it, it would remain invisible to anyone who happened by. Each man pushed a button on his phone, storing the GPS coordinates. At the road, the men stopped and listened for any sign that they were not alone. Hearing nothing, T.J. led the way to the copse of trees and found the car. They entered the car and T.J. paused before starting it. "Allan, time our travel to our destination. We need to know how long it will take us to return here." Allan set the clock to zero and clicked the button to begin the time. T.J. then accessed the navigation app on his phone and clicked the saved destination for the lab. The display read "calculating route." He checked his surroundings one last time for any visitors and started the car. He eased onto the road and began following the blue dot that would lead them to their destination. When he stopped the car, he said, "Mark the time."

Allan replied, "Time marked. It took us twenty-eight minutes."

"Good. I had estimated a thirty-minute drive." He backed the car into a secluded spot, leaving it facing out so it would be ready to go when they returned. "Let's move it."

The team had decided that they would leave the car a half mile from their destination and hike the remaining distance. They covered it in seven minutes, staying off the road in the shadows. When they reached the alley, T.J. held his hand up. "Allan, check left; Lance, check right." T.J. stared down the alley. When he had 'clear' from the others, he moved hurriedly down the alley, his men closely following. As soon as he reached the door, he saw what he had hoped to see; the locks were on the outside of the door so that deliveries could be made without someone having to be there. He stood aside and let Lance move in. In thirty seconds, he had picked the locks and pushed the door open.

T.J. whispered, "There shouldn't be anyone here at this time of night. Nevertheless, be alert and take no chances. We'll find the DNA location first and then we'll take care of the building. If the diagram was accurate, the clean room is off to the left. He led the way to the door. As he anticipated, it was also locked. He motioned to Lance, who made short work of picking the lock. They entered the room. Shiny new equipment sparkled in the light of their penlights. T.J. quickly located the bones that the Chinese were working on. He spread some liquid on them and did the same with the wall in that area; it was a new noncommercial accelerant that would leave no residue at all. Meanwhile, Allan was using a sensor to locate the wiring behind the wall. He pulled a section of the paneling away from the wall and using insulated tools, he stripped the wiring bare in a couple of places. He looked at T.J., who nodded to him. Using a spark igniter, he started the flame. As soon as he was sure it would stay burning, he pushed the panel back in place. He clicked the igniter once over the bones and they began to burn. Without another word, the three men left, making sure that the doors were locked just as they had been when they had entered.

When they got back to the car, they paused briefly. Lance looked at his watch and said, "One minute." At the end of the minute, there was a sudden explosion from the direction of the lab. "Okay, the chemicals they had stored there just blew. There will be nothing of value left."

Twenty-seven minutes later, they parked the car back where they had found it. Moving to the shore, they retrieved their dive gear and eased into the water. By the time they surfaced two hundred yards into the bay, the boat arrived to pick them up.

Back in their hotel room in Hong Kong, T.J. powered up his SAT phone. When it was answered, he simply said, "Accomplished."

Chapter 67

I asked, "Have you checked in with Dr. Yates?"

Lander replied, "Yes; everything is going well at the lab here. She will be ready to go back to Colorado in a couple of days; actually, she will probably finish up here tomorrow afternoon. She's taken a couple of extra days here, but when she started to use the thermocycler, it blew out. She had to wait for a new one to get here."

Lander's phone interrupted him. He looked at the display and said, "Director Frazier." He answered, "Lander here."

Frazier said, "Mr. Lander. We have an interview set up for tomorrow. You may want to be here; it will be interesting to say the least."

"What time do I need to be there?"

"I'll send a car for you; be ready at seven a.m. Oh, and bring the Kents with you. You all won't be in the room, but will have a front-row seat." He ended the connection.

Lander replaced the phone in his pocket. "We have a meeting tomorrow. Get ready and we'll meet for breakfast downstairs at six. Someone will pick us up at seven. It'll be an interesting day."

The black SUV was waiting for them at seven o'clock. Lander got in the front passenger seat while Cyndi and I took the back one. No one spoke during the short drive to Langley. We exited the car and walked to the front door that was heavily guarded. One of the men checked our IDs while the other kept his eyes on us. His assault rifle was pointed at the ground, but his hand remained close to the trigger. I had no doubt that he could have raised the weapon and fired it before I could get my hand in my pocket. Lander had warned us to keep our hands visible and not to make any sudden movements. We were glad to comply with those directions. After a quick frisk of our bodies, we were directed to enter. Another officer met us inside the door and said, "Please follow me."

After a short distance down the hall, the man stopped and the door beside him opened. Director Frazier walked out and addressed Cyndi and me. "Welcome to Langley. Please." He nodded his head toward the open door and stepped through. We followed him and he directed us to a row of chairs facing a mirrored wall. We sat down and he asked, "Did Lander bring you up to date on our investigation?"

I replied, "Yes. I think he told us all he could, but sometimes he tends to hold back information so he can feel superior."

Frazier smiled at my remark. "So, you know who we've identified as the mole in our government."

"Yes, I couldn't believe it. I'm sure it came as a shock to you, also."

"It surely did. No one would have fingered . . ." The wall lighting up interrupted him. What I had thought was a mirror was actually a two-way mirror. From where we were, we could observe what was going on in the room. I should have known that and won't admit to Lander that I didn't recognize the wall for what it was. "You all can observe, but understand that anything you see or hear is classified and can never be discussed with anyone." He looked at me and said, "Not even in a new book." With that, he left us sitting there.

We watched as he entered the room followed by President Branson and FBI Director Johnson. The President began the conversation. "Harvey, we wanted to bring you up to date on our skeletons' case."

"Has your man, Lander, I think it is, discovered who the murderers are? I hope so. Maybe we can put this behind us and get on with the business of the people." Johnson licked his lips and tried to smile. I could tell he was nervous about being there.

They talked a few minutes and then Johnson just shook his head. "Have you any proof? I can't accept that you really believe that."

Frazier laid out the facts as he knew them. As he talked, Johnson slumped more and more. He suddenly looked to be twenty years older than when he walked into the room. He clutched the bottle of water sitting before him and sipped it. His tongue kept flitting over his lips. Finally, he said, "You know that this will end my career—if it doesn't kill me."

Branson said, "I am really sorry about this, Harvey. We have been friends for many years. I will stand behind you but you know what the outcome will have to be."

Johnson slowly shook his head. "I know and I appreciate all that you have done for me. I should have listened to your advice. I didn't and now I will pay the price. Can I remain?"

Branson considered that and looked at Frazier for guidance. Frazier remained quiet and finally Branson pushed the button on his radio. "Come on in." All three men stared at the door and watched the two men enter, led by a large security man with handcuffs around his wrist.

Johnson stood and walked toward the men. He paused at the first man, and then grabbed the second in a huge bear hug. He tried to speak, but no sound came from his throat. Finally, he squeaked, "Son, what have you done?"

The guard led the handcuffed man to the table and pushed him to a chair. Johnson flopped down beside him, wiped his eyes, took a deep breath, and then sat up straight. He looked at his son and said, "Do you want to tell us about it?"

"Tell you about what? I don't know why I am here."

Tim Johnson stared at the men. His insolent glare spoke volumes to us as we watched the scene unfold. His father spoke again. "They know what you've done. It will go easier on all of us if you tell the truth."

Tim stared at Frazier. "You tell me what you think you know. I've done nothing."

Frazier looked at Director Johnson, who nodded his assent. Frazier said, "We know about your role in the act of attacking four excavation sites. We know about the bone segments stolen and shipped to Russia and China. We have Romonov and Ambassador Serhat in custody now and they have admitted their guilt. We know that you were working for a thug in Russia known as The Man."

Tim Johnson had lost his air of insolence and his face was pale. He looked at his father and said, "Dad, I am sorry. No one was supposed to have been killed. I was just obtaining the bone segments and selling them to the Russians. I don't know anything about China's being involved in any way."

Frazier said, "I believe you about not knowing the Chinese were involved. I think that was a side sale by Romonov. How did you become acquainted with The Man?"

The young Johnson spoke so low that we barely could hear him. "I've never seen The Man. I met Romonov at a bar and we began to talk. He knew who I was and said that he could get me a lot of money for helping him. He promised that no one would be hurt. It was just some old bones, so I took him up on it. After I became involved, they forced me to provide them information. They said that if I didn't help them, they would tell my father what I had done. So, I gave some names and dates when things were happening. I talked directly to The Man on a phone."

Frazier asked him. "Did you know what they were going to do with the bones?"

"At first, they were only going to recreate some old animals, but I learned that The Man was going to take it to another level."

This was new information. Frazier asked, "What did he mean about this?"

"I honestly don't know; he never told me. I wasn't on his top tier of workers or friends. I do know that he had some other scientist than Leonid working on that part."

"Who was the other scientist? The American?" This from Frazier.

"No, he had another Russian; I think he was going to modify the DNA to place a cell in it that would allow the giant animals to be easily trained or controlled."

Frazier said, "I thought you just said that you didn't know the next level."

"I was never told exactly, but Romonov let something slip and I think that was what the other man was to do. I don't think even Leonid knew about this part of the plot."

"What was significant about the training of the animals?"

"I don't know. You'll have to figure that out yourself. Really, that's all I know." He sat back and lowered his head.

Director Johnson looked at the President. "Are we through with him?"

Branson said, "Yes, I don't think he can help us anymore."

The son looked at his father and said, "I should have listened to you. I should have taken your advice."

The FBI Director said to his son. "I'll get you a lawyer. Don't talk to anyone else." He motioned to the guard. "Take him out and lock him up." He said to the President, "I'm so sorry." And then he also left the room.

When he had gone, Frazier stood and walked out to where we were. "You all can join us now." We followed him into the room and sat next to Frazier.

Lander said, "Does anyone know about this additional scientist that The Man has brought into the picture?"

None of us knew about him. "Do you think Leonid knows what his role is?" Frazier asked the question for which we feared the answer.

Lander replied. "I don't think so. Even Johnson denied that Leonid was knowledgeable about him."

Branson said, "I'll follow up with President Kruschov on this. He should be able to discover what is going on there. Anything else before we close this meeting? I think we have all the bad guys in the U.S. accounted for. Oh, and we don't have to worry about the Chinese. They have disbanded the project." He smiled as he said this. "I have another meeting. You all stay in here and pick each other's brain. We still need to determine The Man's real goal." He started toward the door and then stopped. He turned and looked at us. "Our country is again in your debt. I appreciate your help. If you keep helping us solve problems, I am going to have to put you on the payroll."

Lander laughed. "Yeah. You'll pay them what you pay me."

Branson laughed and left.

Cyndi said, "I have a question. What did the Director's son mean when he said 'I should have taken your advice'?"

"Director Johnson wanted to help his son get into government work. He and the President are long-time friends. President Branson didn't want to bring him in, but Johnson put pressure on him. To his credit, the young Johnson worked hard and did such a good job that he was continually advancing. When the political position of Assistant Director of the NSF came open, Director Johnson talked the President into appointing his son. That's how he knew about all the projects. Both the President and Johnson constantly warned Tim not to get involved with anyone outside the government and advised him not to talk to anyone about the NSF projects. The lure of big money made him disregard those warnings." That was the longest speech I had ever heard Frazier say.

We sat there for another hour discussing the events, but finally admitted that we had to wait for additional information before we could completely close the case. As we left, Lander said, "I hope that Leonid gets out of Russia before The Man hears about what we have done."

Chapter 68

The next day, we accompanied Dr. Yates back to Colorado. Frazier had agreed that she was now secure enough to shed her "kidnapped" status, so she called her family to give them the good news that she was safe. Late that afternoon Leonid arrived back from Russia. We sat down with the two scientists and brought them up to date on the case. We couldn't tell them everything, but enough was said that they felt secure now. They agreed that what they were working on was important enough that they continue their collaboration. I was glad that the project was going to continue.

We had left the two scientists working in the lab and had just sat down for dinner when Lander's phone buzzed. He looked at the display and said, "Frazier." Because the dining area was crowded, he arose and mouthed, "I'll take it outside." He was gone about almost five minutes before he returned. "Things are moving forward," he said. "The Director has been in communication with President Kruschov and brought him up to date. Kruschov is going to handle the problem in Russia as quickly as possible. By this time tomorrow, I suspect that The Man will have had a fatal accident."

I said, "It would be too bad if he happened to step in front of a stampeding woolly." I smiled as I said that.

Cyndi added, "It would be karma—and well-deserved, I might add."

I said, "Once The Man has been taken care of, as far as we know, all the bad guys will have been either eliminated or taken into custody."

Lander chuckled. "At least all the bad guys in this case; they're plenty more out there."

Cyndi said, "Can you all wait until next year to take on the rest of them?"

Our dinners arrived and we spent the next twenty minutes, almost silent with a little small talk thrown in, enjoying the good food. We ordered after-dinner coffee and Lander and I got dessert. Just as we started to eat it, Lander's phone buzzed again. I said, "Is this Grand Central Station today?"

Lander held up his index finger—yeah, I know it was his index finger—and stepped outside again. He was back within a minute, smiling. "Frazier again?" I asked.

He nodded and said, "The Man, along with his right-hand man, had an accident thirty minutes ago. It seems as if their car lost a wheel and careened off a small slope. The car must have hit a tree or something because both men were dead at the scene."

Cyndi said, "I think we need to talk with Ranger McKenzie and Sheriff Spencer. How much can we tell them?"

Lander considered this for a moment. "I agree we need to talk to them. We'll tell them that we have word that Dr. Yates has been found and her kidnappers killed. We can tell them that the kidnappers were the people who attacked the camps and stole the bones."

"What do we tell them about the bones?"

"Just that they were recovered along with Dr. Yates and have been returned to the NSF."

I said, "I'll call McKenzie and see if we can meet with him and the Sheriff in the morning." I powered on my phone and hit the contact number for the Ranger. "McKenzie. Phil Kent here. How are you doing?"

He said, "Fine. How are the Kents and Lander doing? Are you all back in Tennessee now?"

"No, we're not. We're still in Durango and will probably go home in a couple of days. Hey, listen. Could we come over to your office in the morning and meet with you and the Sheriff?"

"You're not bringing more trouble, are you? We've had enough for a year or two."

"No, in fact, we have some good news."

"In that case, be here at ten o'clock. I'll get the Sheriff here."

"Sounds great. We'll see you tomorrow."

I ended the call and said to Cyndi and Lander. "Ten o'clock tomorrow morning. He had the nerve to ask me if we were bringing him more trouble."

We all laughed at that until Cyndi said, "Knowing you two, that was a legitimate question."

The beautiful weather continued the next morning as we drove to our meeting. Actually, I drove, Lander slept, and Cyndi toyed with her iPad; at least, they did after they finished their coffees. As I parked the car, Lander roused and started to say something. I beat him to it. "I know. Good job driving, Kent." He gave me a thumbs-up and we left the car and entered the ranger station.

"Well, look who showed back up. I thought we had gotten rid of you all." The sheriff reached for our hands.

Lander retorted, "Just hoping, huh?"

Both the Sheriff and McKenzie laughed at that. We followed them into the office and took seats around the conference table. Lander asked them. "Have you all heard any more about Dr. Yates?"

The Sheriff shook his head and said, "Ha! The FBI hasn't given us the time of day. We've heard nothing."

"I was afraid of that. That's why we wanted to meet with you today. Dr. Yates has been rescued and she's fine. Her kidnappers were all caught and are either in custody or dead."

McKenzie asked, "How do you know this?"

I looked at Lander and replied. "Lander worked with one of the Washington bigwigs when he was in Special Forces. They have kept in touch over the years. When he found out that Lander was here when Yates was kidnapped, he called him to interview him. Then, yesterday, he called Lander back and told him that the case had been solved and that Dr. Yates had been found alive and well."

The sheriff looked a little peeved. "Were they going to bother calling us to let us know?"

Lander spoke quickly. "My friend knew we were still out here and he asked us to come by and tell you. I had told him how helpful and efficient both of you were and he wanted you to get the good news about Yates face-to-face and not over the phone. I expect that at some point in the near future, you will get a formal communication from him."

"We didn't like being shut out of the investigation, but I'm glad Yates was found safe." McKenzie scratched his scraggly beard. "Hmm. Sounds awful coincidental that you all are here until the case is solved and then you are just happening to be leaving the next day."

"What can I say? We were planning to leave earlier, but Cyndi finally got a chance to do some shopping. We also saw a lot of places that we originally didn't plan to visit." I knew Cyndi wouldn't mind me using her shopping as an excuse in this matter.

"Did you get to go to Superstition Mountains? I know you wanted to do that."

Lander answered the Sheriff. "No. We didn't. I guess that will have to wait for another trip out here?"

"You're not planning to come back here, are you?" We all looked at McKenzie. He smiled and we knew he was joking . . . I think.

The Sheriff had to add to this. "If you do, give us advance warning so we can call in reinforcements."

We all stood and Cyndi went to them and hugged them. That got them back on our side and we all shook hands and we left.

When we got to the car, Lander said, "Hey, Kent. You lie pretty well. Good job back there."

Cyndi chimed in. "Yeah, just another skill he's learned from you, but one he better not practice at home—not if he wants to keep his life." However, she followed the implied threat with a playful smile.

"I didn't really lie; I just didn't give them all the information. When are we leaving for home?"

"Let's get flights for tomorrow morning. We need to get back; I know that Chelsea has missed us." Chelsea is our Cocker Spaniel. Although she makes some trips with us, we had left her at home this time; our grandson is staying at our house and taking care of her. "And that will give us one more time to get in a training run tonight." With all that was going on here, we hadn't been able to run our normal schedules, but we did enough hopefully that will allow us to take advantage of the extra oxygen when we get back to our normal altitude.

Chapter 69

The next few months were relatively calm. Lander was teaching his classes and I'm sure they were a little more exciting than last year's version. I was teaching an online class and working on my next novel. Cyndi was busy doing much of the research for the book. She also serves as my first reader and keeps me on track with my characters. We were relaxing one night when my phone rang. I glanced at the display and said, "Lander."

Cyndi said, "Don't dare answer it! It'll be trouble."

I laughed and answered it anyway. "Hey, Lander. How goes it?"

"Great. Get ready. We've got a trip to take. Cyndi is coming, too."

"Whoa! You call me after several weeks of no contact and start giving us orders." We had completed our marathons and then had gotten busy with our normal schedules.

"Yeah. I guess I am. We fly out of Chattanooga Friday afternoon at five twenty-three. We need to be at the airport by four o'clock. I'll pick you all up at three-thirty."

"Better make it three-fifteen. You know that Cyndi will have to stop at Starbucks on the way out."

He laughed. "You're right. But Lisa will have to do that also. She is going with us this time." Lisa was Lander's wife and also a good friend of ours.

"Are you going to tell us where we're going?"

"No. I like secrets, especially when they're mine. Take casual clothes and also one dress outfit. Pack for about five days. You all need a break; I know you have been working hard. Oh, I guess you better take your hiking boots." He said, "See you then," and hung up.

Cyndi said, "What was that all about? What does he want you to do now?"

"Not me. Us. He's picking us up Friday afternoon at three-fifteen. Pack clothes to be gone five days; mostly casual, but one dress outfit."

"Can you tell me where we're going?"

"Nope."

"What do you mean, 'nope'?"

"Just nope. I can't tell you because I don't know."

"You told him that we would go on a trip with him, but don't know where we are going?"

"You're right. He wouldn't tell me. But it must be somewhere safe. Lisa is going with us." I thought that might help Cyndi accept the idea. She doesn't normally like surprises, especially when they include unknown destinations. Lander and I could get in a car and just go where the winds and roads take us and enjoy it, but that's not Cyndi.

Finally, she said, "This better not be another adventure. We're just now getting over the last one."

I knew what "adventure" meant. I smiled and said, "I promise. It will be a relaxing trip. You'll enjoy it." I'm not sure she believed that and I'm not sure I did. I could never tell with Lander.

Friday afternoon, we left Chattanooga on time. I had looked at my ticket and the final stop was Phoenix Sky Harbor International Airport. Less than an hour later, we landed at Atlanta; we had a layover there of almost two hours. Lander still would not give us an agenda and, if Lisa knew, she wasn't telling. We landed in Phoenix a little before nine o'clock that night and Lander led us to a waiting car. We placed our luggage in the back of the red Explorer and Lander jumped into the driver's seat. I remember thinking, "Is Lander actually going to drive?" He started the car and accessed the navigation. After a minute, he stepped back out of the driver's seat and said, "Okay, Kent. You're driving. Just follow the blue road."

After driving east on I-85, we turned onto Highway 60, still heading east. We stopped in Mesa for a quick meal and then resumed our trip. In less than thirty minutes, the car's navigation app announced, "Your destination is two hundred yards ahead." I had seen signs announcing the town of Apache Junction and I pulled into the parking lot for a Motel 6.

Lander said, "We'll stay here tonight. Be ready to leave tomorrow at nine o'clock."

Cyndi said, "And what should we wear . . . or is that a secret, also?"

"Wear your church clothes tomorrow." He smiled, but said nothing else.

We were tired, so we said our 'good-nights' and went directly to our rooms. The next morning, we had the free breakfast and then went back to our rooms to dress. Lander did tell us this morning that we would be staying here again tonight, so we left our bags in the room. The Landers beat us to the car, so he had it already running. He decided to let me drive this time, so I jumped into the driver's seat. "Follow the blue road, Driver," he said.

We started seeing signs for local points of interest: Old Mines; Canyon Lake; Theodore Roosevelt Dam; Globe; and the one that really piqued my interest: Superstition Mountains. I followed the route on the navigation display and turned north onto a small, unmarked road. Ten minutes in on this increasingly rough road, I stopped at a closed gate; a ten-foot high fence stretched to both sides of it as far as I could see. A man carrying an iPad and a high-powered rifle approached the car from the left side of the road; I looked around and another man with his hand on a holstered handgun eased to the passenger side. I rolled down my windows and showed him my hands. He said, "IDs, please." Cyndi was staring at me with that look in her eyes.

We all showed our drivers' licenses. The man checked his iPad and looked closely at each of us and at our IDs. He compared those with pictures on his tablet. He handed our IDs back to us and said, "Welcome. They are expecting you. Go about a quarter of a mile and park directly in front of the main building."

I drove though the opened gate and followed the road around a sharp turn to the right. As soon as we completed the turn, the rough trail was replaced by a smooth concrete road. A minute later, we were staring at a cluster of buildings; I stopped in front of the main building, a huge wooden structure that looked like a plush ski lodge. "Well, this is a surprise," said Lisa.

"Yes, in more ways than one," I said, looking at several vehicles with various media outlets marked on them.

I stopped the motor and we exited the car. The front door opened and Director Frazier appeared. "Glad you all could join us. It's a big day."

We followed Frazier into a huge room. It was beautiful with polished wood walls and had large wooden beams stretched across the ceiling. At the back of the room was an enormous fireplace; the blazing logs crackled and sizzled. One side had floor to ceiling windows that looked out on a picturesque forest of trees with a towering mountain peak standing guard over them. The room was set up for some type of meeting with media personnel scattered all around the setting. The only group more prominent than media included a unit that I recognized as security. Frazier led us to a table at the front and said, "Sit here. We're ready to get started." Close to us was an elevated platform that contained a group of chairs; to the right of the chairs was a huge screen, the type used in presentations. Every chair in the room was occupied; some of those present looked puzzled that we were escorted to front and center.

As soon as were seated, Cyndi between Lander and me, a door beside the stage area opened and others entered. We watched in awe as each one entered. First was Director Frazier; he was followed by Dr. Yates and then Dr. Leonid. Next came Dr. Pasternak. Behind her were two others: President Branson and then President Kruschov. The room erupted in a buzz. I leaned over to Cyndi and whispered, "I agree with Director Frazier; it is a big day."

Cyndi said, "Is that really our President?"

Lander heard her and said, "Yes, it is. And the other man with him is Russian President Kruschov. The man beside Dr. Yates is Dr. Leonid."

Frazier went to the podium and tapped the microphone to be sure it was on. The room grew quiet; all media cameras were on him. "I want to welcome you here today. It is a big day for the scientific community. I know that many of you left important work and traveled many miles to join us; we appreciate it and assure you that you will not be disappointed. First, I want to introduce you to our guests on the platform." He turned to them and said, "Please stand when I introduce you."

"On the far right is Dr. Shirley Yates. Dr. Yates is an American paleontologist. You will hear from her later. Next to her is the renowned Russian biologist who has worked in the Siberian re-creation of the grasslands; you will also hear from him, Dr. Aleksey Leonid. To his left is Dr. Sherri Pasternak; she is in charge of most biological projects at the National Science Foundation. The next two men, I will introduce together. We are especially honored to have them join us today. Our President David Branson and Russian President Alex Kruschov." Both men nodded and accepted the generous applause. They sat down and Frazier continued.

"Today marks a significant milestone for American and Russian biological science. This accomplishment will rank up there with the top ten scientific accomplishments of all time. The project is over my head and I will ask Dr. Pasternak to take over."

Pasternak lowered the mic so she could speak into it without tiptoeing. "Thank you, Director Frazier." She looked at the audience and continued. "We have been participating in a joint effort with Russia and we are extremely pleased to announce a successful conclusion to that endeavor. As a biological scientist, it is the culmination of a dream I have had for many years. I am awed by this, as I am sure you will be. But I am not the architect of the project; I wish I were. Our two guests on this stage are. I will allow Drs. Yates and Leonid to come to the microphone to formally announce their accomplishment." She stepped back from the podium and nodded to the scientists to come forward.

Yates and Leonid moved slowly to the microphone. Leonid gestured to Yates to speak first. She coughed once and cleared her throat. "I feel honored to be in the company of those present here today, not just the Presidents and Directors, but of all you in the audience. You represent the best of our scientific community."

She paused and then continued. "As some of you no doubt know, we had four excavation sites attacked. Most important, several of our comrades were executed during those raids. In addition, the attackers shattered bones and artifacts, so rare that they can never be replaced. I was the principal investigator at one of those sites, a site where an extremely rare extinct animal's skeleton was found. I'll give you more specifics later. But, first, I want to allow Dr. Leonid to explain what he has accomplished in Russia, in a remote area of Siberia." She stepped aside and raised her palm to Dr. Leonid.

He stepped to the mic and flipped the remote on that he held in his palm. The screen came to life, showing a slide of the Russian tundra. "This is a picture of the Russian tundra. As you can see, it is full of large brush and trees. It has evolved to this during the last ten thousand years. Prior to that, it was lush grasslands. Most in the scientific community have believed that this change came about because of climate change, which then caused the large animals that used to graze on those grasslands to become extinct. I'm sure all of you have heard of the woolly mammoth. After years of research, a fellow scientist of mine came to a different conclusion and I agreed with him. Ten thousand years ago, there were large herds of woolly mammoths and other animals that lived on the grasslands. I think they became extinct not because of climate change but because at that time, mankind appeared in the area and developed the weapons to hunt large game. I believe we lost the great herds because they were over-hunted. As the herds declined, the grasslands changed. No longer were there enough large animals to keep the large brush and trees trampled down, so they gradually took over the landscape. The grasslands had kept the permafrost frozen at a constant temperature, but when the landscape changed, it allowed the permafrost to begin to melt. You know what many believe happens then: because of the gases released as the ground thaws, the atmosphere is affected; global warming is the result of ozone depletion."

"I felt that if we re-introduced large animals to the landscape that we could reverse the results. Pleistocene Park was created in Siberia to test this hypothesis. This slide shows the same area now with the large brush and trees gone. You can see that the grass is coming back. But I needed the large animals to keep the area trampled down; the woolly mammoth was extinct. We discovered many skeletons of the woolly in the permafrost, many of them almost intact even after thousands of years. With the advances in technology and the handling of ancient DNA, could we resurrect the woolly? I set out to see. I am happy to report that I was successful." He advanced the slides and then clicked the movie icon in the middle of the slide. The audience saw five woolly mammoths grazing contentedly in the grassland. There were suddenly excited voices all over the room. The media became animated as they quickly uploaded images to their home stations. Dr. Leonid bowed, handed the remote to Yates, and stepped away from the podium. Everyone in the room stood and the room was filled with applause. There was no doubt that the audience recognized the significance of the accomplishment.

Dr. Yates stepped back to the microphone. She paused while the room quieted again. "As you can see, Dr. Leonid has accomplished something that many of us dreamed about for years. During the last several months, since the attacks here, I have been working with Dr. Leonid on a project that was authorized by our respective presidents. The four sites that were attacked included skeletons of extinct animals: a short-faced bear, a saber-toothed tiger, a rare dinosaur—the Epanterias—and a giant. We established three labs—two in the United States and one in Russia—to see if we could replicate the results of the mammoth with other extinct animals. Our first project was the short-faced bear. She clicked to the next slide. This is the de-extincted bear. There are three live ones right now. Two are here on these grounds and one is in Russia. This bear has the potential to grow to be much larger than the polar or grizzly bear. The images you see are bears approximately six weeks old.

"Our next project was the saber-toothed tiger. The tiger is a focus of much legend and speculation. Everyone seems to want them back; they are awesome animals." She clicked to the next slide. "This is a three-week old saber. Again, we have three of them, two here and one in Russia. Our next project will be the dinosaur. It will be the most difficult to de-extinct as it has been nonexistent the longest. We will begin work on it next week."

One of the media persons, a young woman from CNN yelled. "What about the giant? When will you produce one of those?"

Dr. Yates gazed at the Presidents before answering. "We have decided that it would be unwise at this time to attempt to create a giant from years ago. Although there are numerous accounts of giants during the history of mankind, they would be out of place in our current environment. Until we can be surer of their safe reintroduction to society, we will leave those skeletons alone." She walked back to her chair to the tune of applause and sat down.

The two presidents made their way to the podium. President Branson was the first to speak. "This is an awesome accomplishment, one that will go down in history as a major turning point in scientific advancement of the human race. To be able to bring back great animals that became extinct at the hands of men is almost unfathomable. I want to personally add my congratulations to Dr. Yates and Dr. Leonid for their work. I also want to emphasize how important it is to work with Russia in this endeavor. I thank President Kruschov for his willingness to collaborate on such a project."

President Kruschov stepped to the mic. In almost perfect English, he said, "I, too, want to congratulate two of the premier scientists in the world." He raised his hand to Dr. Yates and then to Dr. Leonid. "I hope this successful collaboration will be the gateway to future endeavors. In fact, our governments have agreed that this partnership will continue. Any successful de-extinction will be shared between both countries. Dr. Leonid will be the new Director of Pleistocene Park and, at some point in the near future, we will be ready to show it to the world."

President Branson stepped back to the speaker's platform. "I also want to reveal that we have a similar project to that of Pleistocene Park. You are on the grounds of it now. We have not named it yet; we will have public input in choosing an appropriate label for it. It is also my pleasure to publicly announce today that Dr. Shirley Yates will head the complex." Yates' eyes got big and she began to beam. Branson noticed this reaction and said, "She did not know that until this announcement. We could get no one better suited to head it. Congratulations! It is our hope that the re-wilding of selected landscapes will lead the way to a worldwide acknowledgement that all species can live in harmony."

"There is one other item I want to announce. As has been stated, we had brutal attacks on American excavation sites. Invaluable artifacts were destroyed and scientists were executed. This was carried out in order for those bones with their ancient DNA to be delivered to foreign groups anxious to beat the American scientific community to the successful completion of de-extinction. They might have done that except for the timely intervention of some other guests we have here today. Would Bill Lander, Cyndi Kent, and Phil Kent please stand?" We looked at each other and finally stood. "Mr. Lander is a former special-forces operative and is the leader of this trio who, for the second year in a row, have stepped up and played a major role in assisting the U.S. government in foiling major threats. I can't go into detail, but, as a token of thanks, I want to recognize them with the Presidential Medal of Freedom Award, the highest civilian awards in our country. It is awarded to persons who have made 'an especially meritorious contribution to the security or national interests of the United States.' At a future ceremony, I will also recommend that they receive the Congressional Gold Medal."

President Kruschov stepped back to the podium. "I also want to express the gratitude of the Russian government to these three and will offer to them a special invitation to visit my country and Pleistocene Park. It would not be the success it is without their work the last few months."

All we could do was to stand and blush at the attention. We finally sat down to a round of applause. Cyndi wanted to leave as quickly as the presentation ended, but we were swamped by well-wishers and the media. We finally made it to the platform and shook hands with both

Presidents and thanked them. We hugged Dr. Yates and even Dr. Leonid and wished them well. Dr. Pasternak congratulated and thanked us. She said, "You probably saved my job."

When we arrived back at the motel, Lander said, "What a day! That was impressive. How does it feel to be a celebrity?"

Both Cyndi and I shook our heads. Although we appreciated the recognition, neither of us enjoyed the fanfare that accompanied it.

Lander said, "Tomorrow, Lisa and Cyndi are going to drive to some of the local towns and shop." He pointed at me and said, "You and I are going to hike up into the Superstition Mountains. We may even find the Lost Dutchman's Gold Mine."

Cyndi and Lisa looked at each other. In concert, they said, "Oh, no. What can they get into now?"

I looked at Lander. We both shrugged and I said, "Who knows? The Lost Dutchman's Mine is not the only mystery in those mountains."

The End

#

If you enjoyed this book, please leave a review at the site where you obtained it.

Other Books by C.K. Phillips

Kents/Lander series

Book One: *Comes the Awakening*

Nova Scotia: Beautiful, Idyllic, Peaceful—
Perfect. Until it was not!

When Phil Kent finds a body, an investigation
that connects Knights Templar to a modern Native
North American tribe and an extremist terrorist
group using ultra-modern camouflage begins.
Racing to find ancient treasures buried on Oak
Island, Kent, his wife Cyndi, and ex-special forces
member Bill Lander work with security forces of
Canada and the U.S. to foil the terrorists before
they unleash their devastating attack on major
cities of the world. Along the way, the scientist
who had been developing the futuristic camouflage
is rescued from the terrorist cell who had been
threatening his family in order to force him to help
them. Beginning in Canada, the action spans
several countries before the plan is thwarted.

Book Three: *The Survival Initiative*

Why can't Kent just enjoy a football game . . .

. . . Is it because Lander is with him?

They get through the first half before the explosion.

An explosion that hits home to the protagonists! The opening salvo of a targeted attack on western civilization pulls them into a scheme so vicious that you'll look at the headlines to be sure that it hasn't started.

A plot intended to bring the U.S. and its allies to their knees and catapult them back to the dark ages. You'll be shocked as the protagonists slowly peel back the hidden layers of this conspiracy.

Can the country survive this coordinated assault on its civilized culture?

Made in the USA
Middletown, DE
15 December 2020